Brewing Justice

KEN HUBONA

DEDICATION

To Bob Fraser: friend, wit, and attorney extraordinaire.

ACKNOWLEDGMENTS

My thanks to critique partners John Granderson, Ally Burleson-Gibson, Denise Woods, Kathryn Carson, and Donna Sullivan; to Greg Smith, author of *Agile Writer Method*; and to my editors at *Rare Bird Editing*.

CHAPTER 1

Ricocheting off the plate glass window, the Champagne cork careened into Bob's forehead with a thwack, its sting a welcome distraction from the acrid bile burning his throat. He stumbled back as foam hissed from the bottle onto the sleeves of his Givenchy suit. A cheer arose from the assembled attorneys holding up their fluted crystal stemware.

"I wouldn't take a bullet for the firm," Bob said to the crowd. He rubbed his forehead with the back of his hand and forced a grin. "But to close a deal like this, I'd take a cork."

At six-foot-one, he moved easily among the hooting celebrants, slopping the bubbly into their glasses. Beyond the mammoth oak table that dominated the thirtieth-floor conference room a floor-to-ceiling window provided the revelers a real-life mural of the cityscape and riverfront. Perched atop downtown's most prestigious address, Kravitz & Doyle reigned as the East Coast's premier mergers-and-acquisitions law firm and the juggernaut that employed Bob Baldwin.

"Ladies and Gentlemen," Bob said, addressing the roomful of Armani and Anne Klein suits, Hermès neckties and scarves, and eight-hundred-dollar Brooks Brothers wingtips and Salvatore Ferragamo pumps. "Today we celebrate the consolidation of Worthington Industries and Mountain West Fabricators, the biggest merger in the firm's history." He saluted with his glass. "And the biggest fee." He touched the flute to his lips and washed down the rising acid.

Raising their glasses, the standing assemblage cheered. Only one person remained seated. H. Meriwether Doyle presided at the head of the table, his coiffed silver mane perched atop a ruddy face and gray, wolfish eyes that surveyed his domain. A tall man, even while seated, the firm's sole name partner and the surviving half of Kravitz & Doyle cleaned his nails with the blade of a small red Swiss Army pocket knife. He glanced up and nodded once in acknowledgment of the accolades.

"Worthington Industries and Mountain West will become one family," Bob said, "in a marriage that will benefit all—shareholders and employees alike." Another cork whizzed past his ear and more Champagne flowed. Bob refilled his glass, gulped it down, and pressed his fist into his sternum. It wasn't really a merger, a joining of equals. It was a hostile takeover. Mountain West's board of directors had fought the "consolidation" for twelve months before collapsing under the legal onslaught of the larger industrial behemoth, which is why pulling it off had been such a grind for Bob, and why it had generated legal fees well into the seven figures. And at Kravitz & Doyle, fees were the *raison d'etre*, even though the firm website waxed pious about market efficiency, eliminating redundancies, and growing the economy to help working families.

Working families. Doyle had hijacked that one from a politician pal over a double-malt scotch at the club. For Bob, it conjured images of dad and mom and five children marching single file into the mine with shovels over their shoulders. Perhaps whistling. The reality was much darker. Spouse abuse, child abuse, alcohol and drug abuse. Divorce and broken families. The decimation of whole communities.

But now was a time to celebrate. And as lead attorney on the Worthington deal, Bob got the honors. He held up his glass. He had just made that son of a bitch three million dollars, and if he didn't get a fat bonus on this one, he would go down the tubes. "To Mr. Doyle, the finest rainmaker in the state."

Doyle looked up from his nail maintenance, folded the knife blade, and nodded his blessing as the chorus responded, "To Mr. Doyle." He lifted his as yet untouched champagne flute, tilted it like a scepter bestowing grace on his subjects, and downed the elixir.

The huge fee would be divided among the partners according to their rank.

"What are you going to do with your bonus, Bob?" someone called out.

Bob furrowed his brow. Pay down the maxed-out credit cards, or three-months-in-arrears mortgage payments, or the Porsche and BMW leases. He pushed a smile onto his face.

"I don't have a boat yet."

The crowd loved it.

A bonus. Bob still hadn't received one for either of the last two deals. That never happened when Mr. Kravitz was alive. But H. Meriwether Doyle now ruled absolute, and to challenge him was professional suicide. At least as lead attorney on this one, Bob would certainly be elevated to senior partner, putting him well on his way to retirement at fifty-five with more money than he could spend, to relax and travel the world with his beautiful wife. And the promotion couldn't happen soon enough. As much money as he had made as a junior partner, it all seemed to slip away.

Bob had sacrificed his soul for this too-tan, Botox-injected, surgically jowl-less Satan, and he wanted his payment. As Doyle pushed back his chair, Bob awaited his reward. Doyle rose, but instead of speaking, tapped his cell phone and headed out the door.

Bob marched down the long corridor toward his office. He had worked his tail off on this deal. He didn't make junior partner by drinking Champagne and sucking up to the boss. He got there by putting together deals and making them work. Mountain West had been a tough calf to wrangle, struggling for a year. But Bob's red hot legal work seared the Worthington brand onto the smaller company. And if Doyle didn't give him a fat bonus, Bob would wrap his fingers around the son of a bitch's cologne-reeking neck and squeeze it out of him. Bob needed his money. Living the good life was expensive— a mini-mansion in the burbs, a BMW 650i, and annual European vacations with Heather. Bob had paid his dues. His gray-tinged temples attested to his forty-one years, fifteen with Kravitz & Doyle, basically a slave working eighty hours a week. This deal had to clinch a senior partnership.

At her desk, his secretary Doris held the phone, a hand over the mouthpiece. She mouthed, "American Express."

Bob shook his head.

"I'm sorry. Mr. Baldwin isn't in. May I take a message?"

As she hung up, Bob held out the slice of cake he had carried from the celebration. His hand tremor rattled the plate as he set it on her desk.

"Thank you, Bob," she said. They'd been a team for ten years, ever since he had become a junior partner. At forty, she exuded the confidence of a competent professional woman who wore dated business suits and allowed her hair to become streaked with gray.

She saw the purple mark above his eye and reached out and touched his temple. "Oh, Bob. Let me get something for that." As she hurried off, a hand landed on his back.

"Quite a performance, amigo."

Bob snorted. "A lot of good it did me, George."

The perennially cheerful George Gifford followed Bob into the office and plopped down into a client chair, stretching his legs beneath the front of Bob's desk. His shaggy mane and red bow tie were his personal eye-poke to authority. George did quality work, but he showed up at eight a.m. and went home at five, putting family over firm. So in fifteen years, he hadn't made junior partner due to his poor work ethic.

Bob paced around his desk, throwing his hands into the air. "I just made this firm three million dollars, and the man walked out on me."

George reached for a small wooden cube on the desk. He picked up the polished cherrywood box, put on his reading glasses, and inspected the inlaid panels of teak and mahogany. He rotated it and examined the top, the bottom, and each side. He thumped it with his finger. He shook it, and the contents rattled.

"I'm pretty busy, George."

George began manipulating the faces of the box with his thumbs. He pushed and pulled and twisted the inlaid slats.

Bob sighed and descended into the swivel chair behind his desk. A harsh light bored through the window from the sun-reflecting skyscraper across the street. Folders were stacked on his desk, and his vanity wall was adorned with the accolades of his life—diplomas from college and law school, certificates of admittance to the state and federal bar, and various plaques accumulated over the years. But no photographs, no people, except for Heather's gorgeous face in the small frame on his desk.

"Yes," George called out as a slat moved with a click.

Doris returned with a plastic bag of ice and gently placed the compress against Bob's temple, cradling the back of his head with her other hand. "Why don't you go home, Bob?"

He snorted. "Can't. I have to work these files and keep the river flowing." He made his mouth grin, but he didn't have the energy to force his eyes to follow.

A second click emanated from George's box, and Doris retreated to the outer sanctum.

"The son of a bitch has withheld our bonuses." Bob massaged his forehead with the ice bag. "I need my money."

A third slat clicked, and George lifted the top. "You don't have to put up with it." He pulled out an open pack of unfiltered Camel cigarettes, held it up, and peered over his glasses at Bob. "Seriously?"

Bob snatched the pack and threw it into a desk drawer. "It helps with stress."

George tugged at his bow tie as though tightening the knot of the clip-on. "There's a better way to cope." He put his elbows on the desk, interlaced his fingers, and glanced left and right as though Russian spies might be listening. "I got the lease, Bob." His eyes twinkled. "Second floor of a warehouse on Water Street. It's perfect. And cheap." He held up his hand. George's enthusiasm could not go unacknowledged, so Bob slapped the upraised palm, though his heart wasn't in it.

"I'm happy for you."

"Not *me*. *Us*. I want you to come with me." George had been planning his escape for years.

"George, how many times have I said no?"

"That was before you were getting stiffed. And you hate this place. Hear me out."

Bob exhaled, tossed the icepack into the trash, and leaned back into his chair.

"This is right up our alley," George said. "We know business. We know the law. I have a long list of potential clients I've been collecting. And best of all, it's our chance to do some real good."

Bob groaned. George never stopped harping on his dream to start a boutique law firm specializing in helping entrepreneurs get their businesses off the ground.

"We'll give the small guy a chance to build something. And we get out of this immoral rat race and actually help people." George swung his arm over the files on the desk. "Instead of doing mega-mergers so some CEO can buy a private jet with his twenty-million-dollar bonus, while hundreds of factory workers and truck drivers and clerks lose their jobs."

"George, our work creates efficiencies in the marketplace—"

"Blah, blah, blah," George said. "You don't believe that any more than I do." His palms flew upward. "We ruin lives, Bob, and I can't take it anymore." He collapsed back into the chair. "I've only stayed this long for my kids."

A lawyer at Kravitz & Doyle never saw the debris left behind by his work. Like the B-52 bombardier at 35,000 feet, he pressed the button, flew home, and spent the night at the officer's club and then in bed with his sweetie. Meanwhile, the bombs he released rained down in an inferno of ruined lives. Whole communities were decimated while company executives and investment bankers reaped millions, and lawyers like Bob bought boats.

Bob raised his palm. "We're well paid."

George gave him the stink eye. "More money doesn't make it right. Whether you're a thousand-dollar-a-night call girl or a twenty-dollar streetwalker, you're still a whore."

"So you're asking me to give up a good salary, plus bonuses—"

"Which you're not getting."

"—to help entrepreneurs? What did an entrepreneur ever do for me?"

"Plus, it'll be fun," George said. "Like the great times at PLC."

Bob had to smile. In law school, they had interned at the Poverty Law Center. He loved sticking it to slumlords and usurious money lenders who preyed on the poor. After a landlord threw a mother and three children out onto the street without due process, the man turned purple when the judge awarded the woman $2,400 in damages. "She'll never see a cent," the landlord said in the corridor outside, but he ponied up pronto when Bob put a lien on his building and started foreclosure proceedings.

In truth, that year was the only fun Bob ever had practicing law. But the second summer, he dumped the flaking paint and block walls of skid row for the oak paneling, marble, and good wages of Kravitz & Doyle, recruited by the big man himself, Mr. Kravitz, while George continued sticking it to the man at PLC. George looked like a poverty lawyer then, his hair down to his shoulders and a full beard. And though clean-shaven and pink when he came to K&D, inside he remained a hippie gadfly.

"You'd get out from under Doyle's thumb. You'd never have to see his face again, or suck up to him, or beg him for money he owes you." George was a great lawyer. He should be in a courtroom persuading juries rather than drafting documents in a cubicle. "And you'd have more time at home. Hell, you could even work from home when you didn't have a client meeting."

George knew what buttons to push. As Bob thought of spending the days with Heather, the stress melted away. But when he returned to the present, he frowned. "It sounds great, George, but I can't afford to leave. Heather would never go for it. She likes nice things."

"Bob, if this takes off, you'd be making much more than here in a few years. You and Heather can travel the world."

Bob imagined lying on a beach in Bali, making love to Heather, the most beautiful woman he had ever met. More time with her would be wonderful.

"Besides, it wouldn't cost you a dime. I have the overhead covered for a year."

Maybe Bob *could* tighten his belt for a while. "What kind of draw would we take?"

"No, Bob. I'm talking rent and overhead. No salaries. We won't be able to pay ourselves for a year. It's a start-up."

"I can't live without a paycheck for a year." Or even two weeks.

"Couldn't Heather help? Isn't she in real estate? We plan to live on Connie's salary."

Bob shook his head. "Heather hasn't worked since we married. She's too busy with the housekeeper and yardman and shopping." He looked at the ceiling. "Pilates, aerobics, all her gym activities."

"Can't you economize? Hell, we were all broke in school. Remember how much fun we had?"

He did. Despite the pressure cooker called law school, Bob's years with Abbie had been the happiest in his life. "That was twenty years ago. I have obligations."

"I make half what you do, Bob. Connie and I manage. Even with the kids."

"I want to give Heather the things she wants."

George sighed. "My grandfather worked as a janitor for fifty years. He raised four kids. When he passed, he left them a half million dollars."

"I'm guessing there's a moral here."

"Yes, Bob. It's not how much you make. It's how much you spend. How many movie stars and football players and pugilists made millions, yet died broke and alone?"

Only George would say *pugilist*. But he was right. The lawyers here spent as well as they earned. Mercedes, BMWs, and Corvettes filled the parking garage. They enjoyed beach houses, mountain cabins, ski-in condos, boats at the marina, and vacations to Aspen, Rome, and Bali.

Bob shook his head. "I can't join you, George." He stared at his desktop. "I can't lose Heather, too."

"Okay," George said, rising, "but Abbie didn't leave when you were a broke law student. She left when you came to this place."

George knew where to stick the knife. Bob and Abbie had thrived on her waitress's salary. They lived in a rundown college apartment, ate a lot of macaroni and PB and J sandwiches, and went to the movies twice a year. And they never argued. Until he graduated and joined Kravitz & Doyle. She'd endured his first two years as an 80-hour-a-week associate before she broke.

"I want a husband," she finally said.

"What the hell am I?"

"A ghost," she said, and left him for "a balanced life."

From the doorway, George gave a two-finger salute. "Money doesn't buy love, Bob."

Bob did not hear the ringing phone. Deep into the Jensen file, he weighed options and calculated strategies, undisturbed by the muffled background noise of a busy law office.

"Attorney Robert Baldwin's office. Doris speaking."

Bob's desk phone beeped. "Your wife on two."

As he reached for the phone, his tension oozed away. He punched the button.

"Heather."

"Hello, Robert." Her sultry purr made his heart flutter. Heather's beauty and sensuality held an almost frightening allure. "I miss you," she cooed.

He swallowed hard.

"Will you be home soon? I can't wait to see you."

Bob's nether regions stirred as he anticipated the delights that awaited him. Even after three years of marriage, Heather could still whip him into a frenzy.

"I'll leave right now." He began gathering his files.

"Can't wait," she said. "Oh, there's one more thing."

Bob stuffed files into his briefcase. "What is it?"

"It's nothing really," she said. "Well ... it's the credit card ... the Visa ... the good one." She paused. "I'm here at the mall, and Sadie's Boutique declined the card."

"The Visa?" A lump rose in his throat and threatened to choke off his words. "That card has a fifty-thousand-dollar limit."

"I know. I figured they made a mistake. So they ran it through again."

"And?"

"Declined."

"Heather, what did you buy?"

"Nothing, silly. They declined it."

He took a slow breath. "No, I mean *before* that."

"Nothing," she said. "Well, nothing expensive ... nothing *that* expensive." She smacked her lips. "It didn't *just* happen. I've only been paying the minimum balance. And I might have missed a couple months, I'm not sure."

He laid his head on the desk.

"I was embarrassed, sweetheart. I shop at Sadie's all the time." Her voice lowered to a coo. "So could you have Visa bump the limit again?"

Bob found the view from Doyle's corner office magnificent, looking both south and west across the city. Afternoon sunlight bathed the huge room and massive desk, clear of any indication of work. A leather sofa and chairs, Persian carpet, and large, round coffee table made the space more like a living room than an office. Expensive artwork hung from the walls, top-shelf booze lined the bar in the corner, and a private bathroom hid behind a concealed door. Rumor had a jacuzzi in there, but Bob knew no one who had been inside.

"Come in," Doyle said, sprawled in an overstuffed chair. "You're my number one hit man." With a hand wave, he offered Bob a seat.

Bob took the other chair, avoiding the sofa known as *Henry's casting couch.*

Melting ice cubes tinkled as Doyle swirled them in amber liquid and raised the glass to his lips. "Great score with the Worthington deal."

Bob nodded his thanks. "I think Mr. Kravitz would have been pleased."

"Pleased? The money-grubbing Jew would have shit his pants. He didn't have two nickels to rub together when I met him."

Bob had liked Mr. Kravitz and chafed at Doyle's revisionist history. Solomon Kravitz already operated a thriving one-man show when he hired associate attorney Henry Doyle, forty years earlier. Under Kravitz's leadership, Kravitz & Doyle prospered and grew into a silk-stocking business law firm. Upon the old man's death five years ago, Doyle took unfettered control and rewrote the firm's history to a version more to his liking. He claimed Kravitz spent his days defending drunk drivers in traffic court and bailing hookers out of the city lockup until Doyle showed him how to really make a buck. Doyle would have renamed the firm *Doyle and Associates*, but he recognized the gravitas carried by the Kravitz name.

When the bonuses slowed after Kravitz's death, Bob chalked it up to normal transition confusion and waited for things to return to normal. They never did. And with all the power in one man, confrontation carried risk. But Bob had to act. Bills demanded payment. He had a forty-two-hundred-dollar monthly mortgage, utilities, maintenance, car payments on his BMW and her Porsche, the club dues, the vacations, the credit cards. Payroll withheld half his paycheck for taxes and insurance and medical and on and on. And, of course, he had to provide for his beautiful Heather, for whom a "balanced life" meant shopping, being coifed and pampered weekly at the spa, and in the evening meeting the needs of a hard-working husband. He'd do anything to keep her fulfilled.

Bob cleared his throat and stiffened. "Mr. Doyle, I wanted to ask about the bonuses."

Doyle's grin evaporated, but Bob continued.

"We closed the Myers deal in January and the Penske acquisition two months ago. When Mr. Kravitz was still with us, bonuses paid out immediately when the funds arrived. And now—"

Doyle's eyes narrowed. "I thought you wanted to make senior partner, Baldwin."

"I am, sir, but the delay in payout is causing some hardship. And, of course, now the Worthington bonus is also due—"

"Due?" Blood vessels in Doyle's nose throbbed red and his face blotched, even under the golden tan. "Every partner takes home a substantial draw each month. A bonus is due when I say it's due."

"Yes, sir. I understand. It's just that—"

Doyle leaned forward and interlaced his fingers. "Bob, have you ever wondered how we got that massive oak table into the conference room?"

The change in direction caught Bob off guard.

"We saw that table and wanted it," Doyle said. "What did we do? Get a smaller table? No. We wanted *that* table." He raised his eyebrows. "So, how'd we get it in?"

"The elevator?"

"No. Wouldn't fit. It's a solid hunk of wood cut from one tree, thirty feet long, seventeen hundred pounds."

"Then I don't know."

"We put a crane on the roof, hoisted the table up the side of the building, removed the plate glass window, and brought it into the conference room. That cost twenty thousand dollars."

Bob stared blankly.

"My point is, to get ahead in this business, you have to think outside the box. Be bold. Like you did in the Worthington deal. You get ahead by grabbing the world by the balls and taking what you want, not by following the rules. Otherwise, you're a drone working for someone else, like that loser Gifford."

"George?"

"Yeah. That tree-hugging faggot has been an associate for fifteen years. If he had any self-respect, he'd quit. But he doesn't. Why? Because he's an employee." His face flushed. "He barely makes his two thousand billable hours a year." He pulled out a white handkerchief and sopped the sweat on the back of his neck. "So why do I keep him around? Because we pay him eighty bucks an hour and bill the client two fifty. He makes us a shitload of money."

"George isn't gay, Mr. Doyle. He's got four kids."

Doyle stood. "Stay the course, Bob." He put his hand on Bob's shoulder and shepherded him toward the door. "One more deal like this and that senior partnership is yours."

Bob found himself alone in the hall as Doyle's door clicked shut behind him. His face throbbed with burning blood. One more deal?

CHAPTER 2

"Order up," Lester called through the pass-through as he slid the two plates on the counter and dinged the bell. Grace appeared, slipped another order into the clip, and winked. She grabbed the two plates, spun around, and disappeared into the crowd. Lester's pass-through was his window into the diner.

The restaurant buzzed with morning conversations, clinking of plates and glasses, and the plaintive wail of the cowboy crooning from the jukebox. "My wife ran off with my best friend," he cried. "And I miss him." The smell of bacon and coffee permeated the busy diner. Most of the clientele wore jeans, boots, and work shirts, and cowboy hats outnumbered baseball caps. Two boys wore little league uniforms with *Mountain West Grizzlies* embroidered on the back. The morning sun streamed through the plate glass windows. The beep of the door sounded as more customers entered from Main Street. G&L's Diner was sandwiched within a line of thriving enterprises—a bookstore, flower shop, two taverns. Across the street stood the beauty salon, bakery, and hardware store, and down on the corner, the minimart and doughnut shop. Street parking had even become a problem.

Lester watched Grace hustle about, slinging plates, filling coffee cups, and working the register. A stunner in her youth and still lovely at forty-five, each wisp of gray hair and line in her face wove the tapestry of a hard life.

He cracked an egg in each hand and slid the contents onto the grill. Grease spat in protest of the intrusion on the hot metal. A couple slices of bacon and a spatula full of home fries followed. Three seconds. Truly a thing of beauty. Lester was the maestro, and G&L's Diner the eating and social center of downtown LaPlante, Idaho.

"Order up," Lester said. He wiped his face with his forearm. With a pot belly, thinning white hair, and twenty-year seniority over her, Lester didn't look like a man who would have a beautiful wife.

Grace pulled the popped toast, grabbed the plate and the coffee pot, and spun around. A black-clad man leaned over the counter and held up his hand, stopping her. "I need to see the kitchen, too," he said.

"Go crazy," she snorted with a head tilt. "Look wherever you like. I'm busy." She hurried off with the plate.

The man bulled through the swinging door, past Lester and his ballet of grill-top magic. Luis, yellow rubber gloves to his elbows, whistled as he scrubbed a pot in the sink.

"Where's Hector?" the man said. With *ICE* emblazoned on his black jacket and the front of his black baseball cap, he wasn't a stealthy hunter.

"Who?"

He snorted. "Hector Martinez."

"I don't know no Hector Martinez," Luis said, rinsing the well-worn pot.

The Iceman walked to the screened back door, ajar and gently slapping the jamb to the music of the cool spring breeze. He gazed at the pine forest that started beyond the dumpster and ran down the valley and up the mountain beyond.

"We don't employ no illegals here," Luis said.

Lester saluted as the man stomped out past Grace, wiping a table for four factory workers coming off shift. "What'll it be, boys?"

"How about a kiss, Grace?" the biggest one said.

"My husband doesn't like me kissing the customers."

"When you get tired of the old coot, you know where I live."

"I sure do. With your wife and two kids."

His buddies howled.

"But she wasn't second-runner-up Miss Idaho 1992."

"That's ancient history, Ronnie. Four coffees?"

As the stream of customers rolled in, the front door beeped continuously. Mountain West Fabricators blazed along at full production, running three shifts a day. With so much overtime, some workers turned it down, even at double-time, and the company had to bring in part-timers and temps to meet production quotas. Shift change around here had become a madhouse. Grace had even hired a couple of high school girls to help wait tables.

Luis banged pots in the sink. "Hey, Lester," he said. "How come you call this place G&L? Why is *Grace* the first thing in the name? You're the man."

Lester slid two plates into the pass-through and dinged the bell. Grace grabbed them and stuck up four more orders on the clips.

"She isn't just the first thing, Luis. She's *every* thing." A line of orders hung over the pass-through like a string of mountain trout. "Criminy. I can't keep up. I've never seen it this busy." He opened the refrigerator. "Luis, we're running out of eggs. Head over to the U-Save and get us twelve dozen."

"But I'm not done here."

Lester's head tilted toward the back door. "Hector will finish up." A young man sauntered in, brushing pine needles from his pants.

"Right." Luis snapped off his gloves, handed them to Hector, and hurried out.

Lester's dancing spatula froze. He grimaced and massaged a growing ache in his left shoulder.

Hector walked over. "You okay, Boss?"

Lester waved him off. "My arthritis. I'm fine. Got to cook." A line of orders hung over the pass-through. His forced smile became a grunt of pain as another wave shot through him.

"Let me take the grill, Boss." Hector draped the yellow gloves on the sink. "You take a break." He placed his hand on Lester's back and guided him toward the dining room.

Later, as Lester sipped coffee at the counter, Grace put her hand on his shoulder and kissed his neck.

He looked up from his newspaper. "Who are the suits?" Two men in coats and ties occupied a corner booth, their briefcases on the floor.

Grace shrugged as she refilled his cup from behind the counter. "Don't know. Never saw them before. Lawyers?"

A vein bulged in Lester's forehead as he grunted.

"They ordered poached eggs," Grace said. "So I'm thinking city boys from back East."

Lester combed his fingers through his thin hair. At sixty-seven, he didn't need this aggravation. Most of the diner folks talked excitedly about the Mountain West merger rumors and believed the hype that it would bring great things to the town. As unofficial town elder, Lester normally kept his concerns to himself. No need to cause alarm. He looked up at Grace. "The last company Worthington bought, the town went dead as that moose." The animal's mounted head protruded from the wall.

Lester would do whatever it took to protect Grace. This business had to thrive. And that needed a healthy community. But corporate suits and their lawyer stooges would happily sell out the working man if it would add a nickel to their dividend. "I wonder what they're up to?"

She raised her eyebrows. "Ask them."

"I think I will." He rose from the stool. "I'll welcome them to our friendly town."

As soon as he stood, the shoulder pain became intense. He grimaced and buckled over, his forehead on the counter and right hand clutching his left shoulder.

Grace cradled his head from behind the counter. "Lester?" she said. "Lester?"

She dialed 911 as Hector and Luis raced from the kitchen and laid him out on the floor. He stared at the ceiling, the suits standing nearby. Grace hung up the phone and came to him. She kneeled and cradled his head in her arms. "Don't leave me, sweetheart. Help is on the way."

He stared up at the silk-tied suits observing the show and moved his lips, but the elephant on his chest stopped the words. Grace put her ear to his lips.

He whispered, "What's black and brown and looks good on a lawyer?" Her warm tears fell onto his cheek.

"What, baby?" she said.

"A Doberman."

CHAPTER 3

Heather lounged on the chaise, slathered in cocoa butter and absorbing the first warm rays of the late April sun. Her long, toned legs glistened, stretching from her gold anklet to her sculptured buttocks—bronze hemispheres defined by the string between them. Her bikini top straps hung from the sides of the chaise, exposing a lineless tanned back from hips to blonde ponytail.

Heather was an artist. A fit body was her brush, sensuality her paint, and matrimonial optimization her masterpiece. Previous canvases had been her apprenticeship. She had been trading up since her teens. Bob was her third marriage, not including the annulment at eighteen. Now, at thirty-two, she had a husband on the fast track to great success and, with it, a life of luxury for his loving wife. After years of honing her craft, she had finally bet on a winning horse. Pliant, naïve, and career-driven, Bob had huge earning potential.

Her diamond earrings, worn even at the pool, sparkled. The delicate gold anklet glinted in the sun, and her white bikini accentuated her golden tan. And though clothes, shoes, jewelry, and accessories consumed much of her labor, it wasn't all about shopping. Her craft demanded tenacity, discipline, and time. She had endured braces, teeth whitening, and nips and tucks; spent hours at the fitness center working with her personal trainer; and was coifed weekly at Richard's Pinnacle Salon by Richard himself.

When she got her first whiff of Bob three years earlier, she was already disillusioned with her second husband. It happened at the summer soiree that the firm threw every year. Only the lawyers, staff and their significant others received invitations, but crashing was never difficult for a beautiful woman.

"We're an M and A firm," Bob had said when he discovered her, alone and sitting next to him at the bar. She displayed her bewildered pout. "Mergers and acquisitions," he said. "When businesses buy each other out and consolidate."

She opened her azure eyes wide. "That sounds fascinating." She traced her turquoise nails across his forearm. Within three months, she had divorced number two and was living in Bob's condo.

But even with stunning natural beauty, one did not rise in her craft without eternal vigilance. Someone was always gaining. So, fresh from her Brazilian bikini wax, she sported the "Bermuda Triangle," having been in a traditional mood. Her nails had been bespeckled at the salon by eighty-pound Vietnamese women while she sipped cucumber water. Even the bottoms of her upturned feet, exfoliated by exotic hands and softened with emollient, exuded sensuality.

A swarthy pool boy dipped a net into the water. His muscular arms and legs protruded from the loose Hawaiian shirt and baggy shorts and promised a solid build beneath. His flip-flops slapped the bottom of his feet as he walked around the backyard pool in the lengthening afternoon shadow of the McMansion that Bob and Heather Baldwin called home. He snared a small island of leaves in the net on the metal pole and tilted toward another just out of reach.

Heather opened one eye and sighed. "Go around to the other side. It's closer."

Showing his white teeth, the man grinned broadly. "I can make my pole longer, Mrs. Baldwin." His calf brushed against her shoulder as he passed.

"Don't do that, Ricardo."

She glanced next door where the Simpsons sipped iced tea at a wrought iron table on their back patio. Mike Simpson read his newspaper while Millie glared at Heather. When Millie's lips moved, her husband lowered the newspaper and peered over his reading glasses across the yard. Heather allowed the hint of a smile to grace her lips as she slid on her darkly-tinted sunglasses. She rolled on the chaise and settled onto her back, her golden breasts jiggling, constrained only by string and two postage-stamp-sized patches of fabric draped over the hidden stem of each grapefruit. As Mike's mouth dropped open, Millie leaped up, grabbed her husband's arm, and hustled him into the house.

Several minutes after Ricardo gathered his cleaning supplies and disappeared into the pool house, Heather tied the strap of her bikini top, stood, and did her stretching exercises. She put on the robe and adjusted the neckline. She undid her ponytail and shook her head, sending the blonde locks cascading about her shoulders. Mastering one's craft required habit, perseverance, and discipline. But in addition to keeping herself irresistible to her husband, the mistress-of-the-manor's duties also included handling staff. She yawned, glanced around, and slipped into the pool house.

Bob hissed through clenched teeth. "One more deal like this. That's what Doyle said. One more deal like this." He looked around at the restaurant lunch crowd and lowered his voice. "I've made the man millions."

George pointed with his fork to the pickle on Bob's plate. "You going to eat that?"

Bob shook his head. "I don't think he's ever going to make me a senior partner." His face burned. "Grab the world by the balls, he said." He slapped the table. "I'll grab *him* by the balls." A nearby diner stared and Bob lowered his voice again. "I've had it up to here."

George speared the pickle. "Are things okay at home?"

"Heather? Of course. We're solid. This isn't about her." He leaned forward. "But yeah, what kind of man can't provide for his wife? And how could a woman respect him?" Bob grimaced and swallowed the bubble of bile that had invaded his throat. He wasn't about to let a third-rate lawyer like Doyle screw him over. That aging pretty boy should be a male model pitching Viagra to the senior set instead of having control over Bob's life. "I want my money."

"I'd tread lightly, my friend." George crunched on the pickle. "Remember what happened to Rachel."

A first-year associate, Rachel McDonald had claimed Mr. Doyle made inappropriate advances. Bob liked Rachel, but she suffered the recent misfortune of a liberal arts education, complete with safe spaces and the neutering of sexism. Aging hippie college professors and Volvo-driving, planet-saving, committee-meeting law faculty did not adequately prepare their wards for the real world. Sue Mr. Doyle and get justice? Try getting an attorney in this town to take that case. Even if you did, you'd be up against H. Meriwether Doyle, the most powerful lawyer in the state, friend of judges, politicians, and business leaders, and practitioner of the scorched-earth litigation philosophy. Even the Women's Rights Consortium wouldn't touch it. By the time the dust settled, win or lose, you'd be deader than disco. A week after she filed the discrimination complaint, she found herself unemployed and unemployable.

"She moved to Alaska," George said. He pushed his plate away, pulled out his keychain, and twisted the small Rubik's Cube.

"What's Rachel got to do with my bonus?"

"It's the same lesson. You don't cross Doyle."

Bob put his palms on the table. "I don't care anymore. I've got expenses."

George glanced around and cleared his throat. "There's another, um, *factor*." George was never one to be stealthy, so Bob's attention focused. "You think *you've* got expenses?" George said. "What about Doyle?"

"What about him? He makes a ton of money."

"And he spends a ton and a half. A mansion on the water, a Bentley, a yacht, that not-so-secret love-nest penthouse condo on Fifth. His lifestyle isn't cheap."

"Neither is mine. What's your point? I should feel sorry for the guy?"

"My point is that his extravagances are the reason you're two bonuses behind."

"What are you saying?"

"The man's a thief, Bob. He's been playing fast and loose with the trust account ever since Mr. Kravitz died."

Bob's head spun. "What?"

"He *borrows* client money from the trust account. When a deal closes, he returns the money he *borrowed* from the last deal. Or two deals ago. Then chintzes on the bonuses to make it up. Or eliminates them altogether."

"That couldn't work."

"I know. It's a Ponzi scheme and requires bigger and bigger fees to cover the money already taken. But the fees have continued to grow, thanks in no small measure to your hard work, so he's been able to pull it off."

"But it's unethical. And stupid. He'd be disbarred. He could lose everything."

"Bob, you've been cloistered in this building too long. Powerful men believe they can get away with anything."

Blood drained from Bob's face. "Even he couldn't be that stupid."

George shrugged. "Look at the evidence. How do you think he can afford those trips to the islands, to Vegas, to Europe? And everything is first class."

"Okay. He spends a lot. It's circumstantial evidence. That doesn't make him a thief."

"There's more." George leaned closer. "Betty in accounting. Our kids are in the same school. We've had them over a couple of times."

"Betty wouldn't tell you this."

"Not at work. But after a few wines she becomes, shall we say, loquacious."

"And reveals confidential information?"

"She's a regular blabbermouth. Her husband tries to shut her up. They need both their incomes. Anyway, they came over on Saturday. On the second bottle of chardonnay, Betty dropped a bomb. Doyle issued himself a four-hundred-thousand-dollar bonus three weeks ago." George paused to let it sink in. "And the Worthington fee hasn't even come in yet. He's taking other clients' money, Bob. And he's been doing it for years."

"That's not possible. The Executive Committee has to approve a disbursement over twenty thousand dollars."

"Wrong again, Bob. Doyle has a special executive code in agreement with the bank president, his pal Oglethorpe, which allows him to make withdrawals. Bank software does not question transactions that use the code."

Bob clenched his fists.

"And that's why the bonuses are slow in coming," George said.

"We're going to have it out," Bob said. "Right now."

"That's a losing strategy." George picked up the solved Rubik's Cube and randomized the faces. "It's basic game theory. If you let your opponent know what you're going to do, he can counteract it. You've got to keep him guessing, stay one move ahead. Or better still, several moves."

Bob stood, pushing his chair back with his calves and tossing his cloth napkin on the table. "Screw game theory." He pulled out his cell phone and dialed his secretary. "Doris, tell Mr. Doyle's assistant I'm on my way over. I need to speak to him. Now."

He jogged across the street, dodging pedestrians and the corner hot dog vendor, and into the office building elevator. On the thirtieth floor, Doyle's secretary Martha guarded the gate. "He's in conference. You can't go in."

Bob reached for the doorknob.

"It's locked," she said.

"When will he be done?"

"I don't know, Mr. Baldwin. He's interviewing an associate."

"Since when does he interview? Who is it?"

She glanced around and leaned forward. "It's Susan."

H. Meriwether Doyle rocked in his huge leather chair, rotating slowly left and right on the swivel, admiring the tasty morsel sitting beyond the grand mahogany desk. He wet his lips and squinted over his readers.

"Tell me, Ms. Farrington," he said, "how do you expect to succeed at this firm with a lax work ethic?"

He removed his glasses. His gaze roamed slowly over the petite woman forty years his junior, shifting in the client chair, dwarfed by her surroundings. She had rolled her hair and clipped it back, and had applied no makeup other than a hint of lipstick to her pale face. She could make herself as schoolmarm-ish as she liked, but she couldn't hide those luscious bumps and curves beneath a sexless tweed suit.

"My little girl Winnie had the flu, Mr. Doyle," she said. "She had a 104-degree temperature." She tucked her elbows into her sides, crossed her ankles and pushed them beneath the chair. Her hands clenched and unclenched on her lap as she stumbled over her words.

He leaned forward and stretched his lips across his straight, white, $50,000 teeth. His gaze was drawn to the burgundy scarf, the only color she wore. He liked that. A simple school girl in a modest uniform. "I understand that, of course," he said, "but will the associate review committee?"

She unclenched her hands and began rotating her wedding band. "Shouldn't I be talking to Mr. Baldwin about this? He's my supervising partner."

"Normally, yes. But I've taken a special interest in your career. I can see you have great potential."

Her dossier contained the news of her separation, juicy gossip which had spread through the office like the flu in January, and for the last three months, she had struggled with babysitter costs, school loans, car payments, housing costs, and all the other demands of a young professional living in an expensive city. The report also showed zero social life. Doyle didn't keep dossiers on all employees, only the interesting prospects.

"I believe your six-month probation ends next week," he said, "I could put in a good word if you'd like." His starched white shirt gleamed beneath his crimson power tie, and his pressed suit coat draped from a hanger by the bar. Radiating concern required effort, but his confidence and ravenous appetite did not. "Shall we discuss it over lunch?"

"Mr. Doyle," she said, "of course I would appreciate any help you could give me. I ... I need to keep this job. But ..." her voice trailed off, her gaze fixed on the Persian carpet beneath her feet.

He examined her carefully, letting the silence do its work. When she glanced at the casting couch, and then as quickly away, he knew she understood the price. "I'm afraid you're only averaging fifty billable hours a week." His mouth dropped in a disappointed pout. "New associates are expected to bill sixty."

She straightened up. "Mr. Doyle, I can give you more hours."

He didn't want more hours. He only wanted a few minutes.

"Ms. Farrington." He donned his expression of empathy. "Susan." He rose, circled the desk, and took the client chair next to her, pulling it closer. He sensed no perfume, but her citrus shampoo put them on a tropical beach. "I'm sure we can work this out."

When their knees touched, she recoiled. "Please, no," she blurted out, appearing startled by her own reaction.

His face soured. "I'm sorry we won't be able to help each other." He stood. "Thank you for stopping by."

"But Mr. Doyle ..." she started, but fell mute when he tilted his head and raised his eyebrows expectantly. Her shoulders sagged as she heaved a sigh. She rose and left the office quietly, pulling the door closed behind her with its metallic click. Too bad. She would have been a delightful afternoon diversion.

CHAPTER 4

Private detective David Dawson looked down the bar and raised his glass. The bartender approached, but without the bottle of bourbon this time.

"Don't you think that's enough for tonight, Dave?"

Dave shook his glass, rattling the cubes. The bartender sighed, grabbed the bottle, and poured another double. Dave cradled the glass in both hands, inspecting the brown liquid. He looked up at the bum in the mirror. Salt and pepper stubble may be rugged on a male model, but on that guy, it said *homeless*. Shaving was like working. If you didn't do it every day, you were a bum. Dave had worked every day since his eighteenth birthday. And, until recently, had shaved too.

"I used to nail bad guys, Al," he slurred at the bartender rinsing glasses. "Guys who deserved it. Then I'd go home at night to my beautiful family. I had it all."

Sleuthing used to be fun. He tracked down embezzlers, con artists, insurance defrauders. But in recent years, his cases had devolved into nailing the little guy. Instead of exposing crooks, he had become a hammer for The Man. A powerful political candidate used photographs of his married opponent in a gay nightclub. A large insurance company parleyed an ancient drug conviction against a policyholder into denial of a legitimate claim. And corporate employers were always looking for leverage against trouble-making employees.

Dave finally protested when his boss Frankie asked him to investigate the sex life of a young store clerk. "She's just a kid," he said.

Frankie shrugged. "Business is business."

Dave sucked the elixir through the dissolving ice cubes. Even the booze didn't dull the memory of that one. Marla Wiedelbaum, a nineteen-year-old Shop-N-Go clerk, had made corporate trouble. She kept refusing her supervisor's sexual advances and finally complained to upper management. Dave put together a dossier, including a video of her drunk and slutty at a party. She was fired, shunned by her family, and lost custody of her young daughter when her marriage broke up and her life spiraled out of control.

Frankie praised Dave's great work, but the penetrating blue eyes that peered back from the bar mirror judged him harshly. He downed the last of the brown liquid, paid the tab, and dropped his feet to the floor. He rose unsteadily from the barstool and tottered toward the exit, centering his steps between the neon beer signs in each window. He pulled the door open and the bell jangled as he stepped out onto the dark sidewalk. A cold night wind slapped his face. He pulled up his collar against the assault and walked south on Market Street toward his sleazy apartment, a few hundred steps away.

The detective agency operated out of a storefront down the block toward the wharf in the new, up-and-coming commercial district that had not yet come up. Though decrepit, the neighborhood met Dave's needs: an aging apartment building with economical rents, the tavern close to work, and a minimart on the corner for his grocery needs. He could walk to everything in his life, which reduced his chances of another DUI. Everything, that is, except Tracy.

He twisted the key and the lock clicked. As the door creaked open, a dim hall light raced across the threadbare carpet into the dingy studio apartment. A pizza box lay on the kitchen table. Embedded in the collapsed top, his Detective-of-the-Year award lay where he had tossed it weeks earlier. Tomato-sauce-stained, the plexiglass obelisk was engraved *Dave Dawson*. Frankie had gotten the idea from an employee motivation seminar on late-night television while her live-in girlfriend spent the evening beefing up at taekwondo.

Dave went to the refrigerator, popped a beer, and collapsed on the sofa. He hadn't always lived this way. He used to be Mr.

Suburbia, with a ranch house, two cars, a wife and beautiful little daughter. Backyard cookouts. Yard work on the weekends. Neighbors whose names he knew. But he started bringing home his disgust from work. Then the booze. And then the arguments. Everything fell apart. Acrimonious and exhausting, the divorce dragged out over two years. Dave got Tracy every other weekend and two weeks in the summer. He lived for those moments. She was the only point of light in his life, but a brilliant one. He moved into this dump to be better able to support her. Besides, he didn't need much. A bed, a computer, a refrigerator.

He took a long pull on the cold beer. His laptop dinged an incoming email. Frankie. A link to the local news. *Jailhouse fight sends detainee to hospital. A brawl broke out in county jail this afternoon, sending one detainee to St. Patrick Memorial. Inmate Marla Wiedelbaum, arrested for marijuana possession, is expected to make a full recovery.*

Marijuana possession? This had the vengeful client's fingerprints all over it. When he scrolled down, Marla's face appeared—a gash across her forehead, split lip, a chipped tooth, and hair splayed out like a thorn bush.

He couldn't take any more. He hit *reply* and typed. *I quit.* His finger hovered over the *enter* button when he saw Tracy's picture on the end table. He exhaled and his hand fell to the sofa. Dave needed this job. He needed to support Tracy and wasn't qualified for anything else close to his salary. He had barely limped over the finish line in high school, but his obsession with the burgeoning internet made him a master of online research and a great detective. Without his research skills and tenacity, he'd be slathering hot tar on a roof at minimum wage, wondering at forty-five how long he could keep it up.

He finished the beer and hurled the can. It missed the garbage by a wide margin and clattered across the floor. He reached for Tracy's smiling picture, picked up the frame, and stared at the beautiful child. He had taken the photo last year on her eleventh birthday. They had bowled and laughed and eaten hot dogs and soda. He sighed. He couldn't quit. He'd endure anything for Tracy.

And it wouldn't get better anytime soon. Frankie had snagged the mother lode of clients, Henry Doyle, a sleazebag lawyer downtown who wanted to ruin anyone who crossed him. His firm specialized in business consolidations and insurance defense. But their information needs far exceeded their areas of specialization. They wanted research on opponents, their families, their attorneys. Searches of public documents, marriage and divorce records, criminal offenses, traffic tickets, social media, even bank records. This firm didn't like to lose cases, and information was power. If their opponent had a secret, the client wanted it. And the deeper and dirtier, the better.

"Plus, the guy has a taste for the ladies," Frankie said. "And we're talking young here, okay? The guy's a detective's wet dream."

Dave had worked cases for Doyle to squelch sexual harassment complaints, a cocaine-fueled party in a Plaza Royale hotel room involving underaged prostitutes, parties on his yacht that got out of hand. And of course, the drunk driving incidents. The lawyer even kept tabs on his own people. Dave had recently put together a dossier on one of the firm's own lawyers, "in case she made trouble," according to Frankie. Dave remembered the photo clipped to the file. Her youth, high cheekbones, and smooth skin made her offense easy to guess.

His head fell back against the sofa cushion as his mind swirled in the pool of alcohol. Dave wasn't a detective anymore. He was an advance man for a predator. A pimp.

CHAPTER 5

The morning sunlight from the east-facing window warmed Bob's neck. Its cheery light drove the darkness from his office, but not the gloom. Across the desk, Susan Farrington was vanishing. Already a slight woman, she hunched her shoulders and bowed her head. Even her voice had diminished to a whisper.

"I thought...I hoped you might be able to... you know, as my supervising partner, you could..." A raspy cough choked off the words.

Bob pushed a Kleenex box across the desk.

"I worked so hard to get here. What I sacrificed..."

She drew a tissue and dabbed her puffy eyes.

"I brought home the family paycheck, and Brian stayed home with Winnie. I think he felt emasculated, and I hated being away from our daughter. Plus, one salary didn't cover everything. We fought, he left, and so I have to pay for childcare too. And now this..."

Bob cleared his throat. "The review committee recommended your contract be renewed." He shifted in his chair. "While *I'm* satisfied with your work, the senior partners have the last word. I'm sorry. I tried. There's nothing more I can do."

Bob liked Susan, and he'd enjoy giving Doyle a good eye-poke, but he needed his bonus and wanted that promotion. He couldn't afford to confront him. "I'm so sorry."

"Thank you for trying, Mr. Baldwin. I understand. You've been so kind. It's just that I'll never get another job in this market."

Bob swallowed hard against the lump rising in his throat. "What will you do?"

She shrugged. "Go home to Ohio and stay with Mom and Dad for a while. They love having Winnie in the house. Maybe I can find some work there." She drew another tissue and blew her nose. "I was so proud of being a lawyer. No one thought I could do it." She looked up with a brave smile. "I guess they were right."

Bob reached out to touch her but thought better of it.

"I'll be all right," she said, standing. "Thank you for everything."

Bob jumped up and accompanied her through the door. He wanted to tell her that he understood, that he hated the swine, and that nobody had been screwed worse by Doyle than he had. But he knew the my-problems-are-worse-than-yours approach comforted no one. "I wish you the best."

Doris looked up from her desk with concern. "Good luck, Ms. Farrington. We'll miss you." Then she turned toward Bob. As her withering stare bored into him, he retreated into his office.

On Friday afternoon before the long Memorial Day weekend, Bob struggled out the front door of the office building, his arms sore from the briefcase in one hand and the two accordion files in the other. After four weeks of nonstop work, the Jensen deal was finally coming together. Bob had drafted the documents, worked with Jensen's in-house counsel, and attended numerous negotiations between the merging companies. The mind-numbing work had driven him close to exhaustion, but that senior partnership would be worth it.

George waited at the curb, his hands empty. His wife Connie pulled up in their Prius. George slid into the passenger seat and kissed her on the cheek. She placed her hand under his chin and kissed him back, a love light shining from her soft, almond-shaped eyes.

Connie caught Bob staring, and gave him a quick smile and wave. His head bobbed a return hello.

George put his arm out the window. "Bob, we're going to barbeque tomorrow afternoon, just the family. Why don't you and Heather join us?"

The thought of an afternoon with good friends washed over him like a warm tide. Eating cheeseburgers and chips on a backyard picnic table, kids playing in the yard, Heather in a flowered sundress, holding his arm and laughing.

He sighed. Who was he kidding. Heather would hate it.

"Thanks." Bob raised his folders and briefcase. "But I need to finish this."

George and Connie looked at each other. She slipped the car into gear, and the couple headed toward their weekend. Alone on the sidewalk awaiting the valet, Bob's shoulders sagged under the weight of his load.

On his drive home, black clouds gathered and spit rain against the windshield as fast as the wipers pushed it away. But when he got to the house, the moon peeked through, and Heather met him at the door.

"Let me take those, sweetheart." She set the files on the hall table and handed him a drink. Her robe draped open at the neckline and her long tan legs rubbed against him.

"What's going on?" he said, his suspicion not the only thing aroused.

"Nothing, baby." She kissed him. "I just missed you."

When they last made love, as he lay gasping for breath, he saw their intertwined bodies in the dresser mirror. She stared over his shoulder at the muted television and an emerald bracelet dangling from the wrist of a shopping-channel hand model.

"You're not still upset about the accident, are you?" Heather said.

"Of course not, sweetheart."

As she moved, her silk robe slid across the smooth curves of her round breasts, interrupted only by the rise of her nipples.

"You weren't hurt." He shuddered as he inhaled her perfume. "That's all that matters."

She had totaled her $60,000 Porsche, forgetting to set the brake or turn the wheels toward the curb. While she revitalized at the spa, it had rolled into the river.

"I thought you were avoiding me." She pushed against him and her robe parted. "Let me make it up to you." That night, she gave him her undivided attention.

Later, as he lay spent on the tousled, black silk sheets, staring at the ceiling, he remembered the love light in Connie's eyes when she looked at George as they drove away in the dented Prius.

Bob turned his head toward Heather's half-open eyes. Even now, sated and exhausted, he still desired her. She had beauty, class, and sensuality. But something was missing. As she draped her arm across him, her fingers drawing small circles on his chest, he realized what it was. The light in her eyes shone not with love, but with determination.

"I stopped by the dealership this morning, sweetheart," she purred, kissing his ear. "They have a beautiful 911. Carmine red. It's perfect for me."

After half a night of fitful dozing, capped by an hour staring at the ceiling, Bob gave up on sleep. He tapped his cell phone app to start the coffee and padded downstairs. It wasn't much before his usual 4:30 a.m. wake-up, and he had work to do.

He passed through the living room adorned with fashionable furniture, objets d'art, sophisticated wall hangings, and all the other clutter they had accumulated. He flicked on the kitchen light, poured his waiting coffee, and opened his laptop on the island. Copper cookware hung over granite kitchen counters littered with gadgets—a wine station, a bread maker, a juicer, a rotisserie, and a ten-thousand-dollar Victoria Arduino Espresso Machine that Heather needed for a "complete kitchen." George may have had a loving wife, four kids, and a house full of motion and noise and love, but he didn't have an espresso machine. Only a Mr. Coffee.

A column of creditors filled his inbox with the familiar bills—mortgages on the house and timeshare in Florida, lease payments on the Porsche and BMW, the Visa and American Express, department store charge cards, club dues, doctor and hospital bills for Heather's medical procedures, utilities, and a dozen others.

Without bonuses, his monthly draw from the firm had not covered expenses for some time. George was right. It wasn't what you made. It was what you spent. And Bob had been juggling payments for months. Throw one more bill in the air, and the performer would collapse like a broken-legged ballerina.

An email popped up with a ding. First Fidelity, the lien holder on the Porsche. He tapped a key. *Dear Mr. Baldwin: Global Insurance Group has classified the damage to your vehicle as "total" and has remitted the limits of* *the policy. Unfortunately, our lien exceeds that amount by $9,974. Please remit that sum to satisfy the loan. Thank you for your prompt action.*

His hand trembled. For the first time in his life, he couldn't meet his financial obligations. He leaned forward onto the granite counter and dropped his head into his hands.

Bob lived the same day over and over—the same study, same work, same headache, same pills, same coffee, same tremors. He took a shower, popped a couple antacids to keep the bile down, and kissed Heather's forehead above the eyeshade. He started the car, opened the window, and lit a cigarette. He inhaled several deep drags. It helped with the tremors. He'd figure out something. Heather would understand.

After ten hours at work finalizing the Jensen paperwork, he sent it to Doris.

"Tell Mr. Doyle's secretary it's done," he called through the open door. He massaged his temples. If measured by suffering, this would be his best work. He'd now demand that senior partner's chair. Doyle would have no choice. This deal would bring in millions.

He closed the documents on his screen and opened his financial news feed. *Worthington Industries stock up fifteen percent since announcement of merger with Mountain West.*

His head pounded.

The company announced today that significant efficiencies have been gained by the consolidation of manufacturing facilities. Personnel impacted by the plant closings will receive outplacement services and retraining where appropriate.

His headache grew to an 8.5 on the agony scale. As he reached to shut down the computer, an email appeared with a beep. The subject line read, "Bob, wasn't this one of yours?" He clicked on the link. A news story appeared.

An unemployed Jonesboro man fell from the Tri-city bridge on Tuesday. Anthony Genetti fell to his death at 2 a.m., according to a witness. Authorities do not suspect foul play and have classified the incident as a suicide. Family members confirm that Genetti had been despondent since being laid off from Merckle Manufacturing six months ago, following the company's merger and reorganization. A memorial service will be held...

Bob swiveled to the window and the dreary sky as the fog rolled in. His chest pounded and he gasped for breath. His arms went limp as he crumpled forward and the world became black.

Bob opened his eyes to the pattern of white, acoustic ceiling tiles and the smell of antiseptic. A plastic bag of clear fluid dangled on a stand. He followed a small hose to a needle, the business end of which disappeared under a swath of tape attached to his arm. A hospital. What happened? A heart attack? Stroke? Brain tumor?

He sensed movement and calmed, anticipating Heather's soothing touch. He looked to his right. A white-coated man stood over him. "It wasn't a heart attack," the man said. "Our tests show everything is normal. My best guess is a panic attack." The doctor lifted the chart. "But we'll keep you twenty-four hours to be safe."

Bob glanced around the room. No visitors.

"Someone's here to see you," the doctor said.

Bob's gaze shot to the door, awaiting the sensuous figure.

"Hey, buddy." George sauntered in as the doctor left. "You scared us." He sat in the bedside chair. "Where's Heather?"

Bob shrugged and looked away.

"So, what are you in for?" George's face became serious. "Tell me it's nothing."

"Doc says I'm stressed out."

George snorted. "I've been saying that for years."

An hour later, Heather appeared and George hurried out.

"Sorry," she said. "I called. The nurse said you were resting. So I went to my hair appointment." She examined the tube in his arm, sat, and rested her hand on his chest. "How can I make you feel better?"

Be with me when I need you. Love me. Drive a Chevy. He sighed. "There's nothing you can do. I'll be okay."

She squinted at him. "Are you mad at me?"

He turned his head away. "No, Heather." His Adam's apple bobbed as he swallowed hard.

"What's wrong, baby?"

Tears filled his eyes. His words caught in his throat, but he managed to croak. "Am I losing you, Heather?"

She appeared stunned. "What? No. Don't be silly. I had a hair appointment, and rescheduling Richard takes weeks. He's *very* busy."

"I don't mean that. I'm no good for you like this."

"Bob, you'll be back on your feet in no time."

"What if we can't meet each other's needs?"

Her brow furrowed, then the corners of her mouth twitched upward. "Oh, I see." She glanced at her Cartier, pulled the curtain closed around them, and reached under the sheet and squeezed him. "Have you thought about the Porsche?"

"Good afternoon, Mr. Baldwin. My name is Dr. Alvarez."

Bob closed the Jensen file George had smuggled in.

"Our tests reveal nothing organically wrong."

Bob slipped the folder under the bedsheet. "Then I'm okay?"

"I didn't say that. We just can't detect the root cause of the problem, what caused your collapse. That's why your internist asked that I speak with you. I'm a specialist in stress-related disorders."

"A psychiatrist? Are you saying I had a nervous breakdown?"

"We haven't used that term in years. But stress can manifest itself in many physical forms. It's your body's way of saying 'slow down.'"

"Doctor, I don't need a shrink. What I need is to get out of here. I have work to do. Important work."

"More important than your health?" He donned a sincere look. "How are things at home, Robert?"

"I'm living the dream, *Jason*," he said, glancing at the doctor's nametag. "I have a gorgeous wife, a beautiful house, and drive a BMW 650i."

The shrink interlaced his fingers. "And how's work?

"Great. I made $280,000 last year." Without bonuses.

"Is it fulfilling?"

Bob didn't like the direction of this conversation. "I don't work to be fulfilled. I work for money. Isn't that why everyone works? Isn't that why *you* work?"

"Of course. But we need balance in our lives."

Bob's lips flapped as he exhaled. "You don't understand, Doctor. I have obligations. I have a wife and a home and a mortgage. What would you suggest I do?"

The doctor leaned forward and interlaced his fingers. "I would suggest you modify your behavior. Stress is wreaking havoc on your body. When you got here, your pressure had spiked sky high, 200 over 120. I've given you a prescription for blood pressure meds, which you'll need to stay on for life if you don't manage the stress. The pounding in your temples, the headaches, the tremors and other symptoms are likely to recur. Next time, it'll be a stroke or an aneurysm or a heart attack." He tilted his head. "You need to remove the source of your stress."

"That would require quitting my job."

"What do you do?"

"I ruin people's lives."

"I see. Is a career change possible?"

What world did this guy live in? Forty-one and at the top of his game, Bob worked sixty hours a week just to keep the alligator fed. He couldn't leave. Remove the source of his stress? That would mean making amends to all the people he'd hurt, but he couldn't exactly give Anthony Genetti his life back.

"Okay, I'll slow down. I finished a big case at work this week. I'll have some downtime. I promise."

"Good." The doctor stood. "And it might help the anger issues." He left the room.

Anger issues? Bob wasn't angry, he was broke. He gathered the folders and returned to work that afternoon. His coworkers greeted him cheerfully, Doris had set a fruit basket on his desk, and Doyle gushed over the Jensen work.

"This is outstanding," he said during his sixty-second visit, pumping Bob's hand. He grinned like the Cheshire Cat. "I have a surprise for you."

Bob stopped breathing. His bonuses.

Doyle produced a folder and dropped it on the desk. "Trans-Global Communications. We just got it. They're buying Telecom Français." He beamed. "Our biggest deal ever. And it's all yours. My number one hitman."

Heather sat cross-legged on the great-room sofa, applying fusion-pink polish to a nail as *Flip This House* played on the sixty-inch screen. She found it fascinating how attractive they made an old house with a little creativity and a lot of money.

A key in the latch startled her. She glanced at her Cartier. 6:00 p.m. He never came home this early. Bob walked in without his briefcase or files. That was *very* unusual. She closed the polish bottle and set it on the coffee table. "What's the matter, Robert?"

He collapsed on the sofa next to her and took a breath. "We need to talk."

Uh-oh. Surely he hadn't got wind of Ricardo. But she wouldn't put anything past Millie, the mega-nosy neighbor.

"I'm afraid we have a problem." He wrung his hands in his lap. "A money problem."

Bob never talked about money. Never. He began explaining his cases, and his bonuses, and his draw, and his percentage as a junior partner. He said Mr. Doyle this and Mr. Doyle that, and Associate so-and-so was fired because she wouldn't sleep with him and it wasn't fair, but Bob couldn't do anything about it.

She stifled a yawn as he rambled on. Doyle screwed him out of his bonuses, kept breaking promises, and dumped a pile of work on his desk an hour after Bob had been discharged from the hospital.

He took her hand.

"I didn't get my bonuses, Heather."

"What are you saying?"

"I'm saying things are tight, and we're going to have to take some steps to turn this around."

This did not bode well. They never discussed money, nor did she care to. Did he want to conscript her as an ally in his troubles?

"First, I'm afraid we'll have to skip Europe this year."

Her mouth fell open. "The river cruise? But I already bought my wardrobe. I was so looking forward to it. You and me, alone, floating by medieval castles and sipping Champagne."

He squeezed her fingers. "I'm sorry, sweetheart. It's only temporary. We'll go next year. I promise."

She pushed out her lower lip.

"Next, we have to reduce discretionary spending."

"You mean my clothes?"

"Among other things."

She stood and put her hands on her hips. "Bob, the summer soiree is next month, and I have nothing to wear."

"You have a closet full of evening gowns. You look terrific in any of them."

She tried to glare but wasn't sure if she had it quite right. She'd never had to glare at Bob before. So she switched to the pout. That one she had down cold.

"And finally, the Porsche will have to wait a while."

Bob never denied her, but now the no's rained down.

"So I'll be taking the bus?" That was a good one.

"No, baby, no. We'll get you a car. But the 911s cost a fortune." He massaged her hand. "Maybe a Jaguar. We can probably swing a lease for that."

Heather sighed. She didn't need him to explain. She needed him to fix this. And if he couldn't, she could.

"How can I help, Bob?" She tapped a fingernail on the glass-topped coffee table. "Maybe I can talk to Mr. Doyle."

"You? You barely know him."

She shrugged. "We've met a few times. I think he likes me. Maybe I could persuade him."

"Thank you, Heather." He took her hand. "But I wouldn't want you to do that."

"I'd like to contribute. It's for us."

He shook his head.

"Let's leave it open," she said.

For the next month, Heather doubled up on her hours at the fitness center. On the elliptical, the wrap-around mirrors showed the tight leggings that clung to her sculpted buttocks, and firm thighs and calves. She admired her round biceps, well-defined obliques, and tight abs. She nodded approvingly. Any strategy included looking good. But knowledge was power, so she googled *H. Meriwether Doyle* and read every hit—his legal bio, social activities, news reports. She studied his business, his clients, his professional associations. She ran image searches that yielded pictures of him with politicians, business leaders, and celebrities. Anything and everything. After weeks of research, she was ready. She'd get what she wanted.

CHAPTER 6

A tanzanite-blue BMW 650i rolled to a stop under the pillared portico of the Pinnacle Club. A black-vested valet leaped forward and opened the passenger door. The teenager's eyes grew wide as a long, tanned, shapely leg emerged, a golden anklet resting delicately above a Christian Louboutin pump. He stared, mouth agape.

The owner of the leg cleared her throat, and the valet returned to earth and offered his hand. The shoe clicked on the cobblestone as Heather Baldwin rose into the light.

Her husband stood from the driver's seat, adjusted his cummerbund, and rounded the car. Heather placed her arm around his. This last accessory completed her ensemble. They strode to the entrance. Two equally agog doormen parted the doors, and Heather and Bob stepped over the threshold.

The Kravitz & Doyle Summer Soirée was the social event of the year. The firm pulled out all the stops—uniformed valets, an ice swan sculpture and champagne fountain, a six-piece band playing Sinatra and other tunes of Heather's grandparents' generation. Dozens of tuxedoed men and evening-gowned women laughed, danced, and drank exotic concoctions.

Heather felt the impact of her aura as she stepped into the club. Heads turned and the din of the ballroom ebbed. A woman scowled and elbowed her gaping husband, the clarinet player missed his cue, and a tuxedoed waiter collided with a pillar, launching a tray of canapés onto surprised revelers. Time slowed as Heather floated down the stairs. From an unopened bud at fourteen, to a blossom at eighteen, and to a fully-flowered peach bloom at thirty-two, Heather was at the apex of her beauty. Like the peach bloom, the fruit had ripened to perfection, curvaceous and delicious, and all men salivated for a taste.

At the bottom of the stairs, the crowd parted as the huntress passed. Across the room stood H. Meriwether Doyle, working one of the single women allowed to slip in without an invitation. He spotted Heather. His slack-jawed gaze followed her ample cleavage and long legs, barely covered by a gossamer-thin gown with no hint of undergarments. She glided through the room meeting and greeting others. The stalking cat drew ever closer to her prey. When she judged his anticipation had peaked, she entered his orbit.

"You've met Heather," Bob said.

"Indeed, I have," Doyle said.

"Mr. Doyle," she purred, offering her hand.

"Please," he said, taking it in both of his. "Call me Henry." He brought her fingers to his lips. "Truly a pleasure."

She blushed and looked down. When she raised her gaze, her dark eyes smoldered. "The pleasure is mine," she said, squeezing his fingers.

She sensed Bob's unease as he shifted awkwardly, but it couldn't be helped.

"Any word on the Worthington fee?" Bob said.

"Nothing yet." Henry's gaze did not leave Heather. "But let's not talk shop now. It's time to enjoy the delights of the evening."

"And the Jensen file?"

"Great lawyering, Bob. Work that kind of magic on the Trans-Global deal, and you'll be a senior partner."

Bob's eyes grew wide and his mouth dropped open. Heather's time had come. She turned to Doyle. "Are you going to ask a lady to dance, Henry?"

Doyle placed his hand on her waist. "May I have the pleasure?" His fingers slid down the small of her back as he led her onto the dance floor.

"He's been so angry lately," she whispered.

"He hasn't faced his illness," Henry said. "He's in denial."

Her face blossomed into a smile. "Denial isn't just a river in Utah."

He laughed and squeezed her hand. "Beautiful and clever, too."

She tilted her face upward to within an inch of his. "I don't believe in denying myself." His face pinkened with the flush of desire. "He wouldn't get me a 911 or even a Boxster," she said. "He got me a Jaguar." She pronounced it Jag-u-ar, in three syllables. "It's a Ford, Henry."

A commiserating nod accompanied his fingers drawing her closer.

"I'll bet Mrs. Doyle doesn't drive a Ford," she said, nodding at the woman seated at the bar.

Bob stood frozen on the dance floor, his heart throbbing in his neck. One more deal? Jensen was supposed to get him the partnership. And Worthington before that. It was always *one more deal.* The truth hit him in the solar plexus like an artillery shell. Doyle would never make him a partner. And if bonuses ever came, they'd be dribbled out, small and late. Doyle was using Bob like he used George.

A heat of rage burned his face. He marched to the bar and raised a finger at the bartender. "Scotch. Rocks." It came in an instant. He took a sip and placed the cool glass against his forehead.

"I'd strangle him for you, Bob," a voice slurred, "but I'd have to touch him to do it."

Doyle's wife Pamela, perched on the adjacent barstool, sipped Champagne from a crystal flute. She wasn't drunk, but she wasn't sober either. Though still a beautiful woman, she was north of fifty, and Bob saw the work she'd had done. Her eyes were too open, her neck too taut and forehead unfurrowed. The sun that for years had provided the beautiful tan now claimed its payment—prematurely aged skin that no amount of emollient could repair.

"I heard about the hospital, Bob." She put a hand on his arm. "I hope you're feeling better."

"Thanks." He'd always liked Pam.

Their spouses glided across the dance floor. "Your boss doesn't respect marital boundaries," she said.

Bob shook his head. "I asked her to talk to him." He drained his glass, most of the alcohol absorbed before it got to his stomach. He ordered another. He swirled the amber liquid, clinking the cubes. "It's not what you think."

Pam snorted. "It's not?" She took another drink. "Look around." She swept her arm across the room. "It's an auction, Bob. The goods go to the highest bidder."

Throughout the ballroom, couples in small clusters chatted, the wives clinging to their husbands' arms and the husbands gazing at the lithe bodies of the younger wives and young female associates gyrating on the dance floor.

Heather led Doyle onto the patio overlooking the golf course. As persuasive as she could be, Bob doubted she could flatter Doyle into granting Bob his bonus.

"People are just enjoying the evening." Bob said. "It doesn't mean anything."

"It doesn't? How do you think I became the third Mrs. Doyle?"

Bob downed his scotch. "It's not about my wife, Pam. Your husband broke a promise to me."

She snorted. "He's been breaking promises to me for twenty years, starting with our marriage vows." She sipped her Champagne. "He openly humiliates me now, in front of my friends." She put her face in Bob's and waved a finger near his nose. "He even had a fling with a high school girl, for Christ's sake. They only had one thing in common: they were both seniors."

She drained her glass and Bob signaled for another. "He thinks he can do whatever he wants." Her drink appeared. "He didn't even hide his Viagra." She giggled "So I threw the pills out and filled the bottle with tic tacs." She took a sip. "Now he locks them in the desk with his other secrets. He thinks I'm stupid. I've had a key for years."

As Doyle and Heather returned through the patio door, Pam threw back her drink. "Someone should wipe that smug smile off his face."

She slouched over the bar and slurred badly. He felt pretty loose, too. "Pam, this is about money." He lowered his voice to a whisper. "He owes me $300,000."

"Money?" She waved her hand. "That's easy." She wobbled her flute, spilling Champagne on her hand and the bar. "You just take it." She pursed her lips. "You know, that's a good idea. Make the son of a bitch pay. He's spending *my* money, and yours, on his girlfriends. The trips, the boat, the love nest. I'll hit him where it hurts. In the wallet. Clean him out. He won't have enough left to take his bimbos out for a beer and a taco."

"A divorce?"

"No. Empty his bank account."

Boy, she *was* drunk. But he liked her sweet dream.

"I don't think so, Pam."

She cackled and looked left and right. "Do you want your money, Bob?" She leaned forward and wiggled her finger for him to come closer. "I know where he hides the code."

Bob drove home in silence, Heather holding his hand and staring out the window. At the party, he hadn't seen much of her. This was her night, and he didn't want to hover, so he spent most of the evening talking to friends and their spouses. Pam was a mess. He glanced at his beautiful wife's profile. He would never do that to Heather. In twenty years, he would still love her as much as he did tonight. Perhaps more.

At home, Bob removed his cummerbund and tossed it on the bed. "Did you have a nice evening, sweetheart?"

Heather did not answer. She seemed distracted as she entered the bathroom. The shower came on. He was in bed when it stopped and the bathroom door opened.

"Did Doyle say anything about—" Bob's breath caught as she came out in a negligee.

She slid next to him between the satin sheets.

"You look amazing," he said.

Heather put a finger to his lips. "Shhh."

She attacked him with a brutal passion, a ferocity unknown to him. She had never before finished seeming so exhausted. Or satisfied. He would find a way to give her what she deserved.

He increased his hours at work to late into the night. His headaches and insomnia returned. He researched the Porsche 911. Maybe he could swing it. Carmine red.

Three weeks later, Heather surprised Bob when she entered the kitchen, her terrycloth robe as unrevealing as a nun's habit.

"Heather?" He put his coffee down on the granite countertop and glanced out the dark window. "What are you doing up?"

She perched on a stool across the island. "We need to talk."

He stared at her. "Why? What happened?" Panic welled up.

"I need—" She raised her gaze to his. "I need time to think."

A jolt of adrenaline clobbered him. He grabbed the counter and braced himself.

"I don't understand. Think about what?"

She sighed. "About us, Robert. We need some time apart. I'm sorry."

He moaned, "No," and dropped his head into his hands. "Please, Heather, don't do this." He grabbed his briefcase and fumbled inside. "Look." He came up with a Porsche brochure. "The 911. Carmine red. We can swing it."

She tilted her head with a sympathetic smile, like a mother consoling a child distraught over a lost doll. "It's for the best, Bob."

Bob stood. "I didn't mean it about tightening our belts. Everything's okay. I'll get the money." He reached for her hand. "Please, Heather, you're everything to me."

She pulled away. "You need to go to work."

Driving to the office, fatigue overwhelmed him. He could barely turn the wheel. His temples pounded. Bile rose in his throat. Pam had been right. Doyle wanted to take Heather from him. It wasn't her fault that Bob couldn't provide for her. It was Doyle, tempting her with his wealth and undermining Bob by withholding his. Did he plan it this way all along? The son of a bitch was a monster.

At the office, Bob couldn't work. From his desk chair, he stared out the window at the cityscape below. The rising sun reflected off the river. Office workers hurried into the city. The sky brightened from pink to azure as if nothing had changed.

He only had himself to blame. Doyle had warned him. Grab the world by the balls. Doyle wasn't going to give him anything. Not a bonus, not a partnership, not Heather. He had to take what belonged to him. He should go to Doyle's office and throw him out the fucking window. No one would blame him. But George's words returned. "Game theory. Stay several moves ahead and never betray what you're thinking."

He picked up his cell phone from the desk and dialed.

A barely audible voice answered. "Hello?"

"Pam?"

"Yes?"

"You were right."

"What?"

"Doyle. The son of a bitch is after my wife."

"Who is this?"

"Bob. Bob Baldwin. We talked at the soiree."

"Oh, yes. Hello, Bob."

"I'm ready."

"I don't understand."

"The code. I'm ready to do it."

"I can't do that," she whispered. "Please don't call me." The phone clicked.

As the morning passed, Bob opened and closed files, checked email, and stared out the window. He couldn't concentrate. Doris popped in and out with files, and looked at him with concern.

"I'm going to lunch now, Bob."

As she left, he rested his head on the desk.

Bzzzt.

He looked at the phone. Pam. He pressed answer.

"Take the money," the voice slurred. "Take it all."

A glass broke.

"Oops." She giggled.

"Pam? Are you okay?"

"You get your bonus and I get my revenge." A ten-digit number appeared on the screen. "It's a win-win."

Bob moved to the guest room at Heather's request. On a temporary basis. Once he got his bonuses, he would straighten everything out. His plan was simple. He would wait for the Worthington fee to come in, get into the firm account using Doyle's code, and take the $300K in fees owed to him. Then he'd surprise Heather with the car she wanted, pay down the credit cards, and return to her loving arms. Yes, it sounded mercenary, but Heather liked nice things, and she deserved them. And Doyle wouldn't squawk. He did owe Bob the bonuses and, besides, Doyle had been pilfering from the firm account for years. He didn't need any scrutiny.

On Thursday, the Worthington fee arrived and the funds would clear the next day. Friday morning, Bob knocked lightly on Heather's closed door. Then again.

"Bob, please," she said from within.

He cracked the door open, and a beam of the hall light raced across the carpet onto her tousled sheets.

"I'm sorry to bother you," he said, "but I wanted to tell you I'm going to fix everything. I'll have a surprise for you tomorrow."

"I'm going away for the weekend, Robert. I need time by myself. Please close the door."

His heart sank from her coolness as he pulled the door shut, but she would change her mind when he gave her the car. He knew what she needed.

Being summoned to the corner office didn't surprise Bob. He had finished the Jensen merger, and Doyle always took an interest when a big deal neared the finish line. Bob entered without knocking.

Doyle sat at his desk, a USB key dangling from the computer. He quickly pulled it out and locked it in a drawer. He came around his desk. "I've been concerned about you."

Bob stood, rotating the huge globe. He put his finger on a spot and examined it. "Why's that, Henry?" he said from across the room.

"How's your health? You okay? You're not going to have another, um, event, are you?"

"I'm great."

"You can't let it affect your work." Doyle walked over and put his hand on Bob's shoulder. "Stay the course." He guided Bob toward the door. "Oh, and wrap things up on Jensen next week. I'll be out of town for a long weekend."

"Glad to, Henry," Bob said.

"In fact, I'm leaving for the airport now." Doyle saluted. "You have the con."

By 9:00 p.m., only a few of the most gung-ho associates lingered. Bob doused his desk light, slipped down the darkened hall and into Doyle's unlocked office. He pried loose the ancient desk lock and opened the drawer. A USB key lay in the pencil tray. He fired up the computer, inserted the key, and selected *Kravitz & Doyle Trust Account*.

The screen blinked and refreshed. Wow. The fee had come in, and the account balance showed $3,200,521.67.

After a few keystrokes, a box popped up. *Transfer funds to.* He typed in his new offshore account routing numbers.

Another box appeared. *Enter amount.*

He typed $300,000.

Enter transfer authorization code.

He pulled the slip of paper from his pocket and entered the ten-digit code.

The screen blinked. *Verifying…*

As he waited, he glanced in the open drawer. A word caught his eye. *Porsche.* He pulled out the papers. A lease for a Carmine Red 911. Bob froze. The son of a bitch. Rage rose in his throat. Steady. Focus. Stay on task. He examined the other papers in the drawer. It was Doyle's itinerary. Two round-trip tickets to Bermuda and four nights at the Royal Grand Cay, beachfront balcony. First passenger, H. Meriwether Doyle. Second passenger…

Bob blinked.

…Heather Baldwin.

His vision blurred and skin burned as though scalding water pulsed through his veins. His temples throbbed in agony. As waves pounded the beach beneath the balcony of their luxury hotel room, he saw Doyle touching Heather, pleasing himself with her precious body. He squeezed his eyes shut, but the image remained. He shook in a feverish delirium.

The screen continued to blink. *Confirm Transfer Amount: $300,000.*

With perspiration dripping into his eyes, he entered a "2" after the "3," changing $300,000 to $3,200,000. He didn't remember hitting *Enter.* Gradually, the blinking screen came into focus.

Remaining Balance: $521.67.

He gritted his teeth. Buy her a car with that.

CHAPTER 7

Lester scraped the frying egg from the griddle and flipped it over. It landed with a splat. Like a rivulet from a broken dam, the breached yolk coursed across the metal and surrounded the black bacon that smoldered nearby.

"Damn."

He threw the spatula down. These hands once danced across the stovetop like a maestro conducting the Philharmonic. Now, they couldn't even fry an egg.

"I got it, Boss." Hector left the pile of dishes in the sink and picked up the spatula. He scraped off the mess, cracked a couple of eggs, and dropped bacon and hash browns onto the crackling grease.

Lester's head drooped as he sighed. Beyond the window, Grace scurried about.

"How's Luis's mother?"

"She's real sick, man. He's not coming back." Hector flipped the eggs with style, like a dance. "You going to replace him, Boss? This diner isn't a two-person job."

Two-person. Grace and Hector. Lester no longer counted, as useless here as Luis in Guadalajara. While Lester only took up space, Grace worked fourteen-hour days, waiting tables and helping Hector clean up after they closed, then came home and took care of her invalid husband.

Lester picked up his cane and hobbled through the swinging door into the dining room. He lowered himself onto a barstool, hung the cane on the counter, and unfolded his newspaper. That was his contribution now, sitting on a stool while his wife worked nonstop.

Grace scooted behind the counter and poured him a coffee. He grunted his thanks and looked across the half-full eatery. After the factory closed, most businesses in town slowly died. But the diner survived. And the tavern. People had to eat. And drink.

"How many meals did you give away today?"

She wiped the counter around his mug.

"We're not running a soup kitchen," he said. "You can't work for free."

"Not free, sweetheart. On credit. We keep a tab."

A wisp of graying hair stuck to the perspiration on his beautiful wife's forehead. "Why do you do it?"

Hector called, "Order up," and she reached toward the window.

"Because these people are hurting." She picked up the plate. "Because they're our friends and neighbors." She kissed his bald scalp. "And because I know how it feels."

He opened his mouth to object as she hurried off, but no words came. She knew about hardship. Though her life had begun full of promise as a popular beauty queen, several years in an abusive marriage and then raising a troubled son alone sent her spiraling downward. When Lester met her, she struggled as a waitress, alone and reclusive, leaving her trailer only for work. Though twenty years his junior, she accepted his marriage proposal and became his partner in the business and in life. She had been safe, and that was all that mattered.

But now, with Luis gone, the Iceman lurking, and his own slow recovery, Lester had to worry. Johnny's upcoming parole hearing might be a game changer. Grace's ex had done twenty years for murder. Could Lester keep her safe if that cretin showed up?

More plates clattered in the window. Grace retrieved them and raced away. She was a one-woman show, and he, a eunuch. He couldn't help at the diner, or at home, or in the face of danger. What kind of life was that for her? If he'd bought life insurance when he had the chance, he'd have options. If some accident should befall him, Grace would have been protected. He buried his eyes in his palms. How would he get out of this mess?

Lester needed a miracle.

Bob roared down Interstate 95 in full panic mode. What had he done? Where would he go? How could he have been so impetuous? All his life, he'd been a plotter. That's how he made deals work. Devise a plan and follow it. Why hadn't he stuck to the plan? Take the $300K, *his* $300K, then wire it back from offshore and show up for work Monday morning. Doyle couldn't prove a thing. But Bob had acted on rage. On impulse. With no thought of the end game, or even of what would come next. Confused and plan-less, he raced for who-knows-where. Brazil? Paraguay? Maybe a South Pacific island, with its warm breezes, white sand, and rhythmic waves. Rhythmic waves. The Royal Grand Cay. Doyle and Heather. Tears blurred his vision.

Away from the city lights, the stars were a thousand eyes accusing him. Bob wasn't a thief. He should return the money. But to whom? Doyle would just steal it. Including Bob's share. He shook his head. What a mess.

He needed to formulate a new plan. Concentrate. He squeezed the steering wheel until his fingers cramped. He slowed his breathing. Okay. First, get the money. He hadn't even gone home. He had his briefcase, wallet, and the clothes he wore. Fortunately, he carried his passport in his briefcase.

He drove for eighteen hours. By the time he got to Miami, he knew he would give the money back. He just didn't know *how*.

He caught a plane and landed in Georgetown Saturday night. He cringed every time he used his credit card, a beacon that told the world his location. But he had no cash. Yet. He stayed in a small hotel, and tossed his gray business suit for flowered tropical wear, a straw hat, and flip flops.

On Monday morning, banker Smith, a light-skinned black man or a dark-skinned white man in a white linen suit, greeted him warmly. "Mr. Baldwin, it's good to meet you." He led Bob into a private office. When seated, the banker frowned. "We have a little problem."

Bob's stomach sank.

"We received an amount ten times our agreement. $3.2 million vs. $300K. This isn't New York. It will take some time to assemble that much cash."

"How much time?"

"Three, four days. A week."

"I'm on a tight schedule. You can't do any better than that?"

"Possibly." He cleared his throat. "But that would entail additional fees."

"How much?"

"Another, say, three percent?" It came out as a question. "On top of the agreed-upon ten percent."

When lubricated with cash, the wheels of banking can move quickly. That afternoon Bob walked out of the bank with two cases holding $2.8 million, and over to the fifty-grand yacht charter.

"How about girls?" the captain said.

"No, I only need transportation."

"With no girls, it don't look like a pleasure cruise to customs."

Bob sighed. "How much?"

"Five thousand."

Bob nodded.

"Each." The captain grinned broadly.

Two days later, they crossed under the Sunshine Skyway Bridge into Tampa Bay and docked at the Davis Island Marina. A customs officer checked Bob's passport and tapped on his terminal. Bob held his breath.

"You've been out of the country four days?"

Bob feigned a casual, "That sounds right."

"So, you flew out and cruised back?"

"I'm an M-and-A lawyer. My work is stressful. Sometimes I need a break."

Bob looked at the girls. The customs man looked at the girls.

"Welcome home, Mr. Baldwin." He stamped the passport.

Bob hopped a cab to a lot on Nebraska Avenue and bought a used car. On the passenger seat, he tossed a Chamber of Commerce brochure from the Worthington merger file. Some mountain town in Idaho, small, laid-back, and remote. A perfect place to relieve one's stress. And to disappear.

But what would he do with all this money? Hide it? Live on the run? It wasn't his, most of it, anyway. Whose was it?

CHAPTER 8

H. Meriwether Doyle felt terrific. Back from the most erotic five-day vacation ever, he found himself both exhausted and exhilarated. An acrobat of a woman, that Heather Baldwin knew her stuff. The buzz of the first two drinks soothed him as he poured himself another scotch at the mahogany bar in the corner of his office. And as if things couldn't get better, a huge fee had arrived. He had won the trifecta—sex, drugs, and money. True, Baldwin had not yet wrapped up the Jensen file as ordered, but Doyle wasn't going to let that spoil the moment. The gutless pansy probably went off to lick his wounded ego.

Two partners relaxed on the sofa, each holding a drink. Doyle swirled the cubes to cool the amber liquid and took another sip. "So, Mother Superior assembles the nuns and tells them, 'I have to report there's a case of gonorrhea in the convent.' An old nun in back whispers, 'Thank God. I'm so tired of chardonnay.'"

The three men roared with laughter as a shadow appeared in the doorway.

Doyle glared. "What is it, Githens?"

"There's a problem, sir." The manager of accounting sopped his brow with a handkerchief.

"Gentlemen." Doyle nodded toward the door, and the other two hurried out.

Githens shut the door and stood like a man facing a firing squad. He swallowed hard. "It's the Worthington fee, sir. It's missing."

Doyle froze. "What do you mean, *missing*?" He approached the bow-tied dork. "Four million dollars is missing?"

"Not quite four million, sir, but still—"

"Four million?" Doyle bellowed. He grabbed the weasel by the lapels. "How could four million go missing?"

The miserable worm looked ready to faint. "Someone electronically transferred it the evening it arrived."

"It came in last Friday. You spent a week jacking off before you noticed?"

"Oh, no, sir, I checked it with the bank right away. The withdrawal used an executive code, and the bank let it go through. You were incommunicado, and I wanted to check with you before I took action. I didn't know if the transfer was, um, authorized."

Doyle released the man and went quiet. He walked to his desk, opened the drawer, and spotted the USB key in the tray. "That's not possible."

"There's something else, sir," Githens said, his voice quavering.

Beads of perspiration tickled Doyle's forehead.

Githens cleared his throat. "That's the same day Bob Baldwin disappeared."

Doyle's vision faded to a blurry pink, his head pounded, and a roar of agony reverberated through the office. The little bastard got the code. Doyle would gut him like a fish and feed his entrails to the rats. Son of a bitch.

"We don't know he took the money, Mr. Doyle. We only know it's missing. And he is, too. He could be the victim of foul play."

"We can only hope." Sweat poured down Doyle's face. He strode angry circles about the casting couch.

"Should I call the state's attorney, sir?"

"NO!" Doyle's hand shook as he pointed a finger at the incompetent bean counter. "Tell no one." He headed to his door and yanked it open. "Martha, get me that dyke Fontaine."

CHAPTER 9

Three days after squeaking through customs, Bob approached LaPlante and saw the Mountain West Factory. He recognized it from pictures in the file, but its gate was now chained and padlocked, and weeds grew through the asphalt parking lot. He pulled the ten-year-old gray Honda into the Motel 6 on the highway. It looked closed with only one car in the lot. In the morning, he drove to town and parked right in front of G&L's Diner. The main street had plenty of parking spaces. This sure beat twenty dollars a day at a city parking garage. A homemade going-out-of-business sign hung in the flower shop window next to the diner. Down the street, several other stores appeared closed as well. But the neon beer sign in the tavern across the street flashed its enticing escape.

As he walked in, the bell over the diner door beeped. The quiet and inviting place smelled of breakfast cooking and coffee brewing. He took a corner booth.

A waitress approached with a mug and a pot.

"Coffee?" She dropped a menu on the table.

Bob nodded.

She set down the cup and poured. Her graceful beauty startled him. Close to his age, she wore no makeup with her hair pulled into a simple ponytail, a stark contrast to the exquisitely coifed wives of his law partners.

She stepped to another table. A lone man with his head bowed whispered. Bob heard "Grace" before the voice faded. The man would not meet her eye.

"That's okay, Billy." She put her hand on his shoulder. "We'll put it on your tab. What'll you have?"

Bob ate his breakfast in silence. On the second morning, he exchanged a few words with Grace, and then decided to ask.

"Is there any work around here?"

"Not since the factory closed." She refilled his mug. "This town is hurting."

"Do *you* have any jobs?"

"For you?" She looked at his shiny loafers. "Nothing you'd be interested in."

"I lost my job." Both his hands clasped the mug. "I need something. Anything. I'd work for meals."

Her hard eyes softened. "Can you wash dishes?"

Bob was in the zone, scrubbing pots and staring out the window at the pine forest and mountain beyond. His yellow-gloved hands moved mechanically, washing the plates, rinsing the glasses, and scraping the silverware. But in his mind, he stood by a rocky outcropping, jutting above the tree line. A cool breeze caressed his cheeks and the scent of pine filled the air. The view from this small kitchen window stirred him more than any cityscape had from his thirtieth-floor office. He had stopped shaving the day he left, and the two-week growth of facial hair threatened to become a beard, speckled with gray and adding ten years to his age.

Bob closed the faucet, snapped off the gloves, and draped them over the drying rack. He stepped out the back door into the cool mountain breeze, and down the three concrete steps. The screen door spanked the jamb before coming to rest.

As he lowered himself to the bottom step, a twinge of arthritis shot through his right knee. Rigid, unforgiving concrete pressed against his bottom. His hand reached beneath his dishwasher's apron and came out with a pack of Camel cigarettes, a matchbook tucked within the cellophane. He shook the pack and withdrew a cigarette with his lips, struck a match, and cupped his hands around it as it sputtered and ignited in a bright flash. When the flame calmed to a warm yellow, he brought it near and drew in. The flame curled into the tobacco, and the embers glowed a bright orange. He took a long, slow drag and inhaled deeply. When the nicotine molecules passed through the membrane of his lungs into his blood cells and flowed to his brain, the rush was like the first sip from a mug of steaming coffee on a cold morning. As he exhaled the cloud, the mountain breeze claimed it for its own and carried it away. He placed his hand on his sternum. No more heartburn. He gazed at nature's tapestry and submerged into a trance.

"What'd you pay for them shoes?" a voice said through the screen door.

Bob glanced down at his Gucci loafers. "Those are from a different time, Hector." He held up the pack. "Smoke?"

Hector seemed surprised. "Okay." He bounced down the steps, sat next to Bob, and lit up. "So, where you from, Bob?"

"Back East."

"You come out here to pursue your dishwashing career?"

Bob smiled. The mid-morning sun painted the rocky mountain crest, and fir trees swayed in the valley below. As they smoked in silence, a flock of honking geese passed overhead toward warmer climes. Bob finally broke the stillness.

"What do you want, Hector?"

The younger man squinted. "From you? I don't want nothing from you."

"No. From life. What do you want from life?"

Hector paused. Then his eyes lit up. "I want a Camaro, man."

"That's all?"

"I don't see you driving no Cadillac. What do *you* want?"

Bob took another drag. The ember on the tip of his cigarette glowed as orange as the sun sliding behind the mountain ridge. When he exhaled the smoke, the wind whipped it until it vanished. What *did* he want? Love that isn't blown away by the first adverse wind.

A voice came from behind. "I don't pay you to smoke." Wearing her waitress apron, Grace's beauty was undiminished by a hard life, and her boss-voice more loving than stern. "We have customers."

Bob and Hector stubbed out their cigarettes on the concrete and marched up the steps like contrite children.

CHAPTER 10

"Ow." Dave winced and brought his bleeding finger to his lips. His attempt to dislodge a jammed stapler with an unfolded paper clip had caused another injury. "Son of a bitch." He opened a desk drawer and pulled out a Philips screwdriver and needle nose pliers.

"You can get another stapler from the supply cabinet, Dave."

"Hell, no. This bastard won't beat me." He disassembled the device, fiddled with it until he unstuck the jammed mechanism, and methodically reconnected each part. Then he tested it on a sheaf of papers with a flurry of palm whacks.

"You're one tenacious bastard, Dave. That's why you're my number one boy."

Dave glanced up. Frankie Fontaine looked sharp in her black suit, pink shirt, and purple silk tie, topped off by her short-cropped black hair, graying at the temples. On the wall hung a poster of Humphrey Bogart in a trench coat with turned-up collar, one eye peeking from beneath the brim of a black fedora, and a smoking .45 automatic Colt pistol in his hand. Her tough-broad persona had built a thriving business. Her business name, *Frances Fontaine & Associates, Private Investigators,* painted on the glass door, mirrored the style of Sam Spade's office. With equal parts show business, financial acumen, and a laser focus on the client, she had built a thriving detective agency. But she checked her moral compass at the door.

"We provide information," she liked to say. "What the client does with it is not our concern."

A year earlier, Frankie had dragged Dave to the pitch that had snagged the Kravitz & Doyle account.

"My stepfather had his way with me when I was thirteen," she told Doyle. "My mother lived in fear and didn't protect me. I ran away at fifteen and never looked back. I got my education on the streets."

Dave had to stifle a snort. Frankie's upbringing more resembled Ozzie and Harriet in suburban Shaker Heights, Ohio. Plaques and photos of her life proudly adorned her office. She played softball and soccer and served as president of the math and chess clubs. She went to Amherst and got a degree in accounting, enjoyed good health, a thriving business, and a live-in girlfriend.

"But you don't want to hear about my life," she told Doyle. "It's not pretty."

"How do you deal with the stress?" He leaned forward and drooled over the salacious story.

Frankie assumed her steely glare. "I go to the gun range every Saturday and unload a few clips into a silhouette that looks like my stepfather."

Doyle had hired her on the spot.

"How do you do it?" Dave said as they left Doyle's office.

"It's advertising." She shrugged. "A little puffery is expected."

The sleazeball even worked out a kickback to bilk his own firm. K&D paid the agency thirty percent above market, and Frankie remitted to Doyle twenty percent.

"And the kickback?" Dave said.

"Signing bonus," she said. "Hey, it's a win-win."

Frankie plopped down on the corner of Dave's metal desk. "Lose the stapler, Dave. I've got a front-burner job for you." She winked. "It's Doyle."

Dave groaned. "What'd the pervert do now?"

"Missing person." She dropped a manila envelope on his desk. "Top priority. Chop chop."

Dave oozed into the plush client chair like an old man settling into a warm bath. Doyle's luxuriously appointed office emitted a feng shui that seduced one into submission. The bar, the couch, the view. This guy knew the ropes. But twenty years of sleuthing had taught Dave that things were not as they appeared and that uncovering the truth required an eye for detail. Like Doyle's coifed and lustrous white mane that waved back to touch his collar, a golden-tanned face too taut for sixty-something, and a mouthful of sparkling teeth, straight and white. With his Armani jacket and Hermès silk tie draped over a bar stool, Doyle exuded casual elegance in an open-collared dress shirt hinting of cologne, manicured nails glistening with clear polish, and emerald cufflinks that matched his tie.

"You said Mr. Baldwin took important information," Dave said. "What information?"

"Why do you need to know that?" Doyle said, his voice deep, rich, and resonant. He might have been in radio. "Just find him." He paced in front of the massive window.

Dave took a breath. "Because if I know *why* he left, it helps me figure where he might have gone, and that's how I find him. You *do* want me to find him?" Dave didn't take any shit from a degenerate like this guy, whale or not.

"Track his credit cards. Or cell phone. Can't you do that? You people are supposed to be pros."

"He stopped using them. He's off the grid. Electronically, at least." Dave tilted his head and waited for an answer.

"He's a thief, Mr... What's your name again?"

"Dawson. Dave Dawson."

"Bob Baldwin stole money from me, Dawson. A lot of money. And I want it back."

Dave pulled out a small notepad. "Have you reported the theft?"

"No. I don't want the police involved. At least not yet. We need to keep this quiet." Doyle towered over Dave. "I just want the son of a bitch back so I can crucify him."

Dave scribbled *Can't reveal theft. Why not?* He appreciated a case to sink his teeth into, tracking down an embezzler, but this Doyle was no prize either. "Help me understand. Why would a partner making a big salary plus bonuses steal from the partnership? From himself essentially. Why kill the goose that lays the golden egg?"

"Because he wasn't a *senior* partner yet. And that made his drawers chafe." Doyle walked to the bar and poured himself a drink.

Dave scribbled *No drink for the help.*

"And because his wife threw him out and he cracked."

Dave didn't need to ask why. He had done his research. Doyle kept an apartment in the city where he crashed at night when the workload supposedly kept him from returning to his suburban mansion, and sometimes all week. In fact, the place was a love nest for his many dalliances, the latest being Mrs. Heather Baldwin.

"He stole a big fee that came in. For a merger we handled."

"Did he work that deal?"

"He participated, but the large deals are under my direction. Worthington Industries, you've heard of them. They bought out a smaller company."

"What company?"

Doyle scowled. "Have Martha check the file." He showed Dave the door.

Martha tapped on her computer. "The Worthington merger," she said. "Here it is. Mountain West Fabricators, LaPlante, Idaho. Would you like a printout?"

Dave had been waiting an hour when Heather pulled into her driveway.

"Sorry I'm late," she said. "Would you mind?" She handed him several packages.

He eyed the Jaguar.

"It's a lease," she said.

He followed her into the house and set the boxes down on the marble tile flooring in the foyer. A circular staircase led to the second floor.

"Nice place."

"Thank you," she said, as she walked into the living room and sat on the sofa. She crossed her legs, clasped her hands on her lap, and tilted her head. Her stare said *Get on with it, I'm busy.*

He pulled out his notepad. "When did you discover that your husband had left?"

"Oh, I don't know. Friday?"

"Didn't he live here?"

"Downstairs."

"He was gone a week before you noticed?"

"We keep different hours."

Bob stared at her, waiting.

She expelled a gust of air. "I was out of town. When I got back, he had left."

She seemed rattled. Go for the jugular. "Mrs. Baldwin, do you know your husband's senior partner?"

She cleared her throat. "Mr. Doyle? We've met."

Beyond the back window, a man skimmed leaves from the pool and glanced toward the house. Heather stood, swished the curtains closed, and spun around.

"Mr. Dawson, Bob and I are separated. We can each do as we please. I'm hiding nothing."

Nobody's hiding nothing.

Dave rang the bell and watched through the glass as a man rose from his easy chair and came to the front door.

"Good morning, Mr. Simpson. My name is Dave Dawson. I'm investigating a missing person. May I ask you a few questions about your neighbor?"

"Police?"

"No. I've been hired by a private party. May I come in?"

A woman raced up. "It's Bob, isn't it. She killed him."

"Millie, please."

"She and that Mexican pool boy. I knew it."

Her husband sighed. "Cuban."

"What?"

"Cuban. Ricardo is Cuban, not Mexican."

"Whatever. She's shameless."

"How long were you Mr. Baldwin's secretary," Dave asked the fortyish woman, impeccably dressed in an older but neat suit.

"Ten years," Doris said. "Since he became a junior partner."

Her hand trembled. He needed to set her at ease. "What's he like?"

Her shoulders relaxed. "He's an excellent lawyer."

"And as a person?"

She smiled. "He's a nice man." She thought for a moment. "Professional. Mature."

"Unlike others here?"

Her eyes widened. She shrugged.

Secretary thinks little of firm's lawyers.

"Weren't you Mr. Doyle's secretary?"

Her eyes cast downward. "That was long ago."

He tried a different tack. "Mrs. Baldwin thinks he went off to lick his wounds. You know, because of their separation."

Doris scowled. When she saw Dave examining her face, it became a mask. "I don't know what to add."

Dave rose to leave.

She held out a hand, then looked left and right. "Mr. Dawson, Bob is an honest man. He must have had a good reason for whatever happened." She hesitated. "Have you talked to George?"

"Personal problems?" George Gifford said. "Yeah, he had personal problems."

Dave's question had lit a fire under Baldwin's friend and former partner.

"His marriage had disintegrated, his boss wouldn't pay him, and he suffered a breakdown. Otherwise, life was swell for Bob."

Dave admired the converted-warehouse-turned-law-office, spacious, sparse, and only a block from Dave's dump. "I'm trying to help him."

"If you want to help him, get Doyle to pay him what he owes, and get him a divorce from his spendthrift wife." He grunted. "As for his health, at least he got himself out of that rat race."

"Where would he go?"

George squinted. "How would I know?"

"Aren't you friends?"

"For twenty years. Since law school." George's steely gaze challenged Dave to call him a liar.

"Is he a person who would disappear? Voluntarily, I mean."

George considered. "I hope so." His eyes saddened. "I don't like to think of the alternative."

Dave placed his yellow pad in the center of his office desk. On the top he wrote, *WHERE IS ROBERT BALDWIN?*

He reviewed his notes and started scribbling.

Boss says he stole money. Wife says their breakup drove him away. Neighbor says wife and pool boy murdered him.

Dave sipped his coffee.

Boss doing wife.

He pulled an earlobe.

Wife doing pool boy.

He wiggled the pencil between two fingers.

Foul play? Doyle offed Baldwin? To get his wife? As a patsy for the theft?

He ran his fingers through his hair. The possibilities were endless.

Best friend quit firm within week of disappearance. Wife living large. Boss won't report theft.

He dropped his head and massaged his eye sockets with the heels of his palms. Interviews were going nowhere. Time to set his nets. He'd already put internet bots on Baldwin, monitoring his credit cards, phone calls, and bank transactions. After Baldwin came through customs a week ago, he dropped off the grid. Dave would have to cast a wider net. He started typing. By the end of the afternoon, search bots scoured the internet for activities of the boss, the wife, and the friend.

CHAPTER 11

8:00 p.m. saw the last customer leave the diner, but Bob couldn't face another lonely evening in his dingy motel room. He missed Heather. He'd been a hermit here for a month, and hadn't had a drink since the summer soiree, a lifetime ago. Maybe a beer would lift his spirits.

He used dirty pool to get Hector to come along. "I'm buying," he said.

The Grizzly Tavern was exactly what Bob had expected—a western roadhouse with a long wooden bar, pine paneling, the dinging of an old-fashioned pinball machine, the clicking of the balls on the pool table, a dart board on the wall, and tables pulled apart to make a small dance floor.

From the end of the dark bar, Bob raised two fingers at the bartender. "Just one," he whispered to Hector when the beers appeared. "I want to stay under the radar."

"You and me both."

The cool brew tingled Bob's throat going down. His tight shoulders relaxed. What was Heather doing right now? He took another pull on the long-necked bottle. A dark shadow descended. Was she still with...*him*? He emptied the bottle. "I need another beer."

They sipped their second and stared at themselves in the mirror. Bob held his hand horizontally in front of his face. It didn't twitch. "I used to have a tremor."

"Like Parkinson's?"

"No, like stress." He pressed the cold bottle against his temple. "I like this town."

The Friday-night crowd started to wander in.

"This is the only place around here that wasn't hurt by the factory closing," Hector said. "People can't pay their rent, but they can afford to drink."

The jukebox volume competed with the growing din of conversation, laughter, and clinking of bottles.

Bob signaled the bartender.

"No," Hector said. "We should leave."

"One more," Bob said as the bartender placed two cold bottles before them.

Three men leaned against the bar next to Bob. One said, "So Darryl and me was fishin' in Donner Creek, and he's taking a leak and a rattlesnake bites him right on the pecker. So I grab the cell phone and call the emergency room and the doctor says we gotta get the poison out right now or he'll die. The doc says, take your penknife, cut an X on the wound, and suck out the poison. Darryl yells, what'd he say? And I tell him, he says you're gonna die."

Bob stifled a guffaw.

The joke-teller signaled the bartender. "Three more," he said with a downward pointed finger circling the bar. "How about you, buddy?" A hand fell on Bob's shoulder. "Can I buy you a beer?"

"Thank you," Bob said, glancing at his watch. "But we have to leave."

Beers appeared before Bob and Hector.

"We gotta go, man," Hector whispered, yanking at Bob's arm. "Under the radar, remember?"

"Okay," Bob said. "After this one."

As Bob's euphoria grew, another bottle appeared.

"I can't let you do that," Bob said. He pulled out his wallet, sheltering it from view. A handful of twenties came out. He took one and stuffed the rest back.

An hour later, a fog engulfed Bob and a pile of twenties lay on the bar before him.

"Let's shoot some pool," someone said, and Bob's new friends picked up their beers and moved to the pool table.

Bob stood, became dizzy, and dropped back down.

"We should go, Hector," he slurred, turning to Hector's empty barstool.

"Is this seat taken?" said a sultry voice.

Bob turned to face a pair of bright red lips, a tangle of blonde hair, and a blouse with the top three buttons undone. Perfume overwhelmed his sinuses.

"I'm Candy," she said.

"I can believe that."

She slid onto the next stool and glanced at the wad of bills crumpled on the bar. "What's your name, big spender?"

"Bob. Bob Smith. But you can call me Bob. Can I buy you a drink?" His gaze roamed up and down her seated figure as he waved at the bartender.

Her gushing over Bob was as sweet as her name. She ran her fingers over his arm, cooed as he bought her another drink, and whispered in his ear.

A man appeared behind them. "Can we talk, Candy?"

She didn't move. "I'm busy."

"I miss you," he said.

Her head jerked to face the man. "Get lost, Darryl. I'm with someone."

Bob stared blankly. Darryl hung his head and shuffled away.

She smiled. "Sorry about that. He's such a loser. These cowboys are all talk. Big hat, no cattle, if you know what I mean."

"Yeah." Bob's head clouded. "No cows."

Bob drifted, immersed in a dark, subterranean lake. He couldn't see. He couldn't hear. The pulsing of the earth's heart coursed through him. Ba-boom. Ba-boom. His head throbbed with each beat. He craved the taste of cool water, but when he swallowed, he gagged, the skin of his mouth and throat sticking, as dry as chalk. He worked his jaw, hoping to coax out some saliva. He tried to open his eyes. His lids seemed stuck together. Finally, one popped open.

A blurry face gradually came into focus. A sideways cherub stared back. The child's face examined him silently. Bob's other eyelid finally broke free. The boy stared until his interest waned and he toddled off through an open door. A TV came on. The whistling introduction to *The Andy Griffith Show*. Bob visualized Opie skipping a rock across the lake.

The left side of his face ached, pressing onto the sheet. A cuckoo clock sprang open and cuckooed seven times, jangling his brain. He groaned. Christ. Late for work.

His eyes roamed the side of the room he faced. Empty beer cans littered a beat-up dresser. A full ashtray lay on the nightstand. The sun blasted through a stained sheet hanging from the window curtain rod. He rolled over to face a naked back, a tangle of bleached blonde hair, and labored snoring. He remembered. Candy.

He looked down. He wore his shirt and one sock. He rose up slowly, lowered his feet to the floor, and waited for the dizziness to subside. His hand touched his face. Deep lines from the crumpled sheet felt imprinted like a wax seal. His cowboy jeans lay inside out on the floor with his Gucci loafers nearby. He quietly rose from the bed, unsnarled and pulled on his pants, and, abandoning the missing sock, slipped into his shoes. He checked his wallet. Seven bucks left out of two fifty. He hurried past the child dwarfed on the dirty sofa, watching Barney Fife practice his quick draw.

He gently pressed the trailer door behind him until the latch clicked, and then hurried away like a man escaping the scene of a crime. He raced past a woman who had paused from watering her flowers, past a faded gray pickup with a shining, cherry-red front quarter panel, and beneath the Mountain View Mobile Home Park sign. He found Main Street, slipped behind the storefronts, and approached the back door of the diner. Ten feet to his right, the dumpster banged. When he pivoted toward the sound, his gaze and the bear's met. He jumped as a jolt of adrenaline slammed him. Racing toward the door, he reached it in a few bounds, grabbed the knob, and flew through.

"A bear. It's a bear."

Hector's apron bore the grease scars of a morning's work at the grill. He called through the pass-through. "Grace. Your bear's back."

A moment later, the dining room door swung open and Grace marched through, her jaw set, anger in her eyes and a pistol in her hand. She tromped out the door, the wind furling her pink waitress apron.

Bob watched, frozen.

"Get away from my dumpster," she yelled, followed by an explosive crack. Metal clanged as the bear clambered out, and leaves rustled as it raced into the woods.

Grace came through the door mumbling with a smoking gun, the pungent smell of gunpowder, and a scowl on her face. "She's not feeding her whole family from *my* trash can." She paused and did a double take at Bob.

He stared back, mesmerized. Her blue eyes pierced his soul. Beautiful, strong, determined. When the spell broke, he shivered, tucked in the dangling half of his shirttail, and snapped on the yellow gloves.

She wrinkled her nose and disappeared into the dining room.

"Did she hit him?"

"Why would she shoot it?" Hector said. "It's only a mama bear scrounging food. It was a warning shot."

"I don't know much about guns." Bob opened the faucet and started scrubbing.

"You don't know much about people either." Hector worked the griddle. "You tossed around money like it was payday, like you're a big shot and they're nobody because they lost their jobs. And grinding against Candy on the dance floor."

Bob's head throbbed from the rising steam.

"She's Darryl's girl. Or was." Hector flipped two eggs with the spatula. "You didn't make no friends last night." He scooped the eggs, bacon, and hash browns from the griddle and onto a plate. "And what happened to 'staying under the radar'? You wash dishes, and you're flashing money like a drug dealer." Hector slid a plate into the pass-through. "You don't know shit about radar, man. You're a lighthouse."

After closing, Bob left the diner for the motel. Hector was right. Bob didn't know much about a lot of things. Like keeping out of sight. Or spending money without a job. Or women.

Under a black, moonless sky, a single pole light dimly illuminated the parking lot next to the Grizzly Tavern. Several men leaned against a pickup, drinking from long-necked bottles. Another pickup pulled out, the gravel crunching and popping until the tires hit the pavement with a squeak, and the truck zoomed away.

One of the men stepped away from the others and started toward him. When he recognized the hulking mass as Darryl, Bob crossed the road and stepped up his pace. The large man crossed, too. Bob's heart raced as he hurried by the closed storefronts. Darryl hopped to the sidewalk in front of him. Bob balled his fists in the adrenaline rush. Fight or flight? Could he even ward off one blow? In his old life, enemies sought to ruin you financially or legally. Here, simple street justice resolved disputes.

Bob ducked his head to hurry past.

Darryl stopped him with the showing of his upraised palm.

Bob raised his arms in front of his face. "I can explain."

"You Bob?" Darryl said.

"I'm sorry man, but she came on to me." His tightly clenched fists ached.

Darryl grabbed the front of Bob's jacket and pushed him against the storefront wall. "Maybe I can't make her want me, but I can sure as hell protect her." He slammed a huge fist into the wall, inches from Bob's ear, cracking the storefront's wood siding. "If you hurt her, you'll answer to me." Darryl's face hovered inches from Bob's. "You understand?"

Bob nodded involuntarily.

Darryl's grip loosened. The rage in his contorted face morphed into agony. Tears welled up. He released Bob's jacket with a jerk and shuffled away, his shoulders slumped. "She meant everything to me."

Bob stood frozen against the wall, staring at the receding hulk.

She meant everything to Darryl. And Bob took her. Because he could. A bigger fish with more money. Just as Heather had been everything to Bob. Candy was Heather, and Bob was Doyle. Instead of escaping the treachery of his old life, he brought it with him. Bob slithered back to the motel.

CHAPTER 12

Bob jerked around all night, stabbed with fitful dreams. Chasing the golden ring in a high-rise prison. Having no purpose. Adrift at sea. Living in poverty. A sultan's harem. Yielding to desire. All peppered with bizarre snippets of Heather and Candy and Darryl and Doyle. But when he awoke, the fever had broken. He threw open the motel room curtains to reveal the pink morning horizon. He slid the pane sideways and breathed deeply as the crisp mountain air poured in over him. The room filled with the smell of the pine forest that hugged the mountain up where his treasure lay buried.

Bob entered the bathroom, started the shower, and stepped into the yellow plastic tub, rust-stained and cracked, its metal fixtures pocked. At thirty-five bucks a night, this fifty-year-old motel was overpriced.

Hot water pounded his shoulders and coursed down his back. He soaped his bearded face, thickening calves, and a belly that grew smaller each day. His now-daily walks to and from work and around town were transforming a body that had grown soft during a career of office life. He threw open the torn shower curtain, stepped onto the cold tile, and toweled off the steamed mirror. His gray-speckled beard had filled in, and his eyes had cleared in the week since he'd quit cigarettes. But he sure could use one.

A faucet dripped onto a brown stain in the sink. He put a finger under the falling droplets. Hot. He reached for his Swiss Army knife, popped the plastic cap off the hot water faucet, unscrewed the

Philips screw, and wiggled off the handle. He pried out the old seal, which dissolved to black grit in his hand, and replaced it with a five-cent washer he'd bought from Ace. He reassembled the mechanism and twisted the repaired faucet snugly clockwise. No drip. Yes. It seemed silly, but the simple pleasure of fixing something exhilarated him.

He pulled on his faded jeans, work boots, and corduroy jacket, and strode from the room. He marched past the old Civic, now a static display for want of a battery, and headed toward town under the brightening sky. Across the highway, a sign proclaimed *Industrial Space for Lease.* The entrance to the closed factory was locked. A chain coiled through the fence and gate like a python squeezing the life out of its prey, its head a brass-colored padlock. A faded sign tilted like a badly-hung picture frame. *Mountain West Fabricators.*

As he passed the closed Tasty-Freeze, the unkempt yards, and gravel driveways with pickups that never moved, his gait slowed and his shoulders drooped. He counted five homes with for-sale signs, one more than yesterday, and two proclaiming "Bank Foreclosure." Colored pennants strung over a closed gas station dangled limply. *Buy here, pay here,* the sign read. *Zero down puts you behind the wheel.* From the trailer park, a baby cried and a man yelled, "Shut that kid up," followed by a slap and a cry and a slamming door. A lump rose in Bob's throat.

The road curved into town, past the shuttered businesses. Bob stopped and stared down at the old man sleeping on the bench. Everything was an accusation. His skillful legal maneuvering had saved the merger. Now, who would save the town?

Bob kept his gaze on his pot scrubbing.

"You were with Candy?" Lester said. "Candy Hoffsteader?" With a grunt, he pressed down the lever, crimping a cap onto another bottle. Ka-Chunk. He stood at the table in the corner of the kitchen, a case of empty bottles on the floor. "Isn't she Darryl's girl?"

"I told him to lay off, Boss," Hector said, sweating before the sizzling griddle. "You seen Darryl's forearms? He worked a metal press before the plant closed."

Lester's face reddened. "You blow into town, plead poverty, then start flashing around money that attracts desperate people and pisses off everyone else. Darryl Wise is a good man. He lost his job like a lot of others." His pitch rose. "The only reason you got a job is because of my goddamned heart attack. If I'd been around, I wouldn't have let Grace hire you."

"Lester," Grace called out through the pass-through.

Lester stopped his capping, pointed at Bob, and hissed, "Why the hell are you here?"

Bob stumbled. "Um, the beauty of this place. The freedom."

"Freedom. Hah. Freedom's in here," Lester said, poking his chest with his thumb. "You brought your chains with you." He jabbed a finger in Bob's direction. "You know what makes people happy around here?"

Bob shrugged. "Money." Same as everywhere.

"Wrong," Lester snorted. "It's about helping your neighbor. Community. Show me a man who thinks life's about money and I'll show you an unhappy son of a bitch."

"Lester." Grace stuck her head in the door. "You're not exerting yourself, are you?"

"No, sweetie." He shoved Bob to the bottle-capper. "I'm showing Bob my brewery."

Lester's clunky beer-making equipment took up a quarter of the kitchen. Bob always had to maneuver around it. And the mash stunk.

"You banned me from the grill, Grace. I need to do something."

"What you need to do is recuperate."

She returned to the dining room, and he resumed capping. Ka-chunk. Ka-chunk. "Love of money is why this town got screwed."

Bob returned to the sink and became lost in his work. Lester's erratic ka-chunking morphed into a steady beat, like the slow chugging of a steam engine. Bob closed the faucet and snapped off his gloves. He took a deep breath. He needed to do it now.

"Lester," he said. "You're a member of the Chamber of Commerce, aren't you?"

"What's left of it. Why?"

"Well, this town has a skilled manufacturing workforce. It has facilities lying vacant. Can't the Chamber attract new business?"

"We've tried. We can't compete. Other states and cities give tax credits and infrastructure goodies. We're too poor. It's a death spiral. The poorer you are, the fewer incentives you can offer, and the poorer you get. And no one around here has any capital to grow." Lester grunted as he crimped on another top.

"Can't you get a machine that does this?" Bob pointed at the manual capping device. "It's too labor-intensive."

Lester's forehead furrowed. "Why would I want a machine? It's a hobby. Don't you do anything just for the fun of it?"

"He did Candy," Hector said.

Bob examined one of the empty bottles. "May I taste it?"

Lester shrugged. "Suit yourself. Some capped bottles are in the refrigerator."

Bob pulled one out, popped the top, and took a tentative swig. He swirled it in his mouth and swallowed. He examined the label and took another long pull. "This is great."

"Of course," Hector said. "It's Lester's Lager."

After staring at the bottle for several seconds, Bob downed the rest of the beer. He looked at the equipment, the tubing, the fermenter. "Would you show me how to do this?"

"You put the bottle here," Lester said, "the top here, and push down until it crimps it on."

"No, I mean the whole process." Bob swept his hand across the table. "Show me how to make beer."

CHAPTER 13

Doyle snoozed on the casting couch, drifting in and out. Through the open door to the outer office, the phone rang. Martha's clickety-clack typing continued through four rings.

"Mr. Doyle's office, Martha speaking."

Doyle stretched his arms.

"One moment, Mrs. Baldwin," Martha said. "I'll see if he's in." The hold button clicked and typing resumed.

Doyle lowered his feet to the floor.

"I'm sorry, Mrs. Baldwin, Mr. Doyle's with a client. May I take a message?"

He could almost hear Heather's voice from here.

"Yes, Mrs. Baldwin. I understand. Important. I'll give him the message."

Doyle relaxed, knowing Martha guarded the gate. She'd been there since the beginning, a pert, part-time high school intern who helped Solomon G. Kravitz open a two-room office on Canal Street. After three tough years, Kravitz and Martha had generated sufficient business to hire a summer intern from Talbot Law, a night school not yet accredited by the ABA. Kravitz did the interviewing but Martha did the choosing. Henry Doyle won hands down. He dazzled her with his gorgeous smile, pearly white teeth, and wavy brown hair. His mediocre grades and undistinguished moot court performance gave Kravitz pause, but Martha overruled him.

Over the years, she had proven loyal, reliable and trustworthy. And the only person in the building who didn't fear Doyle. She knew his peccadillos and didn't care. All great men had them. Look at JFK. Also, he paid her $150,000 a year.

Doyle opened his eyes and smacked his lips to get rid of the taste. In a glass on the coffee table, all that remained of the scotch was melted ice the color of weak tea. He grunted, sat up, and swallowed it. He rose from the casting couch and stumbled into the bathroom. When he came out, he poured himself a Perrier and collapsed into the mammoth leather desk chair. It swiveled under his angular approach. He sipped the cool water, moistening his mouth and throat.

A pink while-you-were-out message appeared on the computer screen. "Mrs. Baldwin," it read, followed by three checked boxes: "called," "important," and "please return call." He grabbed the mouse and deleted the note.

The shelf life of an H. Meriwether Doyle romantic liaison grew shorter with each passing year. His infatuation for Heather had lasted two months, longer than most. And with Baldwin gone a month, she had become a pest. Oh, she was beautiful, enthusiastic, and limber. But at some point, the benefits would no longer be worth the aggravation. Until then, however, he intended to fully utilize the asset.

Dinners and lavish nights out had morphed into late-night trysts at Doyle's high-rise love nest. That she was still Baldwin's wife added a satisfying revenge element, though not compensation for stolen millions. So Doyle's demands had become increasingly unusual. While she had balked at his bringing a third party into the arrangement, she had allowed him to introduce specialized apparatus.

As soon as he had deleted Heather's note, another popped up. Then another. Like whack-a-mole. Another appeared and he quickly dispatched it. Then he froze as he stared at the pink slip. "Artie called. Said you know him." Doyle pulled out his cell phone and punched in a number.

"I told you not to call me at the office. That was the deal."

"Hello, Henry," a rough voice said. "Yeah, that was the deal. Until you stopped answering your cell phone."

"Look," Doyle said. "I've had a bit of a problem here. Last month, some asshole stole a lot of money. Tell your people this week's payment will take a little more time."

The man chuckled. "Henry, you know the rules. Payment is due when it's due. *My people* don't care about your problems."

"I've got some of it," Doyle said. "Ten grand."

The man snorted. "The deal is ten percent a week on the hundred grand you owe. Plus five grand for principal *amortization*."

The moron seemed to like that word.

"Ten grand is barely the weekly juice, Henry."

"I need more time. When we catch this prick, I can pay you in full. We're really close."

Artie wheezed into the phone for several seconds. "Okay, Henry. I don't usually do this, but seeing's how you're a good customer, I'll let you double up on the principal next week. But I'll need an extra two grand for my trouble. That's twenty-two grand next week." Doyle scowled at the phone. "Don't make this a habit, Henry. And I need the ten large today. I'll be up."

"No, no. Don't come here. I'll come to you."

"I'm in the garage. Be here in five minutes."

Doyle went behind the bar, pulled up a throw rug, and spun the tumbler to the floor safe. He opened it, counted ten thousand, put it in an envelope and stuffed it in his jacket pocket. As he rushed toward the door, his cell phone rang.

"I'm on my way," he said.

"Henry? Thank God, I've been calling all day."

Fuck. "Heather, I can't talk now."

"This is important, Henry. My credit cards are locked. Bob didn't pay the bills."

Doyle raced past Martha and pressed the elevator button. "Bob's gone, Heather. He's not paying shit."

"I knew he was upset, but that's not like him."

The doors opened. "Getting in the elevator. Bad reception. See you tonight."

"Anyway Henry, can you help me take care of this until he's back?"

As the elevator doors closed, Doyle hung up.

In the foyer, Heather sat on the Louis XIV chair and drummed her long, bespeckled nails on the glass-topped end table. Her relationship with Henry had progressed satisfactorily.

"Good Lord, woman," he had said, lying splayed across the carpet like a freshly filleted flounder. "Where did you learn that?"

Her lovemaking had been equal parts Kamasutra, Spiderwoman, and Zen.

"When you care about someone," she'd cooed, "giving yourself completely comes naturally." Naturally, plus several thousand hours of aerobics, yoga, and agility training.

She had employed much of her arsenal in their first few meetings, leaving him exhausted and gasping for breath. She should probably be more careful. He was the oldest man she had ever been with, and a heart attack wouldn't do her any good before she got a ring on her finger. Plus, as her most worthy opponent yet, he might require pulling out all the stops. Even the nuclear option.

She went into the kitchen, opened a bottle of chardonnay, and half-filled a stemmed wine glass. She took a sip and set the glass on the marble countertop of the kitchen island, admiring the hanging copper pots, the wine rack, the Sub Zero Professional refrigerator. She loved her kitchen. She took another sip. A truck engine had been rumbling on the street for some time. Metal clanked. She picked up her drink, stepped into the living room, and looked out the picture window. A tow-truck idled in her driveway. A man climbed into the cab and pulled away, dragging her Jaguar.

CHAPTER 14

"I'm out of plates, Bob," Hector called. "Get in here." Dirty dishes filled the sink and covered the adjacent countertop. On the side wall where the beer table had been, a newly cut door led into the adjacent store. A rhythmic ka-chunk emanated from within. Beyond the door, the empty flower racks had been pushed aside. Lester's single brewing table had been dragged in and expanded to three, with plastic brewing containers, clear tubing, and bottles. Bob siphoned beer from the secondary fermenter into bottles, and capped them with the crimper. Ka-chunk. The sharp smell of fermentation wafted into the kitchen.

"Don't make me tell Grace we're out of plates," Hector said.

Bob appeared in the doorway, grinning and holding up a just-sealed beer bottle. He took two glasses off the shelf and put them on the counter next to the grill. He popped the cap, poured the golden brew, and handed one glass to Hector.

Hector sighed and accepted it.

"Salud," Bob held up the glass.

"And happy days," Hector said, mirroring the pose.

Each took a large swig.

"Blah." They both bent over, the rancid brew spilling onto the floor. Bob hurried to the sink and gargled with tap water. Then he stomped through the door and returned carrying a five-gallon plastic container, half-filled with brown liquid. He emptied it into the sink. A pungent odor filled the kitchen.

Hector's hand covered his nose. "No, man, dump it in the woods."

"Three weeks of work down the tubes," Bob said, as he rinsed out the container. "I followed Lester's recipe exactly. I don't get it." Almost two months here, and he had accomplished nothing. If he was to give anything back, he needed this to work. He shook it off as the old depression monster approached.

The kitchen door swung open and Lester stepped in. "What you're not going to get is *paid* if you don't start washing those dishes."

Bob pulled on his gloves, opened the faucet, and began scrubbing.

"And what in God's name is that stink?"

"It's Bob," Hector said. "He's brewing swamp gas."

Lester ambled over to the new door to the flower shop and peered in.

"I followed the recipe," Bob said. "Your exact instructions."

Lester shot a wilting gaze of disgust. "Did you use the precise measurements I gave you?"

"I did."

"In the right order? It has to be in the right order."

"It was."

"Did you allow proper fermentation time? Use a secondary fermenter? Add the priming sugar before siphoning the beer into the bottles?"

"Of course I did. I can follow procedure."

"Did you sanitize?"

"Yes. I washed everything thoroughly."

"Washed?"

"Yes. Washed. I know how to wash. It's my job." He scrubbed another plate with steaming water.

"In the sink?" Lester sighed. "You have to sanitize everything with sanitizer, to kill bacteria. If you don't, when the yeast starts the fermentation, bad bacteria will grow like gangbusters. It'll taste awful." He shook his head. "You're not going to make bilge and call it Lester's Lager. Come on." He led Bob into the flower shop. "Fermentation takes twelve days. Not eleven. Not thirteen. Twelve." He gestured and pointed, talking with his hands. "Log every step so you can track how each variable changes the result. Sanitize everything, including the bottle caps. Use this sanitizer."

Lester began spending several hours each day showing Bob the ropes. He had to rest on a stool most of the time, but his voice remained loud and clear. Three weeks later, Bob, Hector, and Lester raised three glasses of beer. Hector grimaced as they drank. Then he blinked.

"Hey, man, this ain't bad." He poured himself another.

"That's how you make beer," Lester said.

Bob took another sip. "You could sell this."

"It's a hobby, not a business."

"Maybe it should be."

Lester waved his hand. "You're on your own. I'm going to take a nap."

When Bob finished bottling the batch, Hector stood, hands on hips, staring at the flotilla of capped bottles that covered the table. "What are you going to do with all this beer? Drink it yourself?"

Bob picked up a case with a follow-me head tilt.

Hector groaned. "Lester won't like this," he said as they slid out the back door, carrying two cases of Lester's Lager. At the Grizzly Tavern, they set them behind the bar.

"From Lester," Bob said to Cal, the glass-rinsing proprietor.

That evening, Bob scrubbed his zillionth pot, sweating from the rising steam despite the October chill outside. Lester, perched nearby on his stool by the grill, read the paper. His cell phone rang. He checked the ID and punched speaker. "What's up, Cal?"

"I need to talk to you about the beer your boys brought over," the phone speaker said.

"The beer?" Lester looked over.

Bob put his head down, vigorously scrubbing a pot.

"My boys?" Lester looked at Hector, scraping the griddle with intense focus.

"Yeah," Cal said, "the two cases they brought this morning."

Lester scowled. "Not a problem. We'll take it back. Or toss it."

"Toss it? It's all gone. I need more."

And so, Bob delivered another two cases the next week. Cal sold out within a day. With only weekly batches already in the three-week pipeline, Bob expanded production to two batches a week, then four, ultimately producing two cases a day before they ran out of space. By mid-November, the flower shop overflowed with a battalion of buckets, barrels, and bottles.

"We're hidebound," Bob said. "We need more room."

Lester remained nearby. He claimed to be "protecting the brand," but he seemed to enjoy watching. One day, as he stood, tilted against the door frame, arms crossed and stone-faced, Bob took his picture, stylized the photo on the café computer, and sent off for labels. They soon adorned each bottle of Lester's Lager.

Bob massaged his aching shoulders and rotated his head as he watched Lester and Cal through the pass-through.

"You should have done this years ago," Cal said, slapping Lester's back as they sat at the counter. "This could be a thriving business. Lord knows the town needs one. Why have you kept this a secret?"

"It's a hobby. I don't have a license to make and sell beer."

"Get one. My customers love it."

When Grace pushed open the kitchen door, Bob was at the sink. She stepped behind him. "Thank you, Bob," she said.

His legs became wobbly as he gazed into her kind face.

"For giving Lester this. He needed a boost." She reached out and touched his arm. "I'm grateful." She smiled sweetly and returned to the dining room.

"I wish I had a woman like that," Hector said. "A good woman makes all the difference in a man's life."

Bob swallowed hard. And just like that, he knew he was in love.

CHAPTER 15

As Doyle reclined in the swivel chair, sipping scotch, his desk phone squawked. "Mr. Doyle, your three-o'clock is here."

He whacked the button. "Send him in."

He didn't even remember the appointment. Probably another sniveling partner complaining about his bonus. Doyle snorted. He built this firm from a two-room walk-up. Every dime that came in belonged to him, to do with as he liked. If he chose to share some with employees, they needed to be grateful, not arrogant and entitled. If they didn't like it, start their own firm instead of feeding off the leftovers from his table. Jackals skulking about, waiting for the lion to finish eating before they got their scraps. Everybody wanted a piece of him. All the freeloaders. Including the women. Especially the women. Shaking their asses in their tight suits, and then expecting to become a partner. I am woman, hear me roar. Hah.

And the preppy young lawyers that showed up waving their Ivy League degrees that daddy bought for them, their tight suits, and hair gelled up to here. The world is your oyster, their bubble-world kept telling them. Wrong. The world is *my* oyster. Your job is to work your ass off and bill the client 2,500 hours a year at $260 per. I pay you a hundred fifty thou and keep the other half million. I have your oyster right here. He gave his package a shake.

A squat man appeared in the doorway. An open black leather jacket revealed a Hawaiian shirt painted in tropical birds and coconut palms. He looked around and whistled approvingly. "This is the first time I been in your office, Henry," Artie said. "I was beginning to think you was ashamed of me."

Doyle stood. "How'd you get in here?"

"Is that any way to greet a pal?"

"I told your goombah boss I'd have the money on Friday. Now get the hell out."

"I'd be careful if I was you, Henry. Mr. Giantelli is a sensitive man."

Doyle didn't care. What could this low-life do? A bagman with an eighth-grade education. Doyle wouldn't hire him to clean his toilet. "I got my own problems."

"That you do, Henry. And right now, it's the weekly fifteen large."

Doyle's head throbbed. Another leech wanted a piece of him. "Fuck off, Artie. I'll have it on Friday."

"Sounds like you got anger issues, Henry. That's not good for your pressure." Artie's eyes scanned the room. He approached the bar, poured himself a drink, and took a sip. He held the glass up, examined it, and gulped the rest down. "You got an envelope for me, Henry?"

Making the fifteen-grand-a-week payments had been a struggle. Until now, incoming fees had covered it, but the pipeline always slowed during the holidays. He'd have to stall this ignorant goombah. Doyle came around the desk.

"I told you, someone stole from me. We'll get him soon, and you'll get what I owe. All of it." No more of this ten-percent-per-week interest shit.

"Henry, payment is due when it's due. If you're late, there's a penalty. Like at CitiBank."

Penalty? What was this retard talking about?

"You ready, Henry?"

"What?"

A lightning-fast jab caught him in the right eye, sending him back against his desk and the lamp crashing to the floor. For a bulky, squat man, Artie's speed startled him.

"What the fuck?" Doyle steadied himself against the desk. "I told you an asshole stole from me."

"But *he* ain't the asshole that owes us money." Artie headed for the door. "Friday. Fifteen grand." He passed Martha as she hurried in. "Youse have a nice day, Madam."

Doyle retrieved his glasses from the carpet, the right lens shattered, and walked to the bar mirror. His red right eye was already swelling, with a cut beneath.

Martha shook her head. "I'll get ice."

"First, get Fontaine."

Doyle stared at the bull dyke across the desk, with a gray Armani suit nicer than his. Two buttons, slim cut, crisp white shirt, lime silk tie with diamond stick pin, and matching cufflinks. He couldn't imagine a woman under that getup.

"The bastard's been gone three months." Doyle's voice stayed measured, but rage hid a millimeter below the surface. He held his voice in check only because he wasn't quite sure what he was dealing with here. She held a fedora in her lap. "What the hell are you people doing over there?"

"We're close, Mr. Doyle," she said. "We're really close."

She squinted and tilted her head, peeking past the makeup to spot the bruising beneath his dark glasses.

"You've been saying that for months. That's not going to cut it anymore, Fontaine."

"He's a slippery one, Mr. Doyle. This one doesn't want to be found."

"Isn't that your job? To find people who don't want to be found?"

"We're working the case twenty-four/seven."

He picked up his drink and headed to the bar. "Ms. Fontaine, let me explain it to you. I did not hire you to *work the case*. I hired you to *find* him. Do you understand the difference?"

"Of course, Mr. Doyle. I only meant to assure you that we have pulled out all the stops. We have interviewed everyone he knows. We are monitoring his known contacts. He'll make a mistake soon, and we'll have him."

He refilled his glass with cubes and a splash of scotch. He held up the glass and examined it, then poured some more. "I'm not interested in your efforts. Only results. And I haven't seen any."

"We have our best man on it, Mr. Doyle."

He took a long sip. "Yes, I met Columbo. He needs a new suit."

She chuckled. "Dave Dawson is a skilled professional."

This woman was good. She seemed to enjoy the game, using psychology, salesmanship, and flattery. When he summoned her, she scurried over. When he suggested incompetence, she calmly laid out their strategy. And when he insulted her, she commiserated with his misfortune. Like a chess match, each move was thoughtful, dispassionate, and purpose-driven. And, well played, a pawn can checkmate a king.

"You're absolutely right," she said. "Baldwin is slippery, and our inability to find him promptly is an embarrassment. But we will. Soon. And here's what we're doing to find him—"

With lips pursed and eyes boring into her, he raised his hand. "Here's how it's going to work, Ms. Fontaine. You're going to have his location on my desk within ten days. If you do not, your services will no longer be required. On this case, or any other. And the firm will expect a full refund for the fees you have been paid."

"Of course, Mr. Doyle. I'm ashamed of this lapse."

He snorted. He doubted anything could shame her. "Your feelings don't concern me."

"We'll have that information in ten days. I guarantee it."

"I'm disappointed," he said. "But I'm not unreasonable. Find him in ten days, and there's a ten-thousand-dollar bonus in it for you." He cleared his throat. "With the usual finder's fee, of course."

"Of course. Thank you, Mr. Doyle. We won't let you down." She rose. Her shoulders drooped as she dragged herself out the door and past Martha.

He saw her waiting for the elevator, her spine now erect and shoulders straight. And she was whistling.

Dave's head was buried in his computer when Frankie danced in and tossed her fedora onto the coat rack. "The whale's got his knickers in a bunch, Davie boy. We have to produce."

After three months, Dave had run out of tricks. "It's like fishing for an eel. You can't grab him. He's hiding in the coral. You lay your net and wait for him to swim into it."

"The client's tired of waiting. We've got to show him results."

He wants results?

"Okay." Dave tapped some keys and a file popped up. He scrolled through a few pages. "On August 1st at 6:35 p.m., $3,200,000 wire transferred from the Kravitz & Doyle trust account at First National to the Royal Bank of George Town, Grand Cayman. That night, Baldwin's credit card purchased gas in Virginia, South Carolina, and Florida. On day two, he abandoned his leased BMW in the Miami airport parking garage, hopped American flight 2431 to George Town, Grand Cayman, and stayed two nights at the Prince Edward Hotel. On August 4, he chartered a yacht and crew from Sunshine Adventures, sailed to Tampa, passing through customs at 4:50 p.m. on August 6, five days after he left. His passport hadn't been flagged because no one reported the theft to the authorities. Baldwin walked through customs in Tampa and disappeared. No credit card transactions, no cellphone, no contact with anyone that we can ascertain. He's off the grid."

Frankie tightened the knot on her necktie, looking in the wall mirror.

"Plus, this whole thing stinks to high heaven, as does everything Doyle touches. Why hasn't he reported it? How did a junior partner get access to that kind of money? Doesn't the firm have financial controls to prevent that sort of thing? And why does a top-producing partner chuck it all and kill the goose that lays golden eggs?"

Frankie removed her jacket and hung it on the coat rack.

"So, we laid our nets," Dave said. "When he comes out for food, we'll have him. He'll make a mistake soon enough."

She sat in the chair next to Dave's desk and brushed her trousers. "Soon enough isn't good enough. We have a deadline. The whale's putting the screws to us."

"Yeah, and I know why. He's in hock up to his ears. To loan sharks. My sources say his nut is fifteen grand a week."

She rested her elbow on the desk and her chin on her hand. "How do you know that?"

"You said it yourself, Frankie. I'm the best."

"That you are. Nevertheless, we have to find this guy and we have to do it in ten days. Otherwise, the whale walks. *I* can't afford that and *you* can't afford that. That's why all leaves are canceled until we find Baldwin. We are now on this 24/7."

"No can do, Frankie. I've got Tracy for Thanksgiving. We're taking a road trip up to my mother's."

"Dave, I had to do some serious groveling. I barely saved the account. Losing Doyle wouldn't do either of us any good. His firm is twenty-five percent of our business. Lose him and there'd be some serious cuts around here."

"I haven't had a long weekend with Tracy since summer. She's growing up without me."

Frankie shrugged.

"I promised. I'm not going to give up my time with my daughter for that slimeball."

"Lose this job, and how would that impact your relationship with your daughter?"

Frankie was right. Dave needed this income to provide for Tracy. She was all that mattered. If canceling Thanksgiving plans made him a horrible dad, he'd just have to suck it up. As his breath drained from him, he dropped his forehead to the desktop.

Dave coasted the beater to a stop in front of his old home. He shut off the engine and sat quietly as the November winds whipped the last of the oak leaves from their trees. His chest had ached all night. How would he tell her? He hadn't even told her mother yet. Or his.

That pervert Doyle snaps his fingers, and Dave couldn't take Tracy to Grandma's for Thanksgiving. It sickened him.

Right when he had worked up the courage to open the car door and head for the house, his beautiful child came running across the lawn.

"Hi, Daddy," the twelve-year-old said, as she jumped into the passenger seat, throwing in a backpack emblazoned with the latest tween idol.

Dave forced a smile.

"I made a T-shirt for Grandma." She reached into the pack and pulled out a turkey-emblazoned shirt. "See." She held it up.

He didn't speak.

"What do you think?"

The words choked in his throat. "I can't..."

She tilted her head and furrowed her brow. "What's the matter, Daddy?"

He swallowed hard, reached over, and hugged her tightly. His ex watched them from the living room window.

"Daddy, is Grandma okay?"

Tears welled up in his eyes. "I love you, Tracy."

"I love you, too."

Dave rubbed his eyes with his sleeve. What had he been thinking? He'd patch things up with Frankie later, but this moment would never come again. A warm tide washed over him.

"You ready, Squirt?"

"Ready, Daddy."

"I'll need to stop by my place to pick up a few things."

He started the engine.

"Road trip," they both called in unison as the car squealed onto the open road.

After their Thanksgiving feast at his mother's house in the mountains, they played board games, assembled puzzles, and enjoyed old TV shows.

"Your Daddy's favorite," Grandma said, as they mocked *The Brady Bunch*. "He was in love with Marcia."

They laughed and ran through the woods and ate burgers and shakes at the town's fifty-year-old carhop. They drank cocoa and sang and snuggled around the orange glow of the fireplace as the dry logs crackled and popped.

When he returned Tracy to her Mom on Sunday night, a black void pulled at his chest.

"Goodbye, Squirt," he said, kissing her forehead.

Doyle's ten-day deadline came and went, and Baldwin wasn't found. The bonus didn't get paid, and the Kravitz & Doyle account was lost. As usual, Frankie handled it like a consummate professional.

"When I gave him the news, Doyle went ballistic, red and sputtering. He said he'd sue me for malpractice and fraud and dressing like a man."

"Good thing he didn't stroke out," Dave said, hoping to lighten the mood.

"Why's that?"

He smiled at the black humor of her indifference.

She stared blankly.

He raised his palms. "He'd be dead. Or incapacitated."

She shrugged. "It's coming anyway. The man's a walking powder keg."

Not only had the agency lost its biggest account, but it also had to return the fees earned.

"So, Dave, until you get your mojo back, you're on shit detail." She relegated him to investigating Shop-N-Go clerks, burger flippers, and other minimum-wagers making corporate trouble.

And she halved his salary.

CHAPTER 16

Bob sat on the bottom kitchen step, gazing into the woods and clutching the steaming mug with both hands. Cold concrete pressed against his rump, the muscles now lean and taut from months of walking, hiking in the woods, and the long hours on his feet in the diner and brewery. His thick corduroy jacket insulated him, the warm collar up against his neck, protecting him from the frosty breeze. He never tired of this view. The woods, the valley, the mountain. He sipped from the mug, its rising steam and his breath combining into small clouds in the November chill. The hot coffee soothed and warmed him all the way down.

Rustling leaves caught his ear. Shuffling toward him along the back of the empty stores, the homeless man of Main Street stopped to inspect each garbage can. His face and hands were dirty, his layered clothing ragged, and his boots worn and flapping. He carried a large, black plastic garbage bag slung over his shoulder. Against the majestic pine forest behind and mountain above, the bum was a stain on the tapestry.

As the man moved closer, one can at a time, Bob remained still, hoping he might pass without spotting him. He hated fending off bums seeking a handout. He never felt pity or compassion, only annoyance, even anger.

When the man stopped and peered into the diner's dumpster, not thirty feet away, Bob saw clearly the filth—hair and beard matted like a wild dog's winter fur, hands scabbed, and face lined with the scars of a hard life.

He was struggling to pull out a cardboard box when he spotted Bob and froze. Their gazes locked.

Get a job. Bob's knee-jerk reaction came whenever he spotted a bum angling toward him in the city. But this wasn't the city. "The bear is a magnificent creature," Lester had said. "But you don't see her struggle. She's like the people around here, living in a paradise, proud and free, but digging in the garbage for food."

Bob rose and went into the kitchen. He returned with an insulated coffee mug, a huge muffin, warm from the oven, and a blanket draped over his shoulder.

The man eyed him warily.

Bob held out the muffin.

Like a stray dog, the outcast approached, hungry but afraid. He tentatively reached for the muffin, then snatched it and devoured it, crumbs cascading from his lips. His eyes shone with his humanity. When Bob offered the coffee, the man took it, breathed in the steam before taking his first sip, and groaned in pleasure.

Bob tilted his head, offering a seat on the other side of the wide step. Even at three feet, the man's powerful body odor overwhelmed. He accepted the blanket, draped it around himself and over his head like a hood, and dropped to the step.

They sat quietly, sipping their coffee. Finally, Bob rose, put his hand on the man's shoulder, and jogged up the steps. He stopped abruptly. Lester stood in the doorway.

Bob scooted past and resumed his duties at the sink.

"We need some ice out here," Grace called through the pass-through.

Like a synchronized water ballet, Hector dropped the spatula and Bob snapped off his rubber gloves. They passed, and Bob picked up the spatula from the grill and flipped the frying eggs as Hector disappeared out the door. Three seconds later, the dining room door swung open. An all-black-clad Immigration and Customs Enforcement officer, including an "ICE" baseball cap, blocked the opening.

"Where's Hector Martinez?"

Lester squinted at the intruder. "It's only him."

The Iceman eyed Bob's spatula and apron, and scowled. "Do I have to search the place, or do you want to tell me where he is?" He walked to the pantry door, put his hand on the knob, and jerked it open. He stuck his head into the small closet, then closed the door. "You could save everyone a lot of trouble." He opened the walk-in freezer and stepped in. He reappeared and poked his head out the back door. "A man could easily hide in those woods." He examined the crude plywood door covering the opening into the flower shop. He jiggled the latch. Locked. "What's in here?"

"That's the flower shop next door," Lester said. "They're out of business."

"Last chance. You going to tell me where he is?"

Bob and Lester locked gazes and said nothing.

"Have it your way. Open it."

When Lester nodded, Bob opened a drawer, removed a key, and unlocked the door.

Iceman pulled it open and peered in. "Come on out, Hector."

Nothing.

He snapped his fingers. "Lights."

Bob reached through the door and flipped the switch.

The agent stepped in and searched the storefront. "What is this?" he called from within. "A moonshine still?"

"It's my hobby," Lester said. "I make my own beer."

The man reappeared. "You must drink a lot of beer." He pulled a pad of paper from his shirt pocket, scribbled on it, and returned it to the pocket.

"Okay, G-man," Lester said, holding the door open. "You can leave now." Bob knew Lester hated the federal government. He hated the EPA, the IRS, the DOE, and every other acronym. Two years ago, they made him spend ten grand to make the restroom wheelchair accessible. He still waited for their first wheelchair.

"Lester, please," Grace called out from the pass-through as the Iceman left. "Don't get started. Your pressure."

He exhaled heavily and collapsed into one of the straight-backed chairs in the corner of the kitchen.

Bob sat next to him. "Lester, this is a small operation." He nodded at the flower shop door. "It's well-hidden and we haven't attracted much attention."

Lester shrugged. "So?"

"We have to get our ducks lined up, legally. We can sell all the beer we could make. But we need to get a license."

"Yeah, I've been thinking about that. It should be no problem," Lester said. "I have friends at the Chamber."

Bob shook his head. "We need a *federal* license to brew beer for sale. From ATF."

Lester's temple veins bulged at yet another acronym.

"I figured we'd stay under the radar with a small operation," Bob said. "But now, with Inspector Clouseau sniffing around, he's bound to call his friends."

Lester's face reddened. "If the damned Feds shut us down, they'd have a riot. No, an armed revolution. This is Idaho, after all."

Bob put his hand on Lester's shoulder. "Lester, we can't go on without a license."

Lester raked his fingers through his hair. "I haven't a clue how to get one. And we can't afford to hire a blood-sucking lawyer." He exhaled and his shoulders drooped. "I guess we'll have to shut it down."

Bob remained silent. Could he trust Lester? His gaze skittered about the room. He examined his hands.

"What?" Lester said.

Bob exhaled a huge breath, then leaned closer. "I know someone who can help us." As Lester's eyes narrowed, Bob swallowed hard. "Should I make the call?"

Grace stopped at the pass-through and they both fell silent. She wiped the perspiration from her brow with her forearm, as wisps of wet hair stuck to her face. She grabbed an order and scurried off.

Lester's face turned to steel. "Do it."

"What the hell, Bob?"

Bob squeezed the phone. George sounded great. Parked on a mountain road, ten miles outside of town and several cell-phone towers away, Bob pulled up his jacket collar as the car windshield began to frost in the November breeze.

"You're gone three months. You don't call, you don't write…"

"You're not my mother, George."

"…and now you want to start a business?"

"It's how I'll pay the money back."

"Just come home and return it now."

"I spent some of it. Being on the lam is expensive."

"Then return what's left. We can work out a deal with Doyle."

"It's good to hear your voice, George. How's Connie?"

George sighed. "Bob, this is not a good idea. Come home and we can sort it all out."

"Sorry, buddy. I know I made a bad decision. I wish I hadn't. But now I have to move forward. And this is the best way." The familiar bile rose in his throat. "The only question is, will you help me?"

"As your lawyer, I have to advise against it."

"And as my friend?"

George's long sigh heralded his answer.

"I'll see what I can do."

CHAPTER 17

At her father's desk, Susan Farrington tapped on a laptop. From beyond the study's open double doors came the music of her family.

"One fish, two fish, red fish, blue fish," the gray-haired man read as the two-year-old girl on his lap pointed at the pictures. "Black fish, blue fish, old fish, new fish."

In the kitchen, Grandma banged and clanged as she prepared the family's dinner. Outside the window of the small frame house, Second Street tunneled through ancient oaks, their brown leaves frosted in the brisk, December morning. On campus, atop the hill of this small Ohio college town, Susan's parents were both known as "Professor," but here they were "Grandma" and "Grandpa."

"This one has a little star, this one has a little car. See the little car, Winnie? Say, what a lot of fish there are."

In May, Susan had been culled from Kravitz & Doyle for insufficient billable hours. For two months, she had searched for work every day. But when Winnie's cold became pneumonia, Susan's spirit broke. Divorced and in debt, she went home a failure, ashamed for the money her parents had wasted on her college, law school, and wedding.

"Some are sad, and some are glad, and some are very, very bad."

The computer dinged, interrupting the soothing sounds coming from the living room. A window popped up in the middle of the incorporation document Susan was drafting. A blank Skype square on the screen became George's face. She smiled warmly. She had him to thank for all of this.

"Great work on the Henderson filing," he said without a greeting.

George had left Kravitz & Doyle five months earlier and set up his office in a warehouse on Water Street. The boutique firm provided legal work to start-up companies. Charging only a nominal initial fee in exchange for equity in the business, he would pilot them through the shoals of incorporation, taxation, licensure, and liability. This allowed cash-starved businesses to conserve precious resources, and promised George a potentially large payday later.

His strategy worked, and George hired Susan as a remote attorney. "Bob said you're the best," he had told her. And though she received a small salary, she had no overhead, and was out of the pressure cooker and surrounded by family. Grateful for this holy grail of work-life balance, she produced prompt and flawless work as she strove to repay George's trust.

Susan examined the brick wall behind George that displayed his framed diplomas and a bar association membership plaque. "Nice."

He squinted. "Oh, my vanity wall." He smiled sheepishly. "Connie put it up." His eyes grew serious. "I have a new assignment for you." His face grew larger as he leaned forward. "This is for a special client. A Mr. Hargrove."

"A friend?"

"A friend of a friend. Getting it done quickly is the challenge. The client has an ongoing business and is concerned about being shut down. He needs to get his ducks in a row."

This was common. Many entrepreneurs started a garage business without any outside help. They didn't get a lawyer until absolutely necessary, which meant they were making money and had attracted the attention of local government regulators, who wanted their licensing and inspection fees.

"You'll need to file the incorporation papers and handle licensure requirements. Can you get it done in two weeks?"

"No problem." It sounded routine.

"Dinner's on," her father called.

"Have to go," she said to George. "My life is calling."

When his image disappeared from the screen, she hurried to the table.

After dinner, she opened the client information George had emailed and set to work. She prepared the incorporation documents and filed them electronically with the state division of corporations. Then she researched that state's licensure requirements for the business. State and local licenses were no problem. But this business also required federal regulatory approval, which took six months to a year to process. She couldn't complete it in two months, let alone two weeks.

She dropped her head into her hands, contemplating the impossible challenge. Her shoulders hunched as her palms massaged her eyes. There had to be a way. She owed George too much to tell him the client would have to wait. She straightened up and resumed tapping the keys.

"Pumpkin?"

Someone shook her shoulder.

"Have you been here all night?"

She opened her eyes and lifted her head from the desk.

Her father looked worried.

"I'm okay, Dad." She pushed her hair back and rubbed her eyes. "I can't solve a problem. There's got to be a solution, but I can't see it." She put her elbows on the desk and rested her chin on her palms.

"Then keep digging. That dinosaur bone may be only one centimeter deeper."

"Thanks, Dad." Her father meant well with his pithy metaphors. "But this is more complicated than digging in the ground. It's navigating the federal bureaucracy. I need a certificate quickly, but you have to apply and wait six months."

"That's how your grandfather used to buy cars," he said. "If the dealer didn't have the options you wanted, you'd have to order from the factory and wait." He squeezed her shoulder. "So instead of waiting, he'd buy a used car that already had the options he needed."

Susan's eyes opened wide. She bolted upright. The dark screen flashed to life as she attacked the keyboard.

"Glad to help," he mumbled and wandered off.

After twenty minutes of searching, eureka. The client could buy a business that already had a license. But this would take money. And their clients didn't have money. She sighed. Only one way to find out. She called George.

"To get immediate licensure, the client has to buy an ongoing concern."

"Great idea," George said. "The client has resources. See what you can do."

One of their clients had resources? And in Idaho?

"Chop, chop," George said. "Time is of the essence."

She chop-chopped into researching every brewery in Idaho. Eliminating the larger operations left about twenty microbreweries. She started calling. *I have a client looking to buy. Would you be interested in discussing it? May I see your financials?*

She found little interest, discovering that people opened breweries for the same reason they played golf—for the love of the game. And those interested in selling had wildly inflated expectations of their baby's worth. Making a deal seemed impossible. She wrung her hands. She had to get off this emotional roller coaster.

Her father placed a wedge of pumpkin pie on the desk.

"How goes it?"

"I'm not a creative person, Dad. I'm an administrator. I prepare and file documents. I can't do this."

His hand touched her shoulder. "If you believe you can't, it's certainly true."

He knew how to motivate her. She blinked. Motivate. She had to find a motivated seller. Who was motivated? People in trouble. Desperate people. People divorcing, moving, running a failed business. She jerked up ramrod straight. A few taps on the laptop and bingo. Public bankruptcy court records revealed Cascade MicroBrew of Coeur d'Alene, a small operation struggling to survive under a Chapter 11 bankruptcy filing. Chapter 11 technically was a reorganization, holding creditors at bay while the company restructured and submitted a plan to return to solvency. The company had been in Chapter 11 for some time, with the owner attempting to renegotiate debt repayment with his creditors. But this outfit had sunk so far underwater, no light penetrated. Court documents revealed equipment worth $750,000, but debts of two million. She called the attorney of record.

It turned out the owner, John Bender, a stubborn old coot, also had an overinflated view of his business's worth, and his attorney couldn't convince him otherwise. So creditors forced the Chapter 11 reorganization into a Chapter 7 liquidation. They'd be lucky to get twenty-five cents on the dollar. With the brewery closed, the last step was to sell off the assets.

"The creditors would agree to any reasonable offer, but Bender won't budge," the lawyer said. "And he can drag it out for months."

"Jeez Louise." She couldn't catch a break.

"Plus, the son's urging the old man to fight," the attorney said. "He's sore about losing his job as brewmaster."

The son? What the heck, she'd try anything, even grasping at straws.

"Do you have his number?"

Milo Bender sat stiffly, facing the scowling principal, his knees crowded against the front of the metal desk cluttered with the accolades of a low-level bureaucrat. Beyond the hall-facing window, three seventh-grade boys sat in the bad-boy chairs, waiting to be disciplined. Milo shared the boys' discomfort but, with his receding hairline and sagging chin, not their appearance. He wore a knit tie, cinched tightly in an unsuccessful attempt to close the one-inch gap in the unbuttoned collar of his short-sleeve shirt. Like the boys, Milo had come for his punishment. He wanted his old job back.

After college, Milo had drifted for a decade before landing a job teaching in middle school hell. He taught for five years, enduring the transformation that racked adolescent bodies. He could almost hear their bones crunching as they morphed from children to adults, like werewolves when the full moon shone upon the Cascades. Then, a miracle. His father opened a brewery and offered him a job. Milo had found his dream career. He loved beer. Making beer, smelling beer, drinking beer. He practically lived at the brewery. Until the bankruptcy. Now, fat, forty, and living in his father's attic, Milo was in freefall, from brewmaster to middle school teacher.

Years earlier, in the exit interview with the principal, a rotund disciplinarian of keen memory, Milo had remarked on her temperament, management style, and girth. She was now ready to dispense punishment.

"Sure, Milo, you can have your old job back," she said. "Welcome aboard."

"Milo Bender?"

"Yeah?" Hunched over in the attic eaves, he cradled the phone between his shoulder and ear as he ironed the threadbare short-sleeved shirt.

"My name is Susan Farrington. I'm an attorney."

"Good for you."

The voice paused. "Okay. Um, I'd like to discuss Cascade MicroBrew."

"You want the old man."

"This is Milo, right? The son?"

"OW." He burned himself again. He hated his life.

"I understand you enjoy your work," the voice said.

"Teaching? Who told you that?"

"No. Brewing."

Milo stopped ironing.

"Do you have a few minutes? I'd like to discuss a business proposal."

Milo had a few minutes.

"Mr. Bender, I represent a client who is interested in buying Cascade MicroBrew corporation. The offer pays creditors fifty cents on the dollar, and gives your father $25,000 walk-away money."

"So?"

"So, if the bankruptcy proceeds, he'd get nothing. But he won't agree."

"What's it to me? I've got my own problems."

She cleared her throat. "In addition, we're prepared to offer you a two-year employment contract to continue as brewmaster, contingent on relocating."

The iron crashed to the floor. Redemption from middle-school hell.

"We had hoped you might help persuade your father."

Persuade him? He'd push him into a fermenting vat.

Two days later, the old man capitulated and they finalized the agreement.

CHAPTER 18

Bob flicked off the kitchen light and entered the diner, empty except for Lester, seated at the counter.

"She lets me lock up," Lester said, staring at his aging face in the mirror. "That's my contribution." He pinched an inch of sagging neck skin.

Bob slid onto the next stool. "Thinking of a facelift?"

"What for? It'd be like wearing tight jeans instead of comfortable sweatpants."

Bob liked Lester more each day. He should tell him now, but he hesitated. Bob had been blown over when he heard the cost of the license. A million bucks. He had expected five figures, not seven. Would there be enough left to complete the plan? Besides this, there would be the cost of leasing space, start-up expenses, and salaries. And they'd need operating capital until profits started to roll in. He glanced around. No one was nearby.

"I made the call."

Lester stared into the mirror.

"About the license," Bob said. "The beer license."

Lester lifted his coffee mug and sipped.

Bob admired Lester's mastery of silence. "What do you think?"

Lester inhaled a deep breath. "I think this town is dying, and if we don't do something, we'll all be like Ralph."

Bob stared.

"Ralph Hayden. You gave him a muffin."

Ah. The homeless man.

"And my blanket." He took another sip. "Did you get it?"

"The blanket?"

"No, the license."

Bob shifted on the stool. "There's a complication."

Lester raised his eyebrows.

Bob decided to give it to him straight. "Getting a license takes six months to a year." He cleared his throat. "There's a workaround, but it will cost a little money."

Lester swiveled on the stool and swept his hand across the diner toward the windows and Main Street beyond. "You see any money around here?"

Bob raised his gaze to meet Lester's. "It would only cost you ten thousand. And I have some savings."

"You want to be partners?"

Bob shook his head. "No. It would be in your name."

Lester stroked his unshaven face.

"I have, um, liabilities," Bob said.

"And what's in it for you?"

"A job."

"So, you're asking me to invest ten thousand dollars for a license to brew beer, and hire you to run it?"

Bob nodded. "Some equipment would come with the deal, too."

Lester took another sip and offered his hand. "Not only in my name," he said as they shook. "In Grace's too."

Lester's white pickup scrunched to a stop on the gravel shoulder of the road. A wide-porched, one-story bungalow huddled on the large country lot. Lester leaped from the truck, hurried around and opened the passenger door. As Grace stepped out, he offered his hand. She ignored it and marched across the weed-strewn lawn, Lester hurrying a pace behind, the ten-thousand-dollar check from the just-executed second mortgage on their home protruding from his back pocket. They stepped onto the front porch. A sign, *Saint James Real Estate*, filled the window. Grace stood beside the door, arms folded across her chest. Lester reached around her and rang the bell. Alvin jerked the door open, greeting them with a smile as bright as his plaid sports coat.

"Welcome," he said, opening his arms.

They headed for the two seats before the metal desk. Alvin hurried behind to hold Grace's chair as she descended. A filing cabinet, copy machine, and stacks of paper adorned the office.

Alvin sat behind his desk. "After all these years, I don't believe you've ever been in my office." He spoke to Lester but stared at Grace, grinning.

"I'll get right to it," Lester said. "We're having a problem making the numbers work."

Alvin's forehead furrowed up to his bald scalp. "Seven thousand a month is way below market to lease a facility of that size."

"What market are we talking about?" Lester said. "The LaPlante market? There is no LaPlante market."

"The bank is taking a big loss on this."

"They already took the loss when they foreclosed. Now they're trying to salvage something."

Lester had done his homework. When Worthington Industries had come to town and gobbled up Mountain West Fabricators, it abandoned the leased building as it had the employees. The foreclosure dumped the white elephant on the books of First National Bank of LaPlante, who put it on the market with Saint James Real Estate, where it languished for a year.

Alvin Saint James had seemed surprised when Lester called. Yes, the property was still for sale. Yes, the bank would consider a lease-option. Yes, he'd meet them this afternoon.

Lester leaned forward. "Alvin, the bank is in a tight spot. We could go as high as three thousand a month. You can persuade them."

Alvin stammered, holding up both hands. "You don't understand, Lester. The bank is my client. I have a fiduciary duty to represent their interests."

"You know how to twist arms, Alvin."

"Oh, no, I couldn't do that. I have to give them my honest opinion."

Lester sighed. He really didn't want to do it, but he had little choice. This would cost him. He glanced at Grace and nodded.

She uncrossed her arms, and the scowl became a pouty lower lip.

Alvin's eyes grew wide.

"This is important to me, Alvin," she said.

"But…"

She reached across the desk and touched his hand.

His face flushed. He picked up the phone, dialed, and explained to the bank officer the many reasons why he should agree to the lease. "Lester's financially reliable, and he's the only interested party in a year…a brewery would put money into the local economy and help your other shaky loans…the building isn't even an asset, it's a liability, what with taxes and maintenance and insurance." Alvin was on a roll. "The place is in disrepair, the elements will soon be encroaching if money isn't invested. And God help the bank if some kid spray-painting his school colors at 2:00 a.m. falls off the catwalk. You'll unload a white elephant from your books. Lord knows, you've already got enough of those."

Lester listened to Alvin argue every reason except the real one— to please Grace, with whom he had been infatuated ever since she had led cheers for the high school football team and he had played second piccolo in the marching band.

As they stepped off the porch, Grace's eyes flashed at Lester. "Don't *ever* ask me to do something like that again."

The faded gray Honda Civic crept up the snow-dusted mountain road. Bob glanced in the mirror again, pulled over, and waited. No one followed him. He resumed his trek and found the rock outcropping that marked the turn. He eased the car onto a barely-passable trail through an aspen grove, a single plant connected through its root system, where an individual tree lives a century, but the colony continues for millennia.

A gnawing unease grew in his gut. Once he did this, there would be no going back.

Brush swept across the car sides, and low branches slapped the windshield and roof. He didn't recognize the terrain. Snow had hidden his markers. He had built a column of three stones on the forest floor. The stacked rocks, each smaller than the one below, formed a sign like a boundary marker of an old mining claim. As he had ascended the mountain, the snow grew deeper until it concealed all his waypoints. Had he passed it? Was it still ahead? He might not be able to locate the money until spring. Maybe the snow was karma, telling him not to proceed.

Then he saw it, the tree he had marked with three chops at eye level.

He cut the ignition. As the windshield clouded, he saw Grace, glowing with gratitude for the hope Lester had found. He saw Lester, jaw set in determination to protect her. As Bob's affection for another man's wife grew, he knew he would protect her also. Another reason this had to work.

He sighed. Show time.

Pushing the door open against the encroaching undergrowth, he squeezed out. He popped the trunk, removed a shovel and a hard-shell suitcase, and stepped off the trail into the ancient grove. He counted ten paces to the west of the tree, scraped the snow away, and jabbed the shovel into the earth. Six inches down, the spade hit metal. Careful clearing of the dirt and rocks revealed a strongbox. He dusted the top, snapped two latches, and swung it open.

He pulled a Tracfone from his pocket and swapped it for one of the half dozen identical phones in the box. He opened the large suitcase, reached into the buried metal trunk, and began transferring bundles of cash.

CHAPTER 19

Heather sat on the soft leather sofa, one long leg resting on the other knee and her silk robe falling around her thigh. She lifted the long-stemmed crystal from the glass coffee table and sipped the chardonnay. Through the floor-to-ceiling living room window, the lights of the city twinkled. She inspected her long nails, elegantly manicured and glossed in Bashful Passion. She took another sip and glanced at her Cartier. Henry was late.

She had half a mind to walk out. That would teach him she wasn't about to be treated with disrespect. But she wouldn't. Henry didn't respond to snits. After three months of dating, she had H. Meriwether Doyle charted out like a treasure map. She knew where the dangers were—the quicksand, the alligators, the riptide—and most of all, the location of the buried treasure. He was like most men she had known, but more experienced, and that made him dangerous. He required precise handling.

She liked Bob. Truly. Sweet and generous and pliant, he had even remained faithful in their three years together. When she told him about her and Henry, he couldn't bear the hurt, and ran away.

Henry was an assertive alpha male of large appetites. Life with him would be more challenging, but also more rewarding. The mother lode of husband-quest, he would require a three-step landing process. Step one, leave some things here. Step two, stay a while, which meant move in. Step three, marriage. Like boiling a frog, if you dropped him in hot water, he'd hop right out. But if the water was room temperature and you slowly applied the heat, he'd stay until he boiled.

A month in, she had achieved step one.

A key clicked loudly in the lock. It rattled impatiently before the bolt opened with a metallic snap. Doyle strode in. She rose to meet him, handing him a filled wine glass, and stood close.

"I'm annoyed with you, Henry," she said, playing with the knot of his loosened tie. Then her fingers encircled it and ran down its length. "You worried me."

He grabbed her buttocks and pulled her against him and his breath of scotch.

"Henry, not so rough."

He released his grip, collapsed onto the sofa, and took several quick sips of the wine.

She sighed and sat beside him, crossed her legs, and arranged the robe over her thigh.

Heather had begun to suspect that Doyle was not her exclusive property. At sixty-five, he only had one go a night in him, if that, even pumped up on pharmaceuticals. So she knew when he had expended his energy elsewhere. And bravado provided a clue, suggesting a cover-up. This was a problem. She needed to move on to step two.

As he sprawled against the back of the sofa. She snuggled up at his side.

"I appreciate your looking for Bob for me, Henry," she cooed. Her fingers played with his shirt buttons. "He left me in such a lurch, financially."

"Glad to do it. It's not right that he left you high and dry like that."

She kissed his ear. "Last week, the bank pinned a foreclosure notice to my door, and I thought, why do I need that big house now, anyway?" She checked his face to gauge the reaction. Nothing. She put her hand on his thigh. "If I stayed here for a while, we'd see more of each other."

"No."

His abruptness startled her.

"You can't live here. It's a business expense. For entertaining. And out-of-town clients."

Heather knew the only person ever entertained in Henry's love nest was Henry. "I thought, well, it'd be more convenient," she said. "You know, for a trial period."

"Trial for what? Marriage?"

Heather stifled a gasp. She would never have mentioned the M-word at this stage. But since he had opened the door, she should seize the day.

"We'd make a good team."

Doyle raised her chin with his finger. "Let me explain this." He waved his finger between them, meaning their relationship. "It's like a business arrangement. I bring to the table financial assets and a large income, both likely to grow in the future. I'm what you'd call an appreciating asset. You, on the other hand, bring beauty and desirability. But *they* don't grow with time, they diminish. So, you're a *depreciating* asset."

She might have snorted had she not been a disciplined professional. Instead, she allowed some hurt to enter her eyes.

He took a big swig of wine and continued like an economics professor. "And a depreciating asset is not a buy-and-hold, it's a lease. Marriage is out of the question." Another swig. "Plus, I'm already married. And so are you."

Her lip quivered. "But I left my husband for you."

"Yes, and you left your previous husband for him, and the one before that for him. Don't get dewy-eyed on me."

Her tears flowed and she sobbed into her hands.

Even the black heart of H. Meriwether Doyle was not immune to the performance. He sighed. "I'm sorry, baby." He lifted the wine bottle, refilled their glasses, and downed half of his. "We can't find the son of a bitch. He's got something that belongs to me and I need it back." He offered her a tissue.

She dabbed her eyes, sniffled, and rested her cheek on his chest. "He doesn't have *me*," she cooed.

Doyle drained his glass.

She slid her fingers under his shirt and drew circles in his white chest hair. "I'm sorry, too. I just miss you when we're not together." Her assets would soon be appreciating once she employed the nuclear option.

CHAPTER 20

Bob scribbled on a clipboard in the dark recesses of Sally's Donuts. They had punched a hole in the flower shop wall into the next vacant storefront, formerly a mom-and-pop bakery. Equipment filled the empty space, including tables with fermentation vessels, plastic containers and tubes, and shelves piled with grains and malt and empty bottles.

Bob had received the message a week earlier. *Transaction complete. All corporate licenses and permits still valid. Take possession of assets at your convenience.* He promptly notified Lester, the new president and CEO of Cascade MicroBrew, Inc.

A gas burner had been installed in Sally's so as not to require use of the diner stove. Above each vessel hung a clipboard showing the different ingredients in the batch, the mixing order, and cooking and brewing time. Bob kept experimenting, steeping the wort in different fruits and grains, and keeping detailed records of each result.

"Why do we keep changing the formula?" Hector said. "Let's pick one and stick to it."

Bob tapped the clipboard. "Thomas Edison tested a thousand filaments for the light bulb before he found the right one."

The whitewashed windows of the former doughnut shop darkened as an eighteen-wheeler rumbled to a stop on Main Street. Bob hung up the clipboard, and he and Hector walked through the doughnut shop, through the flower shop, through the café kitchen and dining room, and out into the street. Lester and Grace were already outside.

"Delivery for Lester Hargrove," the driver said, handing him the manifest and opening the back of the truck. Grace's jaw dropped. Hector whistled. Gleaming, plastic-wrapped equipment filled the trailer, including a large metal cylinder at least six feet in diameter and eight feet tall.

"How are we even going to get that through the door?" Hector said. He strained to see past the first. "How many are there? Four?"

"Six," Bob said.

Grace glared at him.

"It's on the manifest," Bob said, pointing at the paper.

Lester stared at the packed trailer, then at the equipment list. "Yeah. Six."

"Lester." Grace enunciated his name much too clearly. "Where are we going to put all this? It wouldn't fit if we bored into every storefront on the street."

"It's going into the Mountain West space." Lester's smile became a wince. "That's why we leased it." He glanced at Bob, who remained mute.

"I see," she said.

Bob gazed at the sidewalk.

"And, Lester," she said. "How did we pay for this?"

"The bank loan?" he said. It sounded more like a question than an answer.

She crossed her arms. "That loan was for ten thousand. This looks like a million." She tilted her head and waited.

"I used my stash."

"What stash is that, Lester?"

Bob and Hector climbed into the trailer to inspect the equipment and escape the line of fire.

"My stash. My savings."

"You don't have any savings, Lester."

Lester looked toward the men in the shadow of the trailer. Bob knew he should offer assistance as Hector disappeared into the bowels of the truck.

"I thought we were buying a license and paying some lawyers." She raised her eyebrows. "Where did we get the money?"

Bob listened from behind the safety of a 2,000-gallon brewing vessel.

"Leverage," Lester said. "We bought the corporation. We are now Cascade MicroBrew, Inc. We got their licenses and inventory and equipment. Everything."

Bob cringed at Lester's rapid-fire blathering.

"By owning the stock, we can continue to operate while the Feds check us out as the new owners." Lester's chuckle came out as a croak. "You're not involved in any criminal activity, are you?"

Her face remained frozen. "I might shoot my husband."

From above, Bob watched Hector push the thick-bristled broom in rapid strokes across the concrete floor. The winter sun angled in through the high windows of the cavernous structure, spotlighting the billowing dust clouds. Hector's coffee-brown eyes peeked out between the black shock of hair falling across his forehead, and the white dust-mask covering his nose and mouth, while Milo's arms flailed about.

"We sweep, we wash, we sanitize," Milo said. "I'm not bringing my equipment into a pigsty." He swept one arm across the expanse of the room toward the six gleaming metal fermentation vessels on the loading dock.

Hector glared at the fat man and snorted. "It ain't your equipment anymore, man. It's Lester's."

Atop the high-school-gymnasium-sized space, a glass-walled office overlooked the employee drama below.

"It may be Lester's equipment," Milo said, "but I'm the brewmeister, the artist upon whose talent the entire enterprise rises or collapses. Verstehen sie?"

Milo's ego was off-putting, but Bob had to agree with his penchant for cleanliness. When they had arrived, the place had been filthy. They found broken windows, debris scattered across the floor, and graffiti on a wall—*Mountain West sucks.*

"We don't start the first batch until the place is spotless," Milo said.

Hector had been cleaning for two days. To any objection, Milo responded, "Wer ist der Baumeister hier?" Speaking Deutsch had probably had not endeared him to his father's employees either, but he seemed to relish the persona of claimed German ancestry.

Hector had complained to Bob. "My ancestors were plotting the movement of the stars while his were jabbing spears into each other," he said. "Where'd you find this diva?"

"It was a package deal," Bob had said. "He came with the equipment."

"You're sending dust everywhere, Pancho," Milo called out as Hector swept a pile of debris into a dustpan and dumped it into a barrel.

Hector glared at Milo and trembled visibly. "My name is Hector."

"Okay, *Hector*." Milo's fat lips stretched taut. "I thought you people knew how to push a broom."

Hector's face flushed and he opened his mouth to speak, but no words came out. "I need some air," he finally said.

He propped his broom against the wall and hurried toward the door, his mask gray with dust. He plunged through the plastic-draped loading dock door onto the elevated platform and into the frigid December air.

Bob watched him sit in a canyon of gleaming plastic-wrapped cylinders, on one of the boxes of equipment still waiting to be moved inside and assembled. Above him, an illuminated sign flashed *Cascade MicroBrew*.

Bob had never run a business, and he didn't know how to herd cats. It took two weeks of cleaning and setting up the equipment before Milo began brewing. When Hector burned the wort on the first batch, Milo waved his hands and raved.

"Dummkopf."

They contaminated the second batch, and it too had to be dumped.

"You see? You see?" Milo said. "You can't brew beer in an unsanitary vessel."

The third was drinkable, but not salable. So, Bob made a tap available, free to anyone with a thirst, a plastic cup, and a strong stomach.

The fourth batch proved to be the charm, a sweet tasting brew with a slight tang. Milo swaggered about as Bob, Hector and Lester sipped approvingly.

Lester decided to call Milo's brew *Pierre L'ours*, after the town's founder, Pierre "The Bear" LaPlante.

"But he's a frog," Milo complained. "Frogs don't know beer."

Known as "The Bear" not for his size, but for the mode of his demise, Pierre LaPlante was a legend and a source of pride for the region, a symbol of this rugged country—independent, self-reliant, and imprudent in the face of danger.

On the label, a threatening grizzly towered over the bearded French trapper, and the poster read, "Enjoy it while you can."

Bob felt the presence of the grizzly. With the extensive cleanup and repairs in the plant, and then the bad batches, they were already two months behind schedule, which had forced him to take several more trips to the mountain. And when they tested the old bottling equipment, it kept throwing just-capped bottles to the floor with a pop and a hiss.

"We'll have to bottle the first batches by hand," Bob told Lester.

"Can we afford more equipment?" Lester said to his business manager.

Bob's gaze remained on the floor as he swept broken glass. This would be his fifth "withdrawal" to meet expenses. The hemorrhaging had to stop.

"I guess," he said.

But their don't-ask-don't-tell policy regarding finances didn't extend to Grace.

"Where's this money coming from?" she said, as Bob awaited his lunch across the diner counter. "Every day it's something else."

"Don't worry, sweetheart," Lester said. He put his hand on Bob's shoulder. "Bob's handling it. He's good."

She grunted and lifted two plates from the pass-through. "What did we get ourselves into?"

Bob handled it all right, by exhuming cash at every turn. Everything took longer and cost more than anticipated. So, when they finally bottled the first successful batch, Bob plunged into his role of guerilla marketer, acutely aware of the limited budget and

KEN HUBONA

dwindling cash. He and Hector visited every minimart and mom-and-pop grocery within two hundred miles, leaving a case on consignment, a poster in the window, and a free six-pack for whoever happened to be on duty.

In LaPlante and the surrounding towns, the crowds at the high school football games were large and enthusiastic, so Bob and Hector put on aprons and gave away samples just off school property, which were consumed heartily by friends, family, and faculty as they entered.

Bob even accepted Grace's invitation to their church, and he corralled Hector.

"I'm Catholic, man," Hector said.

"Catholics can distribute fliers outside." And so they did, at church and every other public gathering.

And everywhere they went, they hung posters.

The local U-Save supermarket and Stop-N-Go minimart on the highway were the first to re-order, the Grizzly Tavern sold well, and even the Cascade MicroBrew name brought with it a small following. But total sales remained modest as overhead grew.

"I'm running out of ideas," Bob said, as he and Lester lunched in the elevated office under Grace's watchful eye.

Lester speared his fork into the salad Grace had brought. He came up with a piece of dangling lettuce and examined it. Across the table, Bob stuffed a meat-filled sandwich into his mouth. Lester dropped the utensil onto his plate and fell back into his chair.

"Eat it," Grace said.

"You know what I want," he said.

"Yes, I do. You want pizza and hamburgers and ice cream. Now eat it."

He sighed, jabbed a tomato slice, and fed it into his mouth. "Why can't I have something good?" he mumbled.

"Because your pressure is too high and your cholesterol is too high and your weight is too high."

Lester snorted. "When God saw that Adam was lonely, he said, I'm going to give you a companion. She will cook and clean for you, and bear your children. She will not nag or whine, and she will wait on you hand and foot without complaint and with a smile on her face. She will be called *woman*."

Grace's slender figure stood over Lester, her hands on her hips.

114

"So, Adam says, sounds pretty good, but what's this going to cost me? And God says, an arm and a leg. And Adam says, too much, what can I get for a rib?"

Grace stared at Lester. "Ha, ha," she said in a monotone. "But mostly I watch what you eat because I love you and don't want to lose you."

Bob's Adam's apple jumped as Grace kissed Lester's balding pate and walked toward the door.

Lester scowled and chewed his lettuce.

As Grace turned to leave, Bob ran his fingers through his hair. He didn't want to ask for help, but he was ready to try anything. "I'm out of ideas."

Grace opened the door. "Wineries have tasting rooms," she said as she went out.

Bob froze and his mouth fell open.

Lester shrugged. "That's not a bad idea." He stared at Bob's lunch. "It's your call."

Bob scooted to his desk and punched the calculator, figuring the cost to build a tasting room at the end of the factory floor and stock it with the necessary bar equipment. Would the hemorrhaging never end? He sighed. "I guess we can do it." He started marking up the blueprints of the factory floor. But this was it. Absolutely and finally. This would be the last trip to the mountain. He had to maintain some escape money.

Lester pointed his fork with dangling lettuce toward Bob's half-eaten roast-beef sandwich, mayo and cheese oozing from the sides. "You going to eat that?"

Bob marshaled his forces and built the tasting room in two weeks. They installed a glass wall, set up the bar, stools, tables and assembled a long list of supplies. They painted over the graffiti, repaved the parking lot, and had a grand opening. Lester called a friend in the highway department to designate Cascade MicroBrew an "attraction," and add its name and logo to the signs on the interstate that paralleled the old road. Motorists could conveniently ramp off at Exit 52 and on again at 68, with a stop for a quick tasting halfway between, the sixteen-mile stretch barely a detour.

Staffing the tasting room would cost even more, but he knew the right people. And it was time to man up. Across the booth, Darryl sat with his arms crossed. Candy tapped her foot against the table leg in a steady pelt.

"I owe you both an apology," Bob said.

Lester watched from his usual stool at the diner counter.

Bob straightened his utensils. "I was in a bad place then, but that's no excuse."

"That's okay, Bob." Candy tossed her blonde tangle. "We're back together now."

"Yeah," Darryl said. "We understand being in a bad place. You didn't have to buy us lunch."

Bob couldn't help but admire these people. "I know, it's just that…" He didn't know how to proceed. He swallowed. "I need your help."

Candy and Darryl looked at each other.

"You need *our* help?" Candy said.

Bob nodded. "Can you sell beer?"

A broad smile blossomed on Candy's face.

Could she ever.

Candy's cleavage, smooth and supple and straining to break free from her Bavarian bodice, gently rose and fell with each breath. Even from his perch, Bob couldn't help but notice. No one could. But that was the whole point.

A middle-aged man across the counter leaned forward.

"And this is *Pierre L'ours*, our signature brew. It's a Hefeweizen," she said, drawing an ounce of the yellow brew from the tap into the crystal. With two fingers on the mini vase, she slid the drink across the inlaid wooden bar with a smile and the hint of a wink. "It's a cloudy wheat ale."

The man reached for the glass and their fingers touched as it passed.

"The cloudiness comes from the suspended yeast, which also contributes to the unique hint of banana and clove."

He took a sip, his gaze never leaving her bodice. The uniform was her idea.

She exhaled as though lost in thought. "Des Moines. I always wanted to go to Des Moines. I hear it's beautiful."

Another glass appeared from beneath the counter.

"And this is our Dunkel," she said, drawing from another tap. "It's a dark lager which we produce in two varieties, the sweet, malty Munich style, and the drier, hoppy Franconian style."

She leaned forward. "May I interest you in a couple of cases, John?"

His slack-jawed stare provided his answer.

"Better make it four," she said. "Since you won't be back to see me for a while." She glanced at Darryl. "John would like four cases. Would you take it to his car, Darryl? He's from Des Moines."

Darryl loaded the beer on the dolly. "That Candy's quite a gal," he said as John stumbled off the barstool, his head twisted for a parting glance.

The tasting room spread the brand like a July fire up a tinder-dry slope. Locals, tourists, and passing businessmen crowded the bar and watched the brewing of beer in the pristine facility. The floor shone, the brewing vessels glistened, and Hector walked about purposefully in a frock with an "Apprentice Brewmeister" patch, checking each container against his clipboard. Like any good actor, Hector ignored his audience, immersed in his role to produce the finest beer this side of Munich.

The front door swung open and closed nonstop. Twenty cars lined the parking lot. Customers entered, and dollies piled with crates of beer exited. Hector checked the equipment, Darryl rolled the dolly, and the two new Bavarian-bodiced girls learned as they watched the experienced professional work the counter.

Candy pushed the crystal to her new customer. "Sioux Falls," she sighed with a far-way gaze. "I always wanted to go to Sioux Falls."

Bob threw his cards on the table. He stunk at poker. Hector did an end-zone dance, his hands over his head.

"Hoo-ah." Hector raked in the coins, still in his apprentice brewmeister frock.

"We don't celebrate money, Hector," Lester said. "Money is for living. Money is for helping your neighbor." He looked at Bob. "Money isn't for keeping score."

"It is in poker," Hector said, stacking his pennies.

In the diner kitchen, the four men sat at a round plywood table, seated on crates of various sizes, remnants of the old brewing operation. A new sheet of wallboard covered the former door to the flower shop, the joints mudded and sanded smooth, awaiting paint. The door had been resealed when the adjacent storefront reopened. The success of the brewery inspired other entrepreneurs, and new businesses peeked out like crocuses in February. The increased traffic from the interstate even created a modest tourist trade. Business at the diner had picked up, and Grace had hired replacements for Hector and Bob in the kitchen and two new waitresses. Even parking on Main Street had become a problem during the day.

Cal, proprietor of the Grizzly Tavern, shuffled the cards. "MicroBrew must have cost a fortune, Lester. No one figured you for that kind of money." He dealt out four hands. "This town owes you a debt of thanks."

"I don't deserve the credit," Lester said. He held a bottle toward Bob. "It's—"

Bob's gaze locked on Lester's, and he shook his head.

Lester took a swig. "It's Grace who deserves the credit."

"You both do," Cal said, tilting his bottle in a toast. "You put a lot of faith in this town."

"Hear, hear," Hector said. "And that was before we tripled production."

During the growth spurt, Hector had presented himself in the perch. "We need more capacity," he said, standing before Bob's desk. "We can't ship it fast enough."

"No," Bob said. "We don't have the resources." He wasn't going to spend the last of it.

"Orders are backlogged." Hector raised his palms. "Do you want to lose our customers?"

So, the six brewing vessels had become twelve, and then eighteen as they expanded across the factory floor. Bob hired twelve employees to meet the demand and retired to his lofty office. Now he *had* to make it work.

The gamblers picked up their cards.

"Three cents," Lester said, shoving the pennies forward. He repositioned himself on the crate that served as his seat.

Bob pushed some coins. "See your three, and raise you a dime."

Hector scowled and dropped his cards. "I'm out."

Cal threw his hand on the table. "Too rich for a bartender."

Lester reexamined his cards. "I'm in." He grinned. "And a quarter."

"I think he's got it," Hector said.

Bob leaned forward and counted the pile of pennies before him. "And thirty-nine cents more." He pushed in his entire stack.

Lester raised his eyebrows. "You sure you want to bet everything?"

Bob shifted his weight on the now-empty metal strongbox. "I'm all in."

CHAPTER 21

At half salary since Thanksgiving, Dave struggled like a pauper to meet his obligations to Tracy. He'd never be able to take her anywhere nice for their two weeks in the summer. Demoted and broke, he spent his days searching the internet for dirt, or taking pictures of couples in dark restaurant booths, or listening at the wall in a motel room, like a common Peeping Tom. And he spent his nights sitting on this barstool.

"I did some superlative detective work today, Al," Dave slurred at the bartender, holding up his glass in a self-salute. "I found a video of Barby O'Toole at a raucous party, howling and drinking and shaking her booty. It was easy. Her Facebook led to a friend's Facebook, which led to the video. People are so stupid."

"Kids," Al said in bartender-brevity, defining all behavior under age thirty.

"So she's a slut and a bad mom and deserves whatever she gets. Just another tart looking for an easy payday."

Al rinsed glasses and put them on the drying rack.

Dave addressed the empty bar, spreading his arms. "I'm at the apex of my career. It doesn't get any better than this." He slapped a twenty on the bar, dismounted the stool, caught his foot, and sprawled out onto the floor.

"I'm okay, I'm okay," he said, raising a hand. He struggled to his feet, limped out of the bar, and stumbled toward home, oblivious to the March chill. Home. Hah. He didn't have a home. With no family, no memories, and no love, the sleazy hole of an apartment was where he crashed each night to sober up. A dump befitting a man in his line of work.

Fatigue overwhelmed him and he dropped to the curb to rest. Dark figures approached in the fog, and a searing pain consumed him.

When he awoke, an ache coursed up his bandaged leg. He groaned and squinted against the bright light. A benevolent shadow blocked the glare.

"You passed out in an alley," Frankie said, "and some punks lit you on fire." She removed her fedora. "Apparently they mistook you for a bum." She eyed him. "I can see the resemblance." She pulled up a chair to the hospital bed and put her hand on his arm. "Davie boy, when are you going to get your shit together?"

He groaned.

"Is the booze more important than your job? Your health? Your daughter?" She picked up her hat and walked to the mirror. "Time for you to make a decision." She put it on and ran a finger around the brim. "See you back at the office." She touched her fingertips to an eyebrow and flicked them up in a quick salute. "Or not."

Dave stared at the ceiling as hospital noises beeped and chirped and buzzed around him. Frankie only cared because he was profitable. Why should he change? Booze made his life tolerable, like that plastic bag dripping the painkillers into him and bringing sweet oblivion.

He awoke to the world's sweetest sound.

"Daddy, Daddy." Tracy ran to him in tears and hugged him.

His ex leaned cross-armed in the door frame.

Tracy remained with her head on his chest for several moments. "I was so scared."

His eyes moistened.

"Promise me you'll get better, Daddy."

He swallowed hard and blinked away the tears. "I will, Squirt. I promise."

They let him out two days later, drugged up, limping on crutches, his right foot wrapped in bandages. He hailed a cab, hobbled into his dump, and collapsed on the sofa.

Tracy or booze. Through the haze, he remembered those words from Frankie.

He struggled to rise and dragged himself to the refrigerator. He opened every bottle of beer, liquor, and wine and poured it down the sink. In a large plastic bag, he threw the empties, and, while he was at it, a year's worth of pizza boxes, fast food wrappers, and empty Styrofoam containers.

At his desk, he flipped on his laptop. The software Dave had installed months ago hummed along, scanning the internet, searching for keywords, including every person linked to Baldwin. Among the bot programs, one monitored public filings of the law firm of George Gifford, Esq., PC.

He hit a link, and lines of data appeared on the screen. After scrolling through them for an hour, a word caught his eye. LaPlante. Where had he seen that? He pulled over a banker's box jammed with files, rifled through it, and came up with a folder. He opened it and found the computer printout Doyle's secretary had given him months before. Mountain West Fabricators, LaPlante, Idaho. He jerked upright on the couch and started typing.

A bankruptcy filing in Coeur d'Alene, Idaho was closed with the purchase of the bankrupt's stock by Lester and Grace Hargrove of LaPlante, represented by George Gifford, Baldwin's pal. Baldwin linked to Gifford, who linked to Hargrove, who linked to LaPlante, which linked to the defunct Mountain West Fabricators, which linked to Worthington Industries, Baldwin's client when he disappeared. Dave dove in to investigate these connections.

The next morning, he leaned against the doorframe of Frankie's office. "My seedlings have borne fruit," he said like a cat burping yellow feathers.

Frankie looked up. "The Burger Chef – Trixie McDougal sexual harassment case?"

"That's lime-sized. Bigger."

"The Murphy divorce?"

"That's a grapefruit. We're talking watermelon here."

"You don't have any watermelon-sized cases, Davie boy."

"I used to."

Her eyes grew wide. "Baldwin?"

He examined at his nails.

"Doyle fired us," she said. "Getting him back would be no cakewalk."

"My research into his finances suggests he may be, um, receptive to a new deal."

Frankie nodded, picked up the phone, and dialed.

CHAPTER 22

Doyle pulled his silver Bentley into his assigned spot in the building parking garage. As soon as he shut off the ignition, his door popped open and a gorilla reached in and pulled him out.

"What the fuck?"

Artie stood before him as two of his goons held each of Doyle's arms.

"We didn't get no money on Friday, Henry."

Doyle surveyed his surroundings. The garage was empty of people.

"I went out of town. On business."

Artie shook his head. "You don't get a pass for that." He half-closed the car door. "I'm sorry it's come to this, Henry. I tried to impress upon you the importance of meeting your obligations. But talk don't seem to work with you, and Mr. Giantelli don't tolerate late payments."

"A big fee's coming in Friday. I'll have it then. Now get the goons off me."

"Put your finger in the door, Henry."

"What?" Doyle struggled against the gorillas. Their grips tightened on his arms.

Artie raised his palms in a shrug. "It has to be done."

"I told you I'll have it on—"

"In the door, Henry."

When this was over, there would be many scores to settle. Doyle put his pinkie in the door frame and braced himself for pain, but not for the sharp jolt of agony that shot through him. As the screech left his lungs and echoed through the parking garage, and sweat poured from his face, he collapsed into the arms of Artie's henchmen. They set him down into the driver's seat of his Bentley, his feet on the ground beside the now-open door.

Artie raised a finger in Doyle's face. "Next week, Henry, your payment will be on time." He patted Doyle on the shoulder. "Better see a doctor about that."

Drugged up and his hand immobilized in a splint, Doyle returned to the office. When he arrived, Fontaine was waiting.

"Didn't I fire you?"

She stood. "Yes, sir. And rightfully so. I let you down, and I'm truly sorry for that."

This woman never ran out of bullshit. What did she want? Forgiveness? She already proved herself incompetent.

"So we kept working the case, pro bono, as it were."

His hand began throbbing. He fumbled the bottle of pain killers out of his coat pocket and downed a couple with a splash of scotch.

"Ms. Fontaine, I have work to do."

She smiled broadly. "Hold onto your socks, Mr. Doyle."

The drama queen paused.

He waited.

"We found him."

Burning hot mercury coursed through the veins of H. Meriwether Doyle. His lust for revenge was a drug like no other. Better than bourbon. Or cocaine. Or sex. Passion overwhelmed him and transported him to Hell's inferno. His mind became a laser, focused on the object of his fury, and the satisfaction of scratching the itch. He would strangle Baldwin with a garrote, the wire disappearing into his neck as his head turned purple, his eyes bulged and his tongue swelled out of his mouth. He'd watch the terror in his eyes as life left them, then piss on his corpse and mount his head on a pike at the city gate, a message for all who would steal from the king.

"Where?"

Fontaine held up a finger. "First, there the matter of reinstating our agreement. After all, we've been working the case for free."

"What do you want?" Doyle knew this freak had him.

"Reinstatement of the contract, return of the fees refunded you in December."

He couldn't even pretend to dicker. "Okay."

She told him Baldwin's location.

"What's he doing in East Bumfuck, Idaho?"

"Probably living off your money, sir."

A guttural growl rumbled from within. "Bring me his head."

CHAPTER 23

Heather locked the bathroom door in Doyle's high-rise condo. Eight weeks earlier, a taxi had brought her and her last suitcases. Like boiling the frog, she moved in incrementally and got away with it. When Doyle realized that she no longer went home, it was too late. Plus, her extreme attentiveness mollified his pique. And with his problems at work, he didn't have the energy to fight her.

She bent forward on the toilet and stared at the paper strip. Blue. She smiled as the color appeared.

She hadn't wanted to employ the nuclear option. Conventional warfare had always been successful. But Henry was her most formidable opponent yet, and big rewards required big risks. Exactly how would this play out?

Henry, I'm pregnant. No, too abrupt. *Henry, we're going to have a child.* And he'd say, *Get an abortion.* Then she'd say, *But Henry, I'm Catholic.* And he'd say, *How do I even know it's mine?* Her lip would quiver and she'd weep softly. He'd sigh and put his arm around her. *We'll work it out.*

As she gazed at the paper strip, the smile evaporated. She and Ricardo had been particularly active before she sent him packing. What if…?

Henry would certainly demand a DNA test when the child came. If it was his, she had her meal ticket for life, even if they didn't marry. But if not, her career would nosedive. She would no longer have the pristine body needed to move up the sugar-daddy ladder or even make a lateral move. She'd be washed up at thirty-three, and back in the trailer park.

But if she aborted, she'd lose her meal ticket eventually anyway. No baby, no wedding, for sure. She had taken to heart Doyle's comments about depreciating assets. In ten years, he'd be richer and she'd be painting her face like Pam, the current Mrs. Doyle. The realization first arrived as a tingling, with no clarity, but as it came into focus, she recognized it. Like the foolish dreams of a million high school football players, perhaps the NFL was out of reach, and her future would be selling life insurance in Peoria. She shuddered at the prospect. No. She hadn't come this far by entertaining negative thoughts, but by problem-solving, by working her craft, and by having a can-do attitude.

She flushed the strip, showered, and, sitting cross-legged on the silk sheets, opened the laptop and tapped the keys. "Prenatal DNA paternity testing." Several websites popped up. Clicking on *Whoze-your-baby-daddy.com,* her eyes widened as she read. *Non-invasive prenatal DNA paternity testing is now available.* Yes! *At eight weeks, a blood sample of the mother contains sufficient DNA from the fetus to determine paternity, by comparing it to the purported father's DNA. His DNA may be harvested from a blood sample or cheek swab...* No way she could get a blood sample, or stick a Q-Tip into his mouth. ... *or hair.* Cutting a lock would be dangerous, even as he slept. She jumped up and hurried into his bathroom. Darn. The neatnik's brush and comb were hairless. She returned to the computer.

Then she saw the solution, but it wouldn't be easy. He'd have to participate. Could she swing it without him becoming suspicious? Of course. It would involve some risk, but she could finesse it.

Doyle came home that evening to an elegant candle-lit dinner and Heather in a silk robe, holding a full wine glass toward him.

"What's going on?" he said.

"Welcome home, sweetheart." She handed him the glass and clinked hers to his in a toast. "To an evening together." They both sipped.

She put down her glass, took off his coat, and loosened his tie. He sipped some more wine. She refilled his glass.

By the time he tasted the crème brulee, he had consumed enough Viagra-laced wine to inflate Snoopy at the Macy parade.

"What's that for?" he mumbled, as she ripped open the foil packet.

"Relax, baby," she said, pushing him back onto the bed.

Later, as he snored loudly, she retrieved the used condom from the bedside trash where he had tossed it. In the morning, she headed to the clinic, where she had blood drawn and sent to the lab to be compared to Doyle's DNA sample. Ten days later, she had the results.

CHAPTER 24

Bob pored over weekly production and sales numbers religiously. In December, when the tasting room opened, sales spiked and they ramped up production. But by March, sales had started a steady decline. With roiling stomach acid, Bob found himself popping antacids like tic-tacs. What had changed? It was spring. If anything, business should have been picking up. By June, production costs exceeded revenues. They were in the red.

Bob leaned against the corner of his metal desk, looking at the high-top sneakers on the Bavarian barmaid.

"The customer can't see my feet," Candy said, scanning Bob's office. "And even if he could, he wouldn't be looking down there." She reached down and rubbed a calf. "I'm on my feet all day, so I got to go with comfort." She put her hands on the back of a metal chair and leaned forward. "But you didn't ask me up here to talk about my shoes." She straightened up. "Sorry. Force of habit."

"No, it's not your shoes. It's sales. I'm concerned."

"Yeah. Me and the girls noticed you've been down in the dumps lately. She stood before his desk, hands on her hips and eyebrows raised.

"It's about the beer," he said. "Why isn't it selling?"

She scrunched up her face. "It *is* selling. Me and the girls move thirty cases a day."

"Yes, but what I mean is..." He fumbled for words. "When we opened the tasting room, sales boomed. We really got our product out there. But now…" He rested his hand on a sheaf of papers on his desk. "Tasting room traffic is down, sales have flattened out, customers aren't reordering." And the remainder of Bob's stash fit in a shoebox in the safe. He ran his fingers through his hair. "There are three girls now, and the sales from the tasting room are about the same as when you worked it alone." He leaned forward and interlaced his fingers. "You're on the front line, Candy. What's the customer saying? Do you know why sales have slowed?"

"Sure I do. Me and the girls don't sell beer. We sell an experience. Fun with a fraulein." She jiggled to make the point. "But when the customer gets home, there ain't no flirting fraulein, there's only the beer. And everybody sells beer. Have you been to the supermarket lately? There's a whole wall of it. And, if you don't mind me saying, Milo's brew ain't nothing special."

She sat down in the metal chair and crossed her legs. Her Bavarian skirt moved well up her thighs. "Now, that Lester's Lager we used to drink at Grizzly's, *that* was special. That citrus tang made me shiver. Too bad we don't make that."

Bob nodded. "Thanks, Candy."

She stood. "We'd like to see more of you downstairs, Bob." She opened the door. "And less of Milo."

From his perch, Bob watched Milo strut through his domain like a reigning monarch, with frequent sojourns into the tasting room where he would don his white frock with a "Brewmeister" patch and strut among the patrons to receive their accolades, like the French chef called from the kitchen by adoring diners. Much to the annoyance of Candy and the other girls trying to move product, Milo would sidle up to the counter, his girth taking the space of three customers, and guzzle beer for an hour as he regaled his public on the art of brewing.

"In the year 1516, Duke Wilhelm IV of Bavaria enacted the Reinheitsgebot, the world's first purity law. It mandated that beer be brewed only from barley, hops, and water, ensuring the purity of German beer. That law is still in effect. Which is why German beer is the finest in the world." Milo so often repeated the speech verbatim, the girls mouthed the words as he spoke. "That's why here at MicroBrew, we adhere to those strict traditional standards," Candy lip-synched to Milo's voice.

His belly impinging four inches onto the counter, he held up his ceramic German stein, adorned with Bavarian castles and dancing maidens. With his thumb, he opened the hinged top, threw back his head, and took a long draft. He sighed as if kissing a lover. "Perfection."

Bob made his pitch to Milo in the perch behind closed blinds. "We need to start making Lester's original formula," he said. In the flower shop brewing days, Lester would steep the wort in a secret formula of fruit, barley, and nuts. He called it *my secret sauce.*

"No," Milo said. He crossed his arms. "Remember New Coke? Some genius college-boy-MBA decided to change the formula after a hundred years of success. Almost ruined the company."

"Sales are declining, Milo."

"You're not going to adulterate my beer and defile five hundred years of brewing tradition."

"I'm the business manager, and I know what the market wants."

"And I'm the brewmeister, and this is my domain." Milo swept his arm across the brewery below. "You stay up here." He tapped his finger on the metal desk. "We're not changing my formula. Verstehen sie?"

Bob's face burned, but he kept his anger in check. Was Milo stubborn enough to scuttle everything with a mediocre formula and declining sales, as he had under his father's watch?

When Bob headed for the diner to enlist Lester's support, he found the ashen-skinned man slouched on a stool, his trembling fingers turning the pages of a newspaper. A cane hung from the counter. The old man's face brightened when Bob slid onto the adjacent stool.

"You look great, Lester." Bob rested his hand on the once-broad shoulder and found only bone under the loose-fitting shirt.

Grace wiped the counter. "Whatever it is, Bob," she said, "you take care of it. We trust you."

For the next two weeks, Bob examined sales daily. As the decline continued, he paced the office, cursed Milo, and peeked through the blinds at the girls working the tasting room. When the phone rang, he picked it up, listened, and hurried out.

Cal shook his head from behind the bar at the Grizzly Tavern. "I'm sorry, Bob," he said. "But this ain't the Lester's Lager you brought me in the early days. That always sold out in hours. I couldn't keep it in stock. But this…" He broke eye contact. "I'm canceling my order."

It hit him like a shot to the solar plexus. Was a three-million-dollar investment and the town itself about to go down the drain? Bob shook his head and gritted his teeth. He knew what he had to do.

Bob awoke early Saturday morning, crossed the motel parking lot and the dark highway, and unlocked the gate under the "Cascade MicroBrew" sign. He entered a side door and climbed the staircase into the office. He opened the drawn blinds to the empty brewery and tasting room below. He threw a switch, and banks of fluorescent lights clicked on sequentially. The spotless brewery floor held eighteen geometrically-positioned brewing vessels, with pipes, hoses and other equipment, and two forklifts parked near the loading dock. The broad window at the far end hid the still-dark tasting room.

The outside door slammed, and Hector strolled in, his arms stretched upward, his mouth in a wide yawn. He spotted Bob. "Why so early, man?" he called, raking the fingers of both hands through his black mane. "Milo's gone for the whole weekend."

Disobeying Milo's orders was not difficult. Each weekend, he went home to Coeur d'Alene. And during the week, he spent much of his time in the tasting room enjoying his celebrity and the elixir of the brewmeister's art. But as much as Milo craved the spotlight, Bob and Hector avoided it. They worked their plan in the shadows of the evenings and weekends.

"The tasting room opens at eleven," Bob said. "I want to be out of sight by then." He unlocked a desk drawer and removed Lester's original formula from the old flower shop days, with the sweet fruit and nut and barley formulations.

Bob and Hector cooked up a batch, brewing the hops and steeping the wort in Lester's secret sauce. The process ran all day, so Bob didn't have the option to stop as unknown eyes peered at him through the tasting room plate glass window.

The next morning, they moved the brew into vessels 17 and 18 to ferment.

Three weeks later, in the early morning darkness, from vessel 17, they filled thirty half-barrel kegs, and from 18, almost 5,000 bottles, filling over 200 cases. Hector fired up the forklift and filled two vans.

Each hopped into a van and set off to deliver the product to their customers. Each keg and case bore a likeness of Lester and the logo, *The Original Lester's Lager.*

In the tasting room stood five kegs for the taps and 100 cases for sale, along with a note for Candy.

Put your sizzle on this.

When Bob heard the shriek from the perch, he peeked through the blinds to see Milo slam his stein down on the tasting room counter. Candy and the girls recoiled, and every customer looked. The huge man raced into the brewery and up the stairs, the office shaking with his approach. He burst in, yelling and flailing his arms. His face became crimson, he gasped for breath, and then he collapsed into the metal chair by Bob's desk.

"I never saw El Gordo move so fast," Hector said later. "He went up the stairs like a water balloon wiggling up a fire escape."

CHAPTER 25

Bob glanced around the room, left, right, over his shoulder. The spectators were an odd lot. A man in a suit, clean shaven with his hair slicked back. An obese woman in yoga pants and a Disney World sweatshirt. An eighty-something white-haired woman who kept dabbing her eyes with a tissue.

"What's this all about, Lester?" Bob said.

"I want to show you something." Lester shifted on the hard, wooden bench.

"I have to get back. The brewery doesn't run itself." It had taken two hours to drive to Boise.

Lester stared ahead grim-faced.

Bob straightened up. My God. Milo's alone without adult supervision. God knows what he might pull. "I haven't got time to waste." He rose.

Lester grabbed his wrist and pulled him down. "You need to see this."

At a table in front, three board members faced a TV monitor. On another screen, positioned toward the gallery, appeared a man in a prison jumpsuit. The chairperson thanked the inmate, who grunted, stood, and disappeared from the frame.

Bob glanced at the wall-mounted plaque behind the commissioners. *Idaho Commission of Pardons and Parole.*

"Are you here to spring someone?"

"No, Bob. Just the opposite."

The chairperson opened the next folder before her. A rigid woman in a tweed pantsuit, her lips pursed taut, sat in the center.

"John Paxton."

A tattooed ogre in an orange onesie appeared on the screen.

"Mr. Paxton, you have served twenty years of a twenty-five-year sentence for capital murder." She looked at her fellow commissioners. Both nodded. "We have reviewed your application for parole from the Idaho Correctional Facility. Would you like to say any words on your behalf?"

The prisoner grinned, showing several gaps in his teeth. Prison tats marred a muscular neck as broad as his shaved head. "Yes, Ma'am. I want to say how sorry I am for what I done. I learned my lesson and if you let me out, I promise to follow the straight and narrow." The female commissioner shuddered.

"Thank you, Mr. Paxton. We will make a decision within two weeks."

The prisoner rose, and another appeared before the camera.

Lester elbowed Bob. "Let's go." In the parking lot, Bob opened the passenger door and braced a hand under Lester's elbow, helping him in. He handed Lester his cane. Bob got in the driver's seat, lurched out of the parking lot and onto the highway.

"Okay, Lester, what's the point? That you have some scary guys in Idaho?"

"That was Johnny Paxton."

Bob shrugged. "So?"

"He's Grace's ex-husband."

CHAPTER 26

Bob strode up the narrow brick walk to Lester and Grace's house, a neat, one-story frame that dated to the town's old mining days. He had never been to their home before, and Lester's invitation had surprised him. Set on a narrow lot on Second Street, a block from the diner, the white two-bedroom had a broad front porch with potted ferns on the rails and a hanging swing. Lester sat in one of two rocking chairs and undulated slowly. When Bob approached, Lester smiled and raised a hand. Bob sprang up the four porch stairs in two steps and took the other rocker. Lester's cane hung on the rail.

"You want some coffee?"

"No, thanks." Bob's chair moved in synchrony.

"Tea? Soda?"

Bob shook his head.

Quaking aspen branches swayed in the mountain breeze and the golden, heart-shaped leaves fluttered like pennants.

"A beer?"

Bob stopped rocking. "Lester, why am I here?"

Lester shrugged. "It's a business meeting. We're here to talk about our business."

"*Your* business."

"Oh, right. *My* business. Well, Grace's and mine."

Like the captive of a toe-tapping tune that sets one's caboose in motion, Bob resumed swaying to the music of the leaves. This meeting would be conducted in Lester-time.

Finally, Lester lifted his cane and tapped the porch rail.

"Milo called me. Some fuss about your *insubordination*."

Bob snorted. "I wouldn't call it a fuss. More like a full-blown tantrum. We adulterated the purity of five hundred years of the brewmaster's art. And when we ramped up production of Lester's Lager from two to nine brewing vessels, half the total, I thought he might hold his breath and explode." Bob shook his head. "Frankly, I don't trust him not to sabotage something."

"He won't do that."

"Why not? He's certainly angry enough."

"Because he doesn't have the courage of his convictions. He's not willing to sacrifice for some ideal. If he really believed in his purity gibberish, he would resign." Lester wrapped both hands around the crook of his cane and leaned forward. "That's what I want to talk about."

"About Milo?"

"No, Bob, about you."

Lester resumed rocking. "Milo is temporary. Always has been. His contract is for two years. If this thing is successful, we might even want to buy him out before then and send him packing. What we need is a long-term solution. And long-term doesn't include Milo. The question is" —he stared at Bob— "does long-term include *you*?"

They rocked in silence as Bob stared at his lap. Finally, he spoke. "I want to, Lester, but…" He sighed. "I may have to go back East. In a year. Or five. Or never. I don't know."

"I see."

"No." Bob wrung his hands. "You don't understand. There may be circumstances beyond my control."

"I understand plenty, Bob. Everyone has a past." Lester pointed his cane at the horizon. "I was a bachelor most of my life, and I've seen a lot of this country. Didn't want to be tied down to any place or anyone. Had a few scrapes with the law. And more than a few with women. When things got too hot, I got in my truck and moved on. I couldn't imagine another way to live. I came back here and opened the diner. Then Grace walked in looking for a job. And that was that." His eyes brightened. "Speak of the devil."

Grace strolled up the walk with a basket. "Bob, what a surprise." I wish I had known you were here. I would have brought you some lunch." She kissed her husband. "Lester, you need to cover up." She entered the house and returned with a bundle in her arms. He scowled as she helped him put on a sweater and spread a blanket across his lap.

"I look like an old man. I'm not dead yet."

"It's chilly, and you need to stay warm." She put a sandwich on his lap and a coffee mug on the rail, and squeezed his arm. "Bob, I'll fix you something inside."

He waved her off.

She looked at Lester, and back at Bob, and put her hands on her hips. "What are you two scheming now?"

"Just talking business about the brewery," Lester said. "Trying to protect our investment."

She snorted. "Oh, yes. The millions from your stash."

Bob examined his shoes.

She smoothed the blanket on Lester's lap and kissed his forehead. Lester brushed back a wisp of her hair caught in the breeze. Her eyes sparkled, and his face radiated contentment.

Bob's lips parted as he gazed at the lovers. When he saw Lester looking at him with a hint of a smile, Bob closed his mouth and looked away.

"Please don't forget your nap," Grace said as she rose and rubbed Lester's shoulder. She bounced down the steps with a quick wave to Bob.

Bob's Adam's apple jumped as he returned the wave.

Lester nodded. "I think we're both in love with the same woman."

Bob shifted in the rocker. "I…"

"It's okay, Bob. I understand. She's easy to love."

The men rocked in silence for several moments.

"Look, Bob, the brewery needs a succession plan. Where will this be in two years? In five? Ten? Milo is no solution. In fact, he's an impediment, with his stubborn refusal to try anything new. You're the only one besides Milo who knows the process."

"Hector's coming along."

"Is he ready?"

"Not yet. He'll need another six months or a year."

"And Darryl?"

"We put him on the floor with Hector. He's learning."

"That leaves you."

Bob shook his head. "I'm sorry, Lester. I can't commit."

A pickup crept up the street. Bob slid down in his chair.

Lester snorted and returned Cal's wave. "Bob, why do you think I went along with all your shenanigans? Your hiding in the diner kitchen, and now in the office behind closed blinds. Parking behind the building. Using the back stairs. Hiding in a motel outside of town. You stayed in the shadows when we bought the brewery, even though it was your deal. And, of course, the money. I didn't know how you made your money and I didn't ask. You're a smart guy, an educated guy, so I let it go. I let all of it go." He raised his hands. "Why do you think I took that risk and looked the other way?"

"To build a successful business and make a lot of money?"

"No, Bob."

"To help the town?"

Lester shook his head.

"Then why?"

"For Grace. She's had enough trouble for one life. Paxton used to hit her, Bob. Even burned her with a cigarette. His initials. JP. Branded her like a cow. She never talks about it, but she still has the scar."

He choked on his own words and stopped to take a breath.

"Then he killed Bobby Wise, a Shop-N-Go clerk, during a robbery. Bobby had a wife and two small children. He didn't argue. He gave up the money. Then Paxton shot him. Twice. Just for the fun of it. And right in front of Bobby's six-year-old son."

Bob expelled a puff of air.

"The sheriff suspected him of two other murders, men who disappeared, but they could never prove it. So they got him for Bobby's murder and sent him up for twenty-five years."

A gust of wind sent the aspen leaves fluttering.

"Grace raised their son alone. Sad to say, the boy was a chip off the old block. He ran away at fifteen and only came back long enough to get money. And Grace always gave it to him, even though she lived from hand to mouth, waiting tables and living in that trailer. He died in a crack house in San Francisco. Weighed a hundred pounds. So now she carries the guilt of that, too. When I hired her, she was wrung out. A beautiful, loving person taken advantage of by those she loved. Why do people do that?" His eyes moistened and he wiped his face with his sleeve.

Bob stared at the street.

Lester cleared his throat. "If anything happens to me, I fear for Grace."

"You'll be okay."

"I'm not worried about *me*, Bob. I've had more than any man is entitled." Lester's face contorted in pain. "But Grace needs this business running smoothly." He fumbled in his shirt pocket, pulled out a small tin, and snapped it open. "She needs someone she can trust, someone who cares about her." He took out a pill and popped it into his mouth. Gradually, he relaxed. He leaned back in the chair, breathing deeply.

"Why are you telling me all this?"

Lester stared into Bob's eyes. "Johnny Paxton got his parole."

CHAPTER 27

His house was dark as Doyle pulled into the driveway. Thank God the old crone wasn't home. The fob chirped as he locked the Bentley and strode up the brick sidewalk. Inside the front door, he flicked on the lights. Christ. Pam lay splayed across the sofa, clutching an empty wine glass. She opened her eyes and struggled to her feet as he shuffled through the mail on the hall table.

"What's this?" He picked up a church brochure. *Find the peace within.* "Did you get another Swami?" The lush got a lot of mail from her Church-of-What's-Happening-Now. He snorted, tossed it back on the table, and went into his study. Grover approached, wagging his tail, and settled at the master's feet.

An hour later, with a soft knock, the study door cracked open.

"I thought this might help you work," she said, peeking in. He scowled at the intrusion into his sanctum. She came in with a steaming mug of coffee and put it on the desk.

He looked at the coffee, then at her. "What do you want, Pam?" He picked up the mug and smelled it.

She stood before the desk, twisting her wedding ring. She drew a deep breath. "I think we should get a divorce, Henry." Her shoulders straightened after she said it as though a yoke had been lifted.

He didn't see that coming. Where'd she get the balls?

He squinted and tilted his head. "A divorce?"

"Yes, Henry." She shifted. "It's been an empty marriage for years. I've been selfish, and I've held on because of—" She swept her hand across the expanse of the house. "This. But it's time for me to be honest. I hold no malice. I want to start a new life. To be true to myself."

Her delivery was as stiff as if she had held note cards. In their twenty-year marriage, Pamela had never confronted him. Not when she had discovered his cheating in their first year, not when he began spending nights away from home claiming work, not even when he jetted off with a new lover for a long weekend.

"And it's the Christian thing to do."

Ah. The church. Doyle leaned back in his chair and crossed his arms. "Well, well, well. I'm surprised at you, Pam. Who is he?" He sneered. "Or is it a *she*?"

"Henry, please. Can't we keep this civil?"

Her pleas were pathetic. Did he really have to explain it?

"I like being married, Pamela." He held up his hand and examined his wedding ring. "It's both a lure and a shield." He raised the top of a lacquered burl-wood humidor. "It makes all those next-Mrs.-Doyle-wannabes try harder to please me at the start, but give up more easily when it's over." Reaching into the Spanish cedar wood interior, he withdrew an Arturo Fuente. He unwrapped the Cuban cigar, ran it slowly over his upper lip, inhaling deeply, and sighed.

"Henry, we lead separate lives now. And we should do so without recrimination."

With his silver cigar scissors, he snipped the cigar tip.

"Recrimination? Is that your vocabulary word of the day?"

She swallowed hard. "We both deserve to be happy."

He flicked the engraved silver lighter and rotated the cigar between his thumb and forefinger, warming the tip just beyond the flame's reach, teasing it, toasting the tobacco and preparing it for the flame's entry, but holding back until the tip smoldered, yearning for the flame. He placed the cigar between his lips, wetting it, and continued to rotate it until the flame could wait no longer. He took several short puffs, drawing the fire, making her reach out and come the final inch to him. The flame curled and engulfed the tip of the cigar, entering it and exciting the embers to a bright orange glow. He threw his head back and his eyes fluttered closed. When he opened them, he sent a column of smoke billowing toward her like a cannon discharge. "No, Pam. We're not getting a divorce."

She bit her lip.

He'd have to release the bloodhounds and see what she was up to. He took another long drag and leaned back in his chair before expelling it.

"The right cigar can be so satisfying."

CHAPTER 28

The warm evening found Bob lounging in the stacks of the LaPlante library, a place he found safe, the books a physical and psychological barrier against the outside world. Just as the mountains had protected him all these months, his weekly visit to this refuge surrounded him in silence, solitude, and the smell of books. A cradle within a cradle. Like baffles of a recording studio, the volumes that filled the shelves deadened all sound.

His fingertips tapped the keyboard of the public computer, hidden in an alcove between Self-Help and the donated VHS tapes and DVDs. *The Fugitive* stared down at him.

The black screen flickered, then flashed to become a panorama of white mountain peaks, triangular green firs, and an azure alpine lake. Two fawns grazed near the shore while the nearby doe stood upright, her ears an erect "V" toward Bob, listening.

He tapped more keys and an email account appeared, with a lone email in the inbox.

He opened it.

"The hounds have picked up the scent."

A shot of adrenaline coursed through him. He found the date sent. Two days ago. His gut cramped. He deleted the message, logged off, and hurried from the building.

Dave surveyed the activity in the bustling tasting room. Customers entered with giddy anticipation and left with cases of beer, loaded on dollies pushed by strapping young men. In this beer-drinker's Disneyland, maidens that appeared imported from a Munich biergarten worked the counter. They drew drafts, tilted across the bar, and wiggled and giggled and flirted. And when the sale was made, each fraulein bid a pouty farewell to the customer by name.

He sat alone at the counter, his lips still, but his eyes in constant motion. Before him, a pretty girl named Candy tousled her golden curls over the nametag on her bodice, inviting one's gaze. Behind her, beyond the glass wall, glistening metal containers towered above, creating canyons on the brewery floor where men worked. One moved among the brewing vessels, reading dials and scribbling on a clipboard. Another wiped down equipment. And another shuttled a forklift back and forth carrying cases of beer through plastic drapes onto the loading dock.

"This is our Dunkel," Candy said as she drew the bronze brew from the tap. "It's a dark lager which we produce in two varieties, the sweet, malty Munich style, and the drier, hoppy Franconian style." She pushed the mini vase across the counter, touching Dave's hand in the process.

He lifted the glass, sipped, and nodded approvingly.

In the brewery canyon, a rotund man in a white smock approached the Latino with the clipboard. The fat man's face pulsed red as he pointed here, then there, then jabbed the clipboard with two fingers. The Latino did not speak, but contempt filled his eyes. Other workers glanced furtively as they went about their duties. When the big man finished his tongue-lashing and turned away, the other snapped to attention with a heel click and a Hitler salute to the fat man's back.

Dave's gaze wandered up the metal staircase to the glass office with blinds drawn. Nobody went up or down. A snatch of light from within peeked through the blinds. A shadow passed and briefly broke the beam.

"This is quite an operation, Candy," he said.

"Busiest it's ever been."

"Has it been here long?"

"No, hon. This used to be a fabricating plant. Made machine parts. Half the town worked here. But it closed down and moved to Japan or Madagascar or someplace. That was a disaster."

The fraulein standing at Candy's elbow and working the next customer glanced at Dave, then back to her bearded biker customer. *Fraulein* may have been pushing it. Older and more reserved, she did not look like the "Brittney" on her nametag. She smiled and filled out the dress nicely, but did not shake her bodice or touch the customer. Lines by her eyes showed a weariness that Dave felt, a fatigue that he shared.

"Darryl can help you with that beer," she said to her biker customer, tilting her head toward the forklift man. "He's moving some to the dock now." She glanced at Dave again and caught him staring. His eyes darted away as he smoothed down his new goatee. "How are you going to fit that on your bike?" Brittney said to her customer as she pushed a wisp of graying brown hair behind her ear.

"I got saddlebags, sugar," the biker said. "Don't you worry none." He patted her hand.

Candy reached for Dave's glass, breaking his spell. "And *this* is our signature brew, Lester's Lager," she said, drawing from another tap. "It's a Hefeweizen. The cloudiness is from the suspended yeast, which contributes to the unique hint of banana and clove."

Dave took a sip. "Ahhhh." He took another. "This is good."

Candy beamed. "Lester's Lager is our own formula. It's wildly popular. Can we carry a couple of cases out to your car for you?"

"I'd like to. It's delicious, but right now I'm just visiting and have no place to store it."

"You sure?" Candy said with a pout, a lean, and a jiggle.

He shook his head. "Lester's Lager? Any relation to Lester Hargrove?"

"One and the same. He owns the place, him and Grace. They're great people. I love working here."

The fat man entered through the brewery door, reached beneath the counter, and withdrew a German beer stein with a hinged top. He sidled up to the counter, compressing the line of customers. "Draw me a Pierre L'ours, hotpants," he said to another attractive young woman down the counter. He tugged his frock to make his brewmeister patch visible to the customers.

Candy turned her back to the man and rolled her eyes at Dave.

"Correction," she said. "I love working for Grace and Lester." She leaned forward and whispered. "Not *him*." Her eyes flicked toward the fat man.

Dave admired her talent. This sharing of a confidence forged a bond between the sales professional and customer. She was a pro, and he believed in rewarding excellence.

"I think I *will* take a case."

She flashed an I-knew-you-would smile and batted her lashes.

He considered capitalizing on their new intimacy, reached for the photograph in his shirt pocket, and partially withdrew it.

She sighed. "Except for the bad seed over there, we're like family here."

He released the picture and removed his fingers from his pocket. He stood and glanced at Brittney. Her mouth edges twitched up, hinting at a smile. Not a salesgirl smile, but one of genuine warmth.

He smiled back and limped outside, the burns on his leg still smarting. A cool mountain breeze caressed his face as he savored the view of pine forest and peaks beyond. Tracy loved the mountains. He shook his head to clear it. He had a job to do. He eyed the Motel 6 across the road.

"Any other hotels around?" he said as Darryl loaded a case into his trunk.

Darryl shook his head. "No, sir. Next one is ten miles up at the interstate."

Dave drove across the highway and stepped into the motel office. A bell over the door alerted the clerk, who strolled in.

"I need a room," Dave said.

With gray stubble and a belly that strained the Polo he wore, the old man produced a card-key.

"Do you know him?" Dave held up the picture.

"Nope."

Dave shoved the photo across the counter. "Mind looking at it before you decide?"

"Don't need to. I don't know nobody."

"You know *him*?" Dave slid an engraved printing of Benjamin Franklin next to the picture of Bob.

The clerk wet his lips, looked around, and picked up the $100 bill and slid it into his pocket. "He checked out last night."

"How long was he here?"

He tapped the computer. "Eleven months."

"You got his name?"

"I take it you're not a cop."

"Private."

"What'd he do?"

"He's been missing and some people are worried about him. You got that name?"

He tapped some more but didn't look at the screen. "Smith. Robert Smith."

"Credit card?"

"Cash."

"What's he driving?"

"Couldn't say."

"He stayed here eleven months and you didn't see his car?"

The clerk shrugged.

Dave took another hundred from his pocket, and folded and unfolded it with the fingers of one hand.

"Honda Civic. Gray." He plucked the hundred from Dave's fingers.

Dave picked up Bob's picture and slipped it into his pocket. "I'd like to see his room."

"Suit yourself." He produced a key.

Dave took it and turned to leave.

"And, buddy," the clerk said as Dave stepped toward the door, "I'd be careful if I was you."

Dave raised his eyebrows.

"Folks around here like Bob."

CHAPTER 29

At the back of the Mountain View Mobile Home Park, an old trailer rested on blocks, apart from the others and obscured by the encroaching forest. On the dented mailbox, the faded lettering read *Grace Paxton.*

Bob lay sprawled out on a tattered sofa, a blanket draped across it and a pillow supporting his head.

"You're welcome to stay as long as you like," Hector said. "Grace lets me live here rent-free. But what happened?"

Bob grunted and rolled over.

Hector stood over him. "I just got my hair cut. Rex came in and said a cop was looking for you at the motel."

Bob bolted upright.

Hector threw his hands in the air. "I knew it. I knew it." He stomped around in small circles. "What'd you do, man?" He stopped. "No, I don't want to know. What did I tell you about the radar?"

Bob dropped his head into his hands.

"What are you going to do?" Hector said.

"I have to leave."

"What? No, no, you can't leave, man." Hector paced three steps before running out of space in the tiny trailer. The other room barely fit a bed, and this one wasn't much larger. "We need you at the brewery. Without adult supervision, Milo will run the business into the ground. Before you know it, we'll be brewing that Milo piss again."

"Milo doesn't choose the formula."

"And that ain't the half of it. Without you and Lester around, Milo turns into Hitler. He says Lester's a has-been. He says Grace pulls the strings and has him pussy-whipped."

Bob's eyes widened. "He said that about Grace?"

"I'm telling you, he's got no respect. He don't like you much either, but he keeps it to himself when you and Lester are around. But on the floor, the man is mean. And he keeps hitting on the girls. We need you there."

"Lester can handle it."

"Lester can barely walk. He never comes in anymore."

"How about you?"

"What about me?"

"Could *you* handle it? If I were gone?"

"Gone?" He stared at Bob. "Man, what did you do?"

Bob's shoulders slumped as he massaged his temples. "It doesn't matter. I just don't know how much longer I can stay here." He took a deep breath. "Hector, you're being groomed to run the place, to take over when Milo's contract ends, if he lasts that long. But whatever happens, the brewery can't be left in the lurch. So you need to get your immigration status in order."

"Jesus Christ, Bob. I ain't got no immigration status."

"I might know someone who can help with that."

"You do?"

Bob nodded. "How's Darryl doing? On the floor, I mean."

"He's coming along. Why?"

"Can you and Darryl run the process?"

Hector stared through the window. "If we have to."

"You may have to."

CHAPTER 30

Thwack.

Doyle's Ping G400 driving wood connected solidly with the ball. That rare moment of joy shot through him as the Titleist sailed straight and true, rising high into the blue, late morning sky. But that instant of satisfaction faded with the trajectory. At the top of its arc, the ball drifted right. Farther. Farther.

Splash.

Concentric circles rippled from the impact site in the lake that defined the right side of the fairway.

"Tough break," the other golfer said.

Doyle shrugged. The best part of practicing law was the golf. As rainmaker-in-chief, Doyle wined and dined and sailed and golfed most days. Or he spent the afternoon or evening in the firm's skybox at the stadium, drinking scotch and regaling major clients with his hospitality and wit. But golf was the best.

Today he played with Tom Bradish, Chief Operating Officer of Worthington Industries. They hopped in the cart and Doyle sped down the fairway.

"So, Tom, how's business?"

"Great." He stared straight ahead.

They stopped at Tom's ball. He drew out a three wood and connected nicely with his second shot. The ball landed on the green.

Why hadn't Tom mentioned his new merger yet?

At Doyle's ball, he duffed the second shot, but with the third, managed to hit the green. Tom two-putted and Doyle found the cup in three. Doyle pulled out a pencil and scorecard.

"I read you're thinking of buying Federated Stores," Doyle said. "Any truth to that?" He winked.

Tom shrugged.

"That's a four for you," Doyle said. "A birdie. Nice shooting. And for me…" He licked the tip of the pencil. "Let's see. One in the water. A two-stroke penalty. Two to the green, then a three-putt." He bit his lip. "Eight." He wrote "6" on the scorecard.

The cart rolled toward the last hole.

"What ever happened to that Baldwin?" Tom said. "The lead attorney on our Mountain West deal?"

Doyle stiffened. "He's no longer with us."

"Where'd he go? He was good."

"He's not practicing law, as far as I know."

The par-three eighteenth hole backed up on the clubhouse. Both men drove the green, and Doyle putted in. Tom lined up his shot.

"So, what's with the Federated Stores deal?" Doyle said. "When are we going to see that?"

Tom missed his putt, and lined up his final shot. "Blake and Sweeney out of Chicago are working that for us," he said and putted out.

Doyle stood holding the pin and staring at his companion. "You're changing firms?"

"Yeah, Henry. I'm sorry about that. The board decided. Our CEO is tight with Sweeney. I talked you guys up, but…" He shook his head.

Doyle's face burned as the blood rushed in. This lying son of a bitch torpedoed him. He swallowed the rising bile, took a few deep breaths, then shrugged. "Sorry to see you go. But, actually, we're overloaded as it is."

This was the third client to jump ship in three months and by far the largest. And the second to mention Baldwin. Was that bastard out there stealing his clients?

In the clubhouse, Doyle pulled his cell phone and jabbed at the screen.

"Frances Fontaine and Associates," said a perky young voice.

"Get me Fontaine." His voice choked with rage. "Now."

CHAPTER 31

Dave spread the bath towel across the bedsheet and rested his leg on it. A well-worn bedspread lay in a heap in the corner where he had thrown it as his first act upon entering the room last night. He reapplied the ointment to his right calf. The dingy room needed some attention as well. Frayed curtains on a bent curtain rod, an old television, an ancient mattress that sagged like an old mare. When these places started springing up around the country fifty years ago, they were all the rage. But time and competition had taken their toll, and this place depressed him. Why would a man like Bob Baldwin, a lawyer making big bucks, living in a mini-mansion with a gorgeous wife, steal a few million and then hide out in a dump like this? It didn't make sense.

Dave wrapped the clean bandage around his salved leg. The burns didn't hurt that much anymore, except when he stayed on the leg too long.

And how did Baldwin know? Eleven months there, and he skipped out with only hours to spare. That wasn't a coincidence. Someone tipped him. But who? Who knew? Doyle? His top partners? Frankie? Dave had better not divulge information to *anyone* until he wrapped this up. And since they liked Bob here, he'd better handle the rest of the investigation on the QT.

He slid into the rental car and sped down the highway. He spent the morning checking the hotels on the interstate, three interchanges in each direction. He put two hundred miles on the car and returned to town with bupkis. Baldwin was either long gone or hiding in town.

"Your destination is on the right," the GPS said. Dave slowed as he approached the Hargrove home. An old man rocked slowly on the front porch, looked up, and waved. Dave raised his hand in response and kept moving. He wouldn't get the answers he needed driving by the Hargrove house, but he knew where to find the best gossip in a small town.

Jack's Barber Shop reminded him of Floyd's in Mayberry, as Jack ran the comb across the top of Dave's head and the scissors snipped the tips of his still-dark hair. When he had come in, three customers sat in cracked Naugahyde and chrome chairs, but the barber spirited Dave to the head of the line. More like a men's club than a business, the place sang with conversation. Jack and the boys talked about the weather, Friday's high school football game, a grandson off to college, a pregnant daughter, a crash on the interstate. Anything and everything, except what might be useful to Dave. After twenty minutes of meandering talk and the world's slowest haircut, Dave decided to prime the pump.

"Where's a good place to eat around here?"

"G&L's Diner," two customers said in unison.

"What's that?"

Jack spun Dave around and held up a mirror. "Grace and Lester's Diner. Up the street."

"Grace and Lester's?"

"Yup, the Hargroves."

"I stopped by the brewery yesterday. I thought…"

"That's theirs too," Jack said. "But that only opened recently. Their diner's been here for years."

"They must do a good business to parlay a diner into a brewery."

"Not really. The diner business was slow when they started the brewery. But they started small, brewing in the next store. Then they moved to the plant."

"Still, that's a big operation. Must have cost a pretty penny."

Jack shrugged as he removed the cape draped across Dave and shook it. "People don't talk much about their finances around here. But some folks may have quite a nest egg squirreled away. You never know."

Dave needed to take another tack. Bankers, lawyers, and realtors stay attuned to financial activity in a town, but which is most likely to blab? "Can you recommend a real estate broker?"

"There's only one," Jack said. "Alvin St. James."

"We have some great deals in town," Alvin said, spinning his laptop around on the desk to show Dave the slideshow. "Here's a cute bungalow on Third, perfect for a single man. What business did you say you're in?"

"I'm retired," Dave said.

"Congratulations," Alvin said. "You're mighty young to be retired. Is that why you're relocating here?"

"Not relocating. I want a summer getaway."

"Well, you picked the perfect spot, Mr. Dawson. Good weather, beautiful scenery, friendly people. A great place to get away."

"I like this one," Dave said, pointing. "Can you negotiate me a good price?"

"Can I negotiate? I can sell ice to an Eskimo. And this seller," he said, tapping the screen, "is motivated."

"What have you negotiated recently?"

Alvin St. James smiled conspiratorially. "A good question, Dave. May I call you Dave? I can see you're a shrewd businessman." He flashed pictures on the screen. "A house on Fourth, a small ranch north of town, a commercial property on Main Street."

Dave worked at driving the conversation in the desired direction. "Anything bigger?"

Alvin gave him a curious look. Then his eyebrows jumped up. "Have you seen the brewery on the highway? That was my deal."

"You sold that place? Wow."

"Well, a lease-option. But it took a lot of work to get the price down. And I negotiated with the bank. Those guys aren't pushovers. But I got the Hargroves a great price." He paused. "Of course, the place needed a lot of work. Now *this* cream puff," he pointed to a house on the screen, "is move-in ready."

"The brewery is beautiful now," Dave said.

"Yes, Lester sank a bundle into the place."

"Did you negotiate the loan for that too?" Dave said, trying to appear impressed.

"No, Lester used his own cash. But rest assured, Mr. Dawson, I can get you a great price for this house."

Dave was beat. He would grab some cold cuts and eat in the room. He roamed the small supermarket and tossed items into the hand-held basket. Bread, baloney, mayo, chips, Ding Dongs.

He spotted a familiar face, but he couldn't place it. She wore jeans and a chemise with a leather jacket. Her long brown hair bounced in a ponytail as she walked past. Then it hit him. Brittney. Without makeup, she seemed older, about his age, with a simple elegance and innocent but world-worn eyes, a far cry from her Bavarian-fraulein come-hither look. As his eyes followed her, he stumbled into the canned stewed tomatoes display, toppling the pyramid.

"I'm sorry," he said to no one in particular. He stooped, picking up cans and rebuilding the display.

"Need some help?" She kneeled beside him and gathered cans.

He checked her finger. No ring.

"Thanks," he said as they stacked the cans. "No work today?"

"It's my day off. We're open seven days and we each get one off."

"That's a long week."

"Yes, but I'm glad to have the work."

They finished the twenty-five-can base of the pyramid.

"I take it you're not shopping for the family?" She nodded at his basket resting on the floor.

"No, only me."

"Me, too." She glanced at his assembled snack food. "That's your dinner?"

He shrugged. "What's the alternative around here?"

"The diner," she said. "They have good home-cooking. Tonight, the blue-plate special is meatloaf."

"Do you work there, too?"

"No, but it's the same every Tuesday. And it includes mashed potatoes, green beans, and iced tea."

"Does it include company?" He tilted his head.

She blushed. "I can't," she said, looking into his eyes. "But thanks."

"Then I guess it's chips and baloney for me tonight."

"And Ding Dongs," she said.

They finished stacking the fallen cans and stood.

"Thanks for the help, Brittney."

"I'm Brittney at work." A shy smile radiated from her. "You can call me Jane."

"Dave," he said, his hand on his chest.

She took a deep breath. "The diner does have great blueberry pie."

Their smiles blossomed in unison.

In the corner booth, they leaned toward each other like teenagers at the malt shop.

"What brings you to our fair city?" Jane tilted her head.

"Business," Dave said.

"In LaPlante? Well, I guess we have arrived. Used to be, everyone was *leaving* town."

"But no more?"

"Not since the brewery opened. People think it will turn things around. They have hope now. I know I do. I couldn't find work for a year." She gazed out the window and sighed. "It's been tough for everyone. My girlfriend owns this place, and they were hurting. No one could afford to eat out. Plus, they gave away a lot of free meals. And then her husband had his heart attack." She shook her head. "Those were rough times for them."

"How does she do it?" Dave said.

"She does it for her husband." She pointed to the framed calligraphy above the booth.

Love is patient, love is kind.
It does not envy, it does not boast, it is not proud.
It is not rude, it is not self-seeking, it is not easily angered,
it keeps no record of wrongs.
Love does not delight in evil but rejoices with the truth.
It always protects, always trusts, always hopes, always perseveres.
Love never fails.
1 Corinthians 13:4–8a

"Love never fails," she said.

A waitress arrived to take their order. "Hello, Jane. It's good to see you here." She glanced at Dave and flashed raised eyebrows and a smile at Jane.

Jane blushed.

"What'll it be?"

"The special," Jane said.

Dave flashed a V with his fingers. "Two."

Iced tea came immediately, and meatloaf not long after.

Dave took a bite. "This is delicious." He dug in, surprised by his hunger.

"I told you so."

When she asked about his work, he glossed over it. He did research, mostly on the computer, but sometimes in the field.

She said she liked to read and watch the true-crime shows on TV. And she was writing a story about the town and the people she knew. Their hardships and joys.

"Really?" he said. "That's exciting."

She beamed. "Oh, it's not that good, but I think it's important. People around here don't get enough credit. They're honest and church-going and hard-working, and yet most don't have much to show for it."

The waitress pulled the window shade to protect them from the bright, setting sun.

Jane had been at the brewery for six months, and before that, a clerk at Mountain West Fabricators for ten years. When they closed, she couldn't find work.

"It was rough. I used to be a stay-at-home mom, so I don't have what you'd call marketable skills. My kids are grown up now and gone. The husband too. Well, he's just gone. He never did grow up. But we're still married. Legally. So you know." She smiled impishly. "I'd call it a common-law divorce. Like a common-law marriage. If you live together long enough, you're married. I think it should be the same for living apart." She shrugged. "But it wasn't all his fault. I'm not a good judge of men."

Dave confessed his divorce *was* mostly his fault, so his ex wasn't a good judge of men either. They laughed and their hands accidentally brushed against one another. More than once.

And when he talked about Tracy, love coursed through his chest. Jane's gentle smile said she understood.

Plates were removed, blueberry pie served, and coffee poured.

Jane would like to move closer to her children, but she didn't care for city life. And besides, she loved it here. He wanted to live in the country with Tracy and teach her to ride horses. Jane always wanted to visit New Zealand. It looked like paradise. But she'd never even been to Canada.

"We're closing, folks," the waitress said, setting the check equidistant between them. "You'll have to continue this elsewhere."

Dave grabbed the check.

"Thanks, Grace," Jane said, as the waitress left.

"Grace?" Bob watched the woman clear a table. "Grace Hargrove?"

Jane nodded.

The old feeling welled up. He wasn't suited to this work. Putting a face onto the name made it too personal. A sweet face. A kind face.

"I heard they owned the brewery."

"They do. But they work here. They have management running the brewery. Milo. And Bob."

"Bob?" Dave said before he could stop himself.

"Yes. Bob Smith. He's the business manager or some such thing. I'm not sure. I just pour the beer and shake the ta-tas." She giggled. "Hey, it's work." When he didn't react to her flirting, her smile evaporated. "Why? Do you know him?"

Dave shook his head.

"Is something wrong, Dave?"

He stared at her for a long moment as a sense of loss overwhelmed him like a black mist. "I like you, Jane." His voice faded.

"But...?"

"I'm so sorry we won't get to know each other better."

She looked down and nodded, then reached out and took his hand. "Thank you for dinner, Dave." She squeezed his fingers. "I hope you find what you're looking for."

Dave collapsed on the sway-back bed. He was now officially a first-class shit. He lay staring at the water-stained ceiling. He thought of Tracy. He thought of Jane. He thought of his sorry life. No, not first-class. World-class.

His cell phone started buzzing. He picked it up. Frankie.

"Where are we on this?" she said with no preliminaries when he answered. "The whale just had a conniption in my ear."

"I'm working it, Frankie."

"It was quite a snit." She giggled. "You would have enjoyed it." She paused. "Anyhow, you need to wrap this up before the man strokes out."

"I'm on it nonstop. Baldwin is well-liked around here. Once again, we're chasing the good guys."

"Don't go dewey-eyed on me. And don't forget who's paying the bills."

"He's hiding, Frankie, and no one's giving him up."

"Everyone's got enemies. Even Jesus had his Judas."

"Exactly. And I'm tired of crucifying innocent people."

"Baldwin isn't innocent, Davie boy. He may be Robin Hood, but he isn't innocent."

Dave clicked off and dropped the phone on the nightstand. His leg throbbed.

Dave knocked on the door, bone-weary from a long day that wasn't over yet. No answer. He checked the room number he had written down at the office. He knocked again, harder this time. He was getting too old for this.

"What?" a voice said from behind the closed door.

"Milo Bender? The manager gave me your room number. Can we talk?"

"What about?"

"I'm looking for a friend of yours."

"Who's that?"

"Bob Smith. Would you open up?"

The door cracked. Cannabis and stale beer odors wafted from the slit in the door.

"He's no friend of mine," Milo said across the chain. "He's just an asshole I work with."

Dave's leg throbbed. "May I come in?"

Milo shrugged. The door closed and the chain rattled. It reopened to rolls of pink blubber extruding out around Milo's tighty-whities and skin-tight T-shirt, like a diapered baby magnified ten-fold. He made no attempt to cover himself, but plopped down in the chair, his legs splayed, and adjusted his package.

Chicken buckets, two-liter soda bottles, and strewn clothing decorated the room. Plus rumpled bed sheets, a full ashtray, and dirty underwear.

Milo must have read Dave's thoughts. "I don't let those Mexicans in here with my stuff when I'm not around. They can clean it when I'm gone. I go home on weekends. Get the hell out of this hick burg."

Dave cleared a spot on a chair and sat. "Where's home?"

"Coeur d'Alene. It isn't much, but compared to this place, it's New York City." He took a long swig of grape soda straight from the large bottle. "I'm the boss, so I don't have any friends here."

There probably wasn't a Milo Bender fan club in Coeur d'Alene either.

"You're the brewmaster, aren't you? I saw you working earlier today."

"Brew-*meister*." Milo pointed at the patch on his stained smock hanging on the door.

Dave shook his head in awe. "What a responsibility. It must be tough having all those people working for you. Like herding cats." He forced a chuckle.

"Yeah, it's lonely at the top." He eyed Dave. "What do you want Bob for?"

"We have some business."

Milo's drooping eyelids rose. "Does he owe you money? You going to beat him up?"

"No, Mr. Bender. I only need to talk to him. Can you tell me where he is?"

"Sure. Third floor on the corner." He pointed upstairs. "I'd like to watch. The son of a bitch adulterated my formula."

Dave shook his head. "He moved. Yesterday."

"That's good news."

"Any idea where he may be?"

"How would I know? Shacked up?"

"With whom?"

"I don't know. One of the bimbos in the tasting room. They're always shaking their booties at every swinging dick that comes in."

Dave thought of sweet Jane, and of pushing in Milo's fat face.

"When does he work?"

"I don't know. He works in the perch, the office above the brewery floor. He never comes down to do any real work. He keeps his own hours. He may be there now, for all I know. Now that I think of it, I knew he was hiding from someone. With those drawn blinds."

Dave rose.

"Can I help?" Milo said. "I'd like to help."

Dave's snorted unintentionally as he left the room.

Dave had staked out the place for two hours when a gray Civic pulled up to the back door of the brewery. A man in a brown corduroy jacket hopped out, fumbled with some keys, opened the door and hurried in. Sometimes you get lucky. Parked on a dark gravel road, fifty yards behind the brewery, Dave was stiff and exhausted and his leg wouldn't quit hurting.

Ten minutes later, the man came out carrying a stack of papers. He put them on the passenger seat, started the car and eased away. Dave followed, without lights initially. The car drove to the Grizzly Tavern and the man walked in, his coat collar pulled up against the wind. Dave entered and approached the man hunched over the bar.

"Hello, Bob."

The man turned. "You talking to me, man?"

It was the Latino Dave had seen on the brewery floor. The one Milo berated.

"Sorry. I thought you were someone else."

CHAPTER 32

Doyle grimaced at the voice of the gap-toothed moron on the speakerphone.

"I'm on my way," Artie said. "For your sake, I hope youse got my money."

The phone clicked off.

Doyle heaved a sigh. He knew what was coming next. Martha picked up her steno pad and pen and stepped toward Doyle's office door. She tapped the doorframe and entered without waiting for an answer, closed the door, and stood blocking it.

"Henry, are you going to let these thugs run your life?"

He groaned. "Please, Martha, don't start with me."

"Grow a spine, Henry. Sol wouldn't have put up with this nonsense." Though five years dead, Solomon Kravitz still loomed large. She shook her head. "I'm glad he's not here to see this."

Doyle dropped his head into his hands.

"We barely dodged a Bar audit of our trust account," she said. "Competitors are stealing our clients, and the partners, the *senior* partners, are openly grumbling about their bonuses."

"Who? Who's grumbling?"

"And we got a sexual harassment case filed against us. The world's in open revolt. No one fears us anymore. What's going on, Henry? You've lost your mojo."

"Martha—"

"We have a sweet deal going here, and you're not going to mess it up." She marched to the desk, steno pad clenched to her chest. "Okay, Henry, here's what we're going to do. We're going to get our three million back, we're going to pay off these goons, and, as a warning, we're going to crucify Bob Baldwin." She leaned forward. "And you're going to stop your whining." Her head tilted. "You think you can keep your zipper up long enough to get that done?"

He grunted.

She marched to the door, stopped at the wall mirror, and checked her posture. Leaning forward, she adjusted a stray hair, and touched her face. Apparently satisfied, she pressed the door latch and left.

Doyle stared at the closed door. He swiveled around toward the city, bustling thirty stories below. She hadn't mentioned the other option.

He walked to the bar, kneeled behind it, and spun the tumblers on the floor safe. When it clicked, he swung the heavy door up and looked at the two items inside. One was a single bundle of cash. Ten thousand dollars. One hundred hundreds. Half an inch thick, the size of an open billfold. A hundred of these made a million bucks and fit into a briefcase. But he didn't have a hundred. He had one. And it belonged in the trust account, along with the fifty other bundles that were no longer in the safe.

The other item was his Glock. His exit strategy. It had been eleven months, and he had to consider the possibility that Baldwin wouldn't be found and that Doyle's three million would never come home. He reached in and grasped the nine-millimeter pistol. He removed it, held it in both hands and fondled it. The Glock's grip fit smoothly in his hand. He popped the clip and admired the ten rounds in the magazine, then raised the barrel to his face and caressed his cheek, thinking of the last time he had seen his philandering old man, stumbling in late and loud, laughing and drunk.

"No one in this world gives you anything, Henry. Don't be a sissy boy sniveling for permission. Take what you want." His father leaned closer, his foul breath overwhelming the ten-year-old. "And there's nothing like a little strange nooky now and again to smooth out the rough spots, son." He winked at the boy.

Later that night, the old man had put a .44 Magnum in his mouth and pulled the trigger.

Fuck it.

Doyle returned the gun to the safe, grabbed the last bundle of cash, and stuffed it into his coat pocket.

Doyle marched through the hotel lobby with its high ceiling, chandeliers, and marble surfaces. Golden elevator doors opened and closed, transporting weary guests to their refuges. A black-suited desk clerk might have been a maître d' as he tapped cheerfully on his keyboard and swiped the card. His forehead furrowed. He swiped the card again. His look of distress deepened. He leaned forward.

"I'm sorry, sir," he said. "The transaction won't validate." He cleared his throat. "Do you have another card?"

Doyle produced one.

"Oh, dear," the pansy clerk said. "That one won't go through, either."

Doyle pulled the envelope from his coat pocket, counted out a thousand dollars, and dropped it on the desk. "Will this go through?"

"Of course." The clerk finished tapping and handed Doyle a card key. "No bags, sir?"

Doyle snorted and turned away. As he headed for the golden elevators, the LaRue twins marched through the lobby, their stiletto heels clicking in unison against the terrazzo floor like a close-order drill troupe. As the blonde hair, thigh-length leather jackets, and long, tanned legs spiked past, nearby Y chromosomes vibrated like compass needles finding north.

They joined Doyle in the elevator, executed an about-face, and stood as the golden curtain closed on their rapt audience.

"Ladies," Doyle said, pushing open the hotel room door, and inviting them to enter with a wide arm-sweep. He slipped the do-not-disturb sign on the outside knob. They dropped their cellphone-sized purses on the entry table and unbuttoned their coats.

"Allow me." Doyle took their jackets, revealing silk chemises and short leather skirts partially covering their buttocks.

He sat between them on the sofa and poured three scotches. The twins tousled their hair and downed the drinks. He poured another three, which disappeared as quickly. He cleared the glass-topped coffee table and prepared a line of white powder with a practiced flurry of taps with his declined credit card. He scraped it into three lines and handed a rolled-up Ben Franklin to Twin One, and another to Twin Two. They leaned forward and the powder disappeared. Bending down to the longest line in the center, he inhaled through the green tube. He jolted upright, shuddered, and shook his head. He leaned back, wiped his wrist across his lip, and leered at one girl and then the other. This was the kind of decision he should be making rather than dealing with sniveling partners, low-life mobsters, and ungrateful women.

"Okay," he said. "Who's first?"

They both reached for him and said in unison, "You are."

The weekend blurred past. On Sunday afternoon, Doyle fumbled to insert a key into the lock of his condo. He hadn't showered, shaved, or cleaned his mouth since Friday, and he felt like it. He had lived on white powder, scotch, and room service. He'd still be there if the twins hadn't gone to church. His wallet contained two twenties, and his coat pocket an empty envelope.

The lock finally clicked and he staggered in. Christ. She was here.

Heather came running up in her white silk pajamas. "Thank God, Henry. I've been so worried."

"Don't you ever go anywhere?" he said.

Her brow furrowed. "Like where?"

"I don't know. Paraguay?"

She grimaced. "Where have you been?"

He snorted and wiped his nose. "Working." He took off the dark glasses, squinted, and put them back on.

"You didn't answer my calls or texts."

"I was busy. Big merger coming up."

He threw his rumpled suit coat onto the sofa and poured himself a scotch. Hair of the dog to smooth out the rough edges. He collapsed on the sofa and winced. He seemed to have hurt his back.

"Henry, we've been robbed."

"Don't be ridiculous. We're on the fifteenth floor."

"My jewelry is missing."

Doyle blinked. "What jewelry?"

"The diamond necklace you gave me. My beautiful diamond necklace." She sniffled. "And the emerald brooch." A tear appeared. "The most valuable pieces I had."

"Yeah, about that." He took another sip. "I returned them."

Her eyes widened. "Why would you do that?"

"Because I needed the cash." Artie had accepted them in lieu of last week's payment.

"You took my jewelry? How could you?" She stormed into the bedroom.

Doyle enjoyed ten minutes of solitude with his scotch.

When she returned, her face had softened. She sat next to him and placed her hand on his knee. "You shouldn't scare me like that." She stroked his thigh.

Splayed out on the sofa, he looked at her hand and snorted. Boy, was she barking up the wrong tree. He could barely find his lips with the glass.

"Henry, I have news." She took his hand and paused. "I'm pregnant."

"Good for you." He pulled his hand away and took another swig. "Whose is it?"

She seemed stunned. "That's not funny, Henry." Her lip quivered.

Of course. Cue the tears. He wasn't about to take any more shit from her or anyone else. When he had fondled the Glock, he had seen into the abyss and survived. They could sue him, jail him, or break his legs. But anyone who messed with him would be sorry. "How do I know it's not someone else's?"

She stiffened her spine. "That's not possible, Henry."

"You have proof?"

"I knew you'd be like that." She dropped the letter on the table.

He picked it up and read. *The submitted sample is consistent with paternity to a high degree of probability.*

"What sample?"

"Yours." She actually looked angry. "The baby is yours."

He didn't need any more of her shit. "What do you want from me? Pam would fight over everything in a divorce and drag it out for years." Maybe that would shut her up for a while.

Her eyes softened. "What if she wouldn't?"

He shrugged, took a long sip of the cold scotch and melted cubes, and rested his head on the back of the sofa. He didn't have the energy right now to tell her it was time for her to get out.

CHAPTER 33

On the trailer sofa, Bob pored through a sheaf of sales reports and financial records.

Hector paced the small room. "He parked on Ajax Road, behind the brewery. Nobody parks there except kids. When I came out, he was still there, and then he followed me." Hector swung his hands and bumped the rake and shovel propped against the wall. He caught the shovel, but the rake whacked the floor, leaving a clod of dirt on the linoleum.

Bob stood and reached for the rake. "Why do you keep these filthy garden tools inside?"

"They belong to Grace. I don't want them stolen. In case you haven't noticed, this ain't exactly an uptown address."

Bob picked up the rake and stood it against the wall. "Jesus, Hector, this must weigh twenty pounds." Heavy iron prongs protruded three inches from the base.

Hector crossed his arms and faced Bob. "You're more interested in my rake than the guy who's after you?"

Bob dropped back onto the sofa.

"Anyway, I didn't want to lead him here, so I drove to the Grizzly."

"How do you know he was after me?"

"I drove your car, man."

"Isn't someone after you?"

Hector shook his head. "I know what my guy looks like."

169

"And?"

"And because your guy said, 'Hello Bob.'"

Bob grimaced. He could run, but for now, sheltering in place would be safer.

"He thought I was you, man." Hector raked his fingers through his hair. "I don't need this heat."

"I'm sorry to bring you trouble, Hector. I appreciate you letting me stay here."

Hector nodded his forgiveness.

"There's something I don't get," Bob said. "There are millions of Mexicans here illegally, and no one cares. Why is someone after you specifically?"

"Because he's a psycho." Hector raised his hands. "He ain't even from around here. He comes up from Salt Lake City, looking for me on his own time."

"Why would he do that?"

Hector shrugged. "He don't like me."

"How does he even know you?"

Hector stopped pacing and sighed. "I stole his car." He plopped down on the sofa. "My brother Carlos and me were working in a commercial laundry in Salt Lake, with about fifteen other guys. Iceman and his merry band of Federales raid the place. I'm in the can taking a leak when it goes down, and I climb out the window. And there's this big white Grand Marquis with its motor running. So I hop in, drive to Ogden, and get on a bus out of town. My brother said the driver took a lot of shit from his pals. They were laughing at him and joking. They said, 'Hey, Chastain, the Mexican stole your car.' That's his name. Chastain. Anyway, he made it his personal mission to get me."

Bob laughed.

"It ain't funny, man," Hector said. He scowled at Bob. Then he laughed.

CHAPTER 34

When Dave sat at the end of the counter, Grace flashed a smile of recognition as she poured the coffee. His gaze stayed on the newspaper, indicating he wanted solitude, and she moved away. He hunched over pretending to read as he sipped his coffee. A dozen customers scattered about talked and ate their lunches. Grace hurried from one to the other, exchanging pleasantries while she worked. She didn't strike Dave as a brewery executive.

The door chirped. A presence entered the diner. More than hear it or see it, Dave felt it. His neck hair straightened, like a cat sensing danger. The din of conversation fell silent, and Naugahyde crunched as customers twisted to see.

Grace reached into the pass-through, spun around with a plate in one hand and a coffee pot in the other, and froze in place. As her eyes widened and mouth dropped open, the plate dropped to the floor and shattered.

Dave sensed the presence approach from behind. He looked at his paper, but his peripheral vision locked in on the man who settled onto a counter stool three down and in front of the gaping Grace.

"Hello, darlin'," he said, more of a growl than a greeting.

Dave had seen shaved heads with tattoos, scarred and crudely drawn. But what riveted his attention wasn't the prison tats. It was the deep scar, jagged and ill-healed, that ran from his cheek, down his neck, and disappeared beneath the black T-shirt. That, and the black eyes focused on Grace like a laser.

"Ain't you going to say hello to old Johnny?"

His gaze moved over her, alert and lingering, as the lion admires the fawn. He rested his elbows on the counter. His biceps and thick neck bulged from the too-small T-shirt, and the well-defined muscles of his chest popped beneath the black fabric.

"How about a coffee?"

She put a mug on the counter, and coffee spilled as she poured.

"Now, now, darlin', no need to be nervous."

She kneeled down and swept up the broken plate. "When did you get out?"

"Yesterday. I was disappointed you wasn't there to meet me." He looked around. "Nice place you got here. G and L diner. You the G?"

Dave stared at the man's rippling shoulders and back.

The broken crockery clattered into the trash.

"Don't make trouble, Johnny."

"Is that any way to greet your husband?"

She shook her head. "I divorced you twenty years ago."

"We'll always be married, 'til death do us part."

"There's nothing for you here, Johnny. Go somewhere else and start a new life."

"Au contraire, babe. This is my home, and I ain't got what you call 'means of support.'"

"The things you did. The people you hurt." She shuddered. "You're not welcome around here."

"Sorry you feel that way." He sipped his coffee. "Cause I'm moving into our trailer."

"It's *my* trailer."

"No sweetheart, it's half mine. Divorce don't give you my property."

"I paid off the mortgage. For twenty years."

"And I thank you for that."

She took a deep breath. "Why are you here?"

"Why? It's my home." His lips parted, showing his jagged tooth. "But I'm not an unreasonable man." He looked around the diner. "I see you done damn good for yourself while I was gone. You got yourself a thriving business. I'm sure we can work something out."

"No, Johnny."

"I only want what's mine." He licked his lips. "You remember the good times we had." He inspected her from stem to stern. "Time has been kind to you, darlin'."

He reached for her arm, and she jerked it away.

Dave clutched the counter. Two customers rose.

She held up her hand toward them and shook her head.

"I'm married now."

"Yeah, I heard about that. I also heard he's an old coot. You a nurse now? I'll bet the geezer don't do for you what I did for you."

"The old coot taught me how to stand up for myself." She reached beneath the counter. "And how to use a gun."

Dave saw her hand trembling.

"Do you want to finish this now, Johnny?"

Johnny's forehead furrowed in the wake of her stern glare. "You got yourself quite the attitude." He smirked. "I guess that comes from wearing the pants in the family." He slapped a five on the counter. "I'll be seeing you around."

When the trailer door handle rattled, Bob sprang from the sofa into the bedroom and slid the curtain closed.

"What?" Hector said to the closed door.

"Open up."

The door squeaked open. Bob looked through the curtain. A hulking man stood outside.

"You need to vacate the premises," the man said.

Bob had seen those prison tattoos on a TV monitor three weeks earlier. Hector stood frozen.

"Ok, Paco," the man said. "I knocked on the door, I asked real polite-like, and now, for the last time, you boys is trespassing. Get out."

Hector, standing inside the screen door, turned his head. "What do we do, Bob?"

The man yanked the screen door open and walked in, brushing Hector aside.

Bob swallowed hard and stepped into the room. "We've got the owner's authority to be here."

A lightning fast jab to the face sent him flying backward into the refrigerator and then collapsing onto the floor. "You ain't got shit."

A woozy Bob felt himself lifted by his belt and the back of his shirt, and then flying out the trailer door into Hector's vegetable garden.

"You too, Paco."

Hector scurried out the door.

CHAPTER 35

Heather lay on the examination table and winced as the chatty nurse slathered the cold gel on her exposed abdomen.

"Have you had an ultrasound before, sweetie?" said the older woman, Eleanor Taki, according to her nametag. "No? Well, it's real simple. First, we put this gel on you to get a good seal between your tummy and the transducer. That's this thing. We don't want any air bubbles to mess up the picture. And don't worry, the gel is water-based. It won't stain you or your clothes."

The woman hadn't stopped talking since she had fetched Heather from the waiting room and guided her to the hall scale. "One hundred twenty-one pounds," she said, tapping the number into her iPad.

"I'm one nineteen," Heather said.

"Not anymore, sweetie."

Once in the examining room, the nurse took Heather's temperature and pressure. "Take everything off, jay-bird naked." She handed her a gown. "The opening in front."

When Nurse Talky returned, Heather lay splayed out like a Thanksgiving turkey being basted for the feast.

"You have such a flat tummy, my dear. This your first? Yeah? I can tell. I've had four. You have to keep the skin supple. Otherwise, you get this." She pulled up her smock to reveal marks stretched across her abdomen like a shark's gills. "But I can see you already know that, hon. You have such smooth skin. And a lovely tan."

The door swung open and the doctor marched in, her hair bunned headache-tight and her neck sporting a stethoscope like an Olympic medallion.

The nurse sprang to attention. "This is Mrs. Baldwin, doctor," she said, and her mouth snapped shut.

The doctor sat on the stool, un-necked the stethoscope, and listened to Heather's heart. She picked up the transducer and flipped a switch. The machine emitted a low hum. She circled the device on Heather's stomach while looking at the monitor. She pointed out Heather's ovaries, uterus, and the jerking mass within.

Heather focused on the screen. "A boy or a girl?"

"At ten weeks, it's still too early to tell the gender," the doctor said. "We'll be able to see more in the second trimester. But they appear healthy."

Heather blinked. "They? My ovaries?"

"No." She readjusted the transducer. Two images came into focus. "Your twins."

"You have a lovely home, Pamela," Heather said, admiring the grand space with its lavish furnishings and artwork.

The women sat on the sofa, facing the silver tea service in the center of the coffee table and a china teacup before each of them. Pam rested with graceful ease, her legs crossed. She lifted the saucer with one hand, the cup to her lips with the other, and took a silent sip. Heather perched on the edge of the cushion, ramrod straight, her teacup untouched.

"Pamela, this is a difficult conversation for me, so I'll get right to it." She cleared her throat. "Henry and I are in love." She watched Pam for her reaction. "I didn't mean for it to happen. It just did." Heather could have been this woman's twenty-year-younger clone. "We want to be together, but not like this." She delivered the close. "We want to get married."

Pam's smile was pleasant and interested, but the silence overwhelmed the large room.

"And there's something else."

The older woman raised her eyebrows, inviting the information.

"We're pregnant."

Pam placed her cup and saucer on the table. "Congratulations, dear." She leaned over and hugged Heather. "I never had children. I envy you that."

"And we're having twins."

"Instant family," Pam said. "Even if you didn't marry, you'd still be entitled to child support for eighteen years. Times two. Not a bad outcome." She sipped and replaced the cup on the coffee table. "Except for one thing. Henry is broke."

Heather's mouth opened. She took a breath and reached for her tea, the cup and saucer rattling. "That doesn't matter to me. We're in love. Besides, it's a temporary cash flow problem."

"I see."

Heather fidgeted with her fingers. "So we're getting married. That's why I'm here. To ask you to grant Henry an uncontested divorce."

Pam sighed. "Heather, may I tell you a story?" She leaned over and opened the drawer on the end table. "As a girl, I used to make jewelry. Metal jewelry." She removed a paperclip and carefully straightened it out. "You can bend a paper clip back and forth with no apparent damage." She demonstrated. "But the damage is there, unseen. It's metal fatigue. Everything appears fine, but the next time you bend it, it breaks in two." She bent the clip again and it snapped. She dropped the two small pieces of metal onto the silver tea tray. "We're like that. If we don't catch our self-destructive behavior soon enough, we break in two." She gazed into the distance. "I was broken and alone in this big house. Nothing but a concubine. But now, He has given me purpose."

"Henry?"

"No, Heather. The Lord." The older woman took Heather's hand. "One day, when the bloom is off *your* rose, and you've become invisible, what will you have left?" Her hand opened to the grand room. "A big house? Wealth? Position?" She shook her head. "Happiness comes from here." She pointed to her heart. "Not from out there." She patted Heather's hand. "When I found the Lord, I found peace. I was content. Happy. And finally able to love." She sighed. "Fifty-five years old, and I found love for the first time. Real love." Her blue eyes peered into Heather's. "I wish the same for you."

Heather furrowed her brow. "So, will you? Let Henry have a quick divorce? Before the babies come. We're in love and your marriage is over."

Pam smiled and shook her head. "Is that what he told you?" She sighed. "I'm not surprised." She put her hand on Heather's shoulder. "I filed for divorce a month ago, Heather. It's Henry who's fighting it."

The cab ride home was a fog. Heather's usual clarity of thought had abandoned her. She stared sullenly through the windshield. The wipers swished the rain, clearing the driver's view, which became immediately obscured. A second later, the wipers swished again. The futile act repeated into infinity. She shook her head. A good night's sleep would clear her mind.

She hopped from the taxi and stepped under the building's canopy. The doorman shifted awkwardly. He opened the door without the usual deferential, "Good afternoon, Miss Baldwin." As she rose in the elevator, she thought of her second husband Brad. Mustang-driving, dark-glasses-wearing, real-estate-magnate-wannabe Brad Romaro. Always chasing the next dream. And always broke.

As soon as she stepped off the elevator, she saw the neon orange flier posted on her door. She approached and read it. *IRS Seizure. Do not enter.* And below. *This property has been seized by the Internal Revenue Service. Entry is prohibited under penalty of law.* A metal box locked the doorknob.

She stood, her mouth agape. Slowly, her face contorted. She shrieked. "Nooooo." She ripped the sign from the door and shredded it in a frenzy. "No, no, no." She collapsed onto the floor, sobbing. She had no husband, no home, no car, and no money. Only the clothes she wore.

After several moments, she took a deep breath and dabbed her eyes. She stood, brushed herself off, and checked her makeup in the foyer mirror. She pressed the elevator button, rode to the lobby, and held herself erect as she exited the building.

"Goodbye, Daniel," she said to the doorman.

CHAPTER 36

Bob lowered the icepack from his black eye.

"Did you see what he did, man?" Hector clomped down the basement steps waving a piece of paper. "Milo outed you."

Bob took the flier. Even in the darkness of Lester's cellar, he could make out the picture well enough. Attorney Robert Baldwin. Clean-shaven, smiling, and younger. But clearly Bob. Archived somewhere on the internet, his old Kravitz & Doyle CV still loomed.

Above the photograph, someone had superimposed, *WANTED*, and below, *Lead attorney, Worthington Industries – Mountain West Fabricators Merger.*

"He made these wanted posters and hung them at the brewery. Is it true?"

Bob dropped the picture.

Hector pushed back his hair with both hands. "Oh, man, this ain't going to help your popularity." He paced in a circle. "Milo's loving it. He says he's helping the detective."

Bob groaned and returned the icepack to his face.

A loud thud shook the floor above, followed by the shattering of crockery. Bob and Hector looked at each other, then ran up the stairs. Lester lay on the kitchen floor amid the shards of a shattered mug and a pool of coffee.

"Call 9-1-1," Bob said. He rolled Lester over and listened at his mouth for breathing. His skin was pale and clammy.

"They're coming," Hector said.

Lester's eyes fluttered, then half opened.

"An ambulance is on the way," Bob said.

Lester shook his head. "Bob," he mouthed.

Kneeling over, Bob put his ear to Lester's lips.

Lester whispered. "Take care of Grace."

Bob drew back and looked into Lester's fluttering eyes.

Lester grabbed the front of Bob's shirt. "She's in your hands now." The old man exhaled a long, slow breath. His grip on Bob went limp, and his open eyes became vacant.

When the two EMTs raced in with the stretcher, Lester was already gray. Bob and a deputy sheriff were performing CPR. Grace sat on the floor, her white skirt and pink waitress apron soaked with coffee. Hector slouched on a kitchen chair. The EMTs worked on Lester for thirty minutes, alternating CPR and chest shocks, Lester's arms flopping lifelessly with each futile chest compression. Soaked in sweat, the older tech put a stethoscope to Lester's chest, looked up, and shook his head. He ran his hand over Lester's face and shut the unseeing eyes. The five men stood as Grace rocked on the floor.

They lifted Lester onto the stretcher and rolled him out. Bob and Grace stood by the ambulance as the EMTs loaded Lester in.

"We'll be right behind you," Bob said. He and Hector would follow in Lester's pickup for the twenty-minute drive to Memorial General. He offered Grace his hand for the step-up into the ambulance. In a trance, she took it, her eyes wet and puffy. Her lips parted.

"I didn't even get to say goodbye."

On Monday morning, Dave pulled up to the brewery, parked in the almost-empty lot, and shut off the engine. It had been three days since he had heard the ambulance racing down the highway. Bob's wanted poster lay on the passenger seat. He unscrewed the top of the antacid bottle and popped a couple of tablets into his mouth. It kept getting worse. He pulled out his cell phone and reread the text message. *I know how to collar the subject. Meet me at noon. MB.* Caller ID showed a local area code. Dave hoisted himself out of the car and trudged up the steps to the tasting room. A sign on the door read, *Closed Today at Noon for the Funeral.* He stepped inside.

"You missed one, Darryl," Candy said.

A tall, young man mounted a step stool and ripped down a Bob-wanted poster.

"He put them everywhere," she said.

"Bob should sue him for libel." Darryl turned to see Dave standing by the door. "We're closed, sir."

Dave saw Jane at the bar. Their gazes met. She smiled and gave a quick wave.

Dave waved back, but looked down as he approached the man on the ladder.

"I'm looking for Mr. Bender," he said softly.

"Milo?"

At that instant, a blubbery arm draped over Dave's shoulder like a slab of wet beef. "Mein freund. We find our man yet?" Milo leered at Jane and the rest of his audience. He reached into a pocket of his smock and shoved a wanted poster under Dave's nose. "I figured once these yokels find out that their hero's law firm made millions on that merger, while *they* lost their jobs, somebody would give him up." He raised his eyebrows. "You're probably wondering how I got your number." He smirked. "Rex at the motel. It's on your registration. Pretty good sleuthing, huh?"

Jane's mouth fell open. Candy and Darryl stared.

"Anyhow, here's the tip. There's a funeral this afternoon. I'll bet our man will be there. He and the deceased were tight, as thick as thieves. That'd be a good place to make the bust, don't you think?" Milo offered a fist, but it went un-bumped.

Darryl's eyes narrowed. "You're the guy looking for Bob?" He stepped off the ladder and moved toward Dave.

Candy grabbed his arm.

"I don't care what this stupid poster says, Bob's done right by me. I got my job. I got my girl." He tilted a dolly back and pushed it past Dave toward the door. "I got my truck." The door shut behind him.

"And he got his self-respect," Candy said.

Milo sneered. "These small-town hicks think the mob rules. They ripped down my posters. They resent people who seek justice." He gave Dave's shoulder a squeeze. "Thank God for people like us."

Jane glared at Dave. He considered leaving. Just walk out and go home. But he knew he'd stay. He'd do even this for Tracy. He swallowed hard and walked toward Jane. "I'd like to explain."

She stood in silence.

"Can we talk?" he said.

"Why?" Her voiced cracked. "Do you need more information?"

"It isn't like that, Jane."

She crossed her arms. "What's it like?"

He wrung his hands. "This isn't something I want to do."

"We lost Lester. You're going to take Bob. What next? Close down the brewery? Is *that* something you want to do?"

Dave couldn't meet her gaze.

"I thought we had a connection." She dabbed her eyes. "But you were using me."

Then he said it. It just came out.

"It's my job."

She stiffened. "It's okay. It's my fault." She tossed her head with careless indifference. "Like I said, I'm a bad judge of men."

Dave held the military binoculars against his face, his fingers steadied against his forehead to eliminate the jiggle of the high-powered lenses. Each face was sharp. The widow stood closest to the casket, her eyes puffy, but her jaw set. Next to her stood Baldwin, his face partially obscured by the neatly-trimmed salt-and-pepper beard, and the sunglasses poorly concealing the dark stain that spilled from beneath them onto his temple. Next to him were Candy and Darryl and the Hispanic man. The one he had followed. All somber, all in black. Spread out around them stood most of the town, some in suits and black dresses, some in work clothes. All remained silent and unmoving.

Dave lowered the binoculars, reached for the bottle of antacids in the center console of the white rental car. How would he do this? It would be tricky, with Baldwin protected by an entourage of bodyguards. Dave popped a couple more tablets and chewed. He snorted. This was just like him. Always the practical tactician. Always working on *how*. Never *why*. Or even *whether*.

"People like *us*," Milo had said. Milo and Dave. Peas in a pod seeking justice. Not like those people down there, family and friends pulling together in sorrowful times, there for each other. He chewed the chalky tablets and swallowed the hard truth. He'd been on the wrong team for years. Even his I'm-doing-it-for-Tracy mantra no longer quelled the roiling acid. And he had actually said, "it's my job."

He snorted and raised the binoculars. Across the cemetery, the tattooed man watched. The bully from the diner. Dave flipped open his pad. Johnny. He leaned against a gravestone smoking a cigarette. His open western shirt revealed a sweat-stained, sleeveless wife-beater T-shirt beneath. He stubbed out the butt on the stone and flicked it in a high arc.

Dave swept the binoculars across the rolling hills of the cemetery. The preacher spoke his final words, passing his fingers across the coffin. The widow stepped forward and placed her hand on the casket. Her lips moved silently. No one stirred. Finally, she turned and others joined her. There were many hugs.

Darryl nudged Baldwin, followed by a head tilt in Dave's direction and some whispered words. Baldwin looked directly at Dave. But instead of bolting, he joined the procession marching toward him.

This was Dave's chance to confront Baldwin. He should do it. He reached for the door handle. The procession approached, Grace clutching Baldwin's arm, Candy and Darryl behind, holding hands, followed by the Hispanic and the entire entourage, speaking softly among each other.

Dave set his jaw. No. He released the door handle. He opened his notepad, scribbled a note, ripped the sheet out, and folded it. He rolled down the window and reached out.

A moment earlier, Darryl had nudged Bob. "White car," he whispered, with a head tilt toward the sedan parked on the crest of the hill. Bob squinted through the dark lenses, but the face was too far away.

"We commit brother Lester into thy loving hands," the preacher said.

Grace stepped forward and placed her fingertips on the casket. Though close, Bob barely made out her words.

"Goodbye, my darling," she whispered. "I love you."

A lump rose in Bob's throat.

She returned to receive the condolences of their friends.

Candy leaned toward Bob. "You should go the other way." She nodded at the white car.

Bob shook his head. "No. Johnny needs to know Grace is protected." Bob had seen Johnny, sprawled against the grave marker. Everyone had seen Johnny.

Johnny wanted to be seen.

"But the cop," she said. "He's waiting for you."

Bob offered Grace his arm. She took it and led the mourners up the hill.

As they approached the car, a hand came from the half-open window, holding a piece of paper. Darryl stopped. The hand thrust the paper toward him. He took it. The arm retreated and the window closed.

Others passed, glaring into the car.

Once seated in the driver's seat of the lead car, Darryl held up the note addressed to "Bob Baldwin."

"That you?"

Bob took the paper, unfolded it, and read. *Please meet me at the library. 10 AM tomorrow. Dave Dawson.*

CHAPTER 37

Bob looked down at Grace's hand, resting on his arm as they sat in the rear seat of the sedan. He longed to comfort her, but couldn't find the words, so he stared out the window as Darryl drove toward the cemetery gate. Ahead, Johnny still leaned against a gravestone, a cigarette dangling from his lips. As they passed him, his eyes squinting against the sting of the rising smoke, he flashed his jagged-tooth smile and made a two-finger salute.

Bob had to offer something. "Maybe I can talk to him."

"You already did that," Grace said, her dark glasses covering her red, puffy eyes. "That's why you and Hector are living in my basement."

"I don't remember him," Candy said from the front seat. "But I heard the stories."

"He left twenty years ago," Grace said. "The kids weren't told the gory details."

Darryl stared straight at Johnny with cold, hard eyes.

"Why is he here?" Bob said. "There's nothing for him here. No friends. No family."

"He's here to take back what's his," Grace said.

"What's that?"

"Me."

Darryl pulled onto the highway.

Bob raised his free arm. "We'll get a restraining order."

"Against a psychopath? What world are you from?"

"From lawyer-world," Candy said. "Didn't you see his wanted poster?" She turned around. "I'm only kidding, Bob. You know we love you. You're a father figure to Darryl."

Darryl's frozen face thawed, and he swatted Candy's lap.

"It's true," she said, grabbing Darryl's hand.

As they pulled up in front of Grace's house, Candy turned toward the rear seat. "You sure you don't want me and Darryl to come in? We'd be happy to set a while."

Grace shook her head.

As Grace and Bob reached the porch, they waved goodbye to the car. "I didn't want to fall apart in front of the kids," she said as she unlocked the front door. In the living room, she picked up Lester's sweater from the arm of a chair and wrapped it around her shoulders. She rubbed her cheek against the knitted collar, breathed in, and settled on the sofa. "The only restraining order Johnny understands is the business end of a forty-five."

She smelled the sweater again. "I'm frightened, Bob. And exhausted. I haven't slept in two nights. I don't know what to do." Her eyes glistened and a tear rolled down one cheek. "I miss Lester. We would have talked about this."

Bob sat on the other side of the sofa.

"But now I'm alone." She looked up. "I mean, it's a comfort to have you and Hector here, but that's temporary. And I don't want to put either of you in danger."

Bob bowed his head.

"I walk to the diner every day. I shop alone. I walk to church. I can't live like that, waiting for him to do something."

When the back door opened, she grabbed Bob's arm. He looked out front and spotted Lester's pickup.

"It's me," Hector said, as he shut the door. He saw them staring. "Sorry." He clattered down the basement stairs.

She sighed and released Bob's arm.

"How dangerous is he?" Bob said.

She shuddered, clenched her knees together, and tucked her elbows, shrinking her body into a sitting fetal position. She took a deep breath. "He wouldn't let me leave, Bob. I lived in fear every moment. It's hard to understand if you haven't been through it."

"Did he threaten you?"

"You've met him, Bob. His mere presence is threatening."

"Why did you marry him?" he said, and immediately regretted it.

"Because he had a Harley and an attitude. And because I was seventeen." She stared at the floor. "He murdered a man, Bob. Maybe more than one. So, they locked him up, then sent him back to us, twenty years older and every bit as mean." She bowed her head. "He did things, Bob." Tears welled up.

A lump rose in Bob's throat. He reached for her. She buried her face against his chest and convulsed in sobs. When the shaking stopped, he continued to rock her.

She pulled away, wiped her eyes, and stiffened her spine. "I suppose I'll just have to shoot him myself." She looked into Bob's eyes. "Thank you for being here." She pulled Lester's sweater tightly around her, leaned over, and put her head on Bob's shoulder.

Her breathing became steady. Bob glanced down. Her skirt had pulled up above her knee, and he saw it. A burn scar desecrated the ivory skin of her inner thigh. Jagged, but clear. *JP.* Johnny Paxton.

Bob's breath caught. His eyes darted away, but he would never forget. As he listened to her breathing in the dark, he knew he would protect her, no matter what it took.

Bob shifted in the upholstered leather chair, cracked and stained, *The Call of the Wild* open on his lap. The glass-walled room had a clear view of the front door. It had been the smoking parlor in years past when LaPlante had a thriving library. But today, the only person he had seen was Miss Pruitt, the librarian for the last fifty years. The room's yellow-stained walls appeared not to have been painted since she arrived.

Movement caught his eye. A man entered the library, stopped at Miss Pruitt's desk, and headed toward him.

"Good morning, Mr. Baldwin," the man said, as he entered the room. "I'm Dave Dawson." He offered his hand.

Bob hesitated, then shook it.

The detective closed the door and sat in the other overstuffed chair.

"I work for Fontaine Investigations. We were hired by Kravitz & Doyle to—"

"I know who you are."

"Okay," Dave said. "Then I guess we can skip the preliminaries. I'm here to accompany you back."

Bob noted the word. *Accompany*. Not *take*. "Why would I do that?"

"Many reasons. But mainly because you have to face the music at some point. This isn't about to go away. Do you want to be in hiding all your life? Don't you want to clean up your mess and get on with living?"

"Excuse me," Bob said. "You're not a police officer. Or a bounty hunter. Is there a warrant out for my arrest?"

"No. There's no criminal case pending."

Bob wasn't surprised. He had always suspected that Doyle wouldn't report the disappeared money because it would expose his own theft.

"I have no authority to make you go back. I had hoped to persuade you. But do you really want the police involved?"

Bob crossed his arms. "By the time Doyle filed charges and got a warrant, I'd be long gone. Maybe Tierra del Fuego. A dollar goes a long way in South America." In truth, his last ten thousand hid in a basement coffee can. "Besides, Doyle won't involve the police."

Dave shrugged. "It could be worse. He could send his mob goons after you. They don't need a warrant."

Bob dropped his head. "Look, I'll lay it out for you. I can't leave. Grace Hargrove's life is in danger, and that trumps everything else." He wrung his hands. "I need to stay and protect her."

"From what?"

Bob sighed. "Johnny Paxton. Her ex. He's out of prison and in town. He's dangerous. I can't leave her while he's around."

"Yeah," Dave said. "I've seen him in action." He rubbed his chin. "Can you buy him off?"

Bob shook his head. "That wouldn't work. He's a psychopath."

Dave shrugged. "Psychopaths like money."

"Not this one."

"Are you sure? When I saw him, he asked about the Hargroves' business interests. Seemed pretty obvious he was sniffing around for money."

Bob gazed out the window.

"Mr. Baldwin, staying here isn't an option for you. Yes, you could run. Or come back with me. But you can't stay here." Dave stood up.

"You need to make a decision." He opened the door. "You have until Friday."

CHAPTER 38

Grover nosed open the study door and approached Doyle seated at the desk. With one hand, the master stroked the chocolate lab's head. His other hand held the phone.

"A paternity suit?" he said. "Are you threatening me?" What a stupid tart.

"No, Henry. What I meant was—"

"Heather, my dear, let me explain the *Presumption of Legitimacy*. It means children born in a marriage are presumed to be the husband's. And the last time I checked, you were still married, Mrs. Baldwin." He leaned back in the swivel chair and rested his feet on the oak desk. "Sure, you and I know Baldwin couldn't spawn a tadpole, but that's the law."

"But the DNA test..."

"Ah. Isn't science wonderful? Yes, you might prove I'm the father. But why would you do that? Let me guess. Child support? Sure, I'll support my kids. I'll feed them, clothe them, and educate them. I'll even house them. In *my* house. I might even let you have weekend custody. But *you* won't see a dime." He hung up.

Checkmate. He knew she had no money to fight him. She didn't even have a place to live. Yes, losing the condo had been a shame, but what choice did he have? She wouldn't leave. If your house has mold and you can't get rid of it, what do you do?

Grover rested his chin on Doyle's thigh and gazed up with loving eyes.

"You give it to the taxman."

Grover's tail thumped against the desk with the pleasure of being addressed by the master.

It was well past time to cut her loose anyway. The cellulite on her ass had already started. He'd banish her back to the sticks to hustle drinks from shit-kicking cowboys. He rubbed Grover's ears. The twins part had surprised him. But maybe that wasn't such a bad thing, spreading his seed. He'd take the kids and hire a live-in nanny to raise them. A young one.

The computer screen lit up. He swiveled around and logged into his account at First City National. He pressed his thumb against the ID pad. Fingerprint security had replaced the USB key. He rose, pulled the drapes to the study windows, and returned. He checked the balance of the firm's trust account. A few deposits had come in. Thank God. He'd transfer another fifteen thousand, barely enough to keep Artie from inflicting more damage on Doyle's bruised body. But two huge fees would be here soon. The Bradley fee, about five million, and Baldwin's stolen money, three million and change. Then he'd be back on top.

He tapped the keys and entered the amount. A red box flashed. *Executive authorization code.* He unlocked the desk drawer, slid it open, and felt for the envelope taped beneath. With practiced fingers, he slid a card from its sleeve and typed the ten-digit number. The screen flashed green. *Transaction approved.* He returned the card to the hidden envelope.

"There are two kinds of people, Grover." He reached behind him and spun the large globe. "Those that grab the world by the balls and make things happen. And those looking for a handout." He stroked the dog's throat. "When we get our money, should we chop off Baldwin's hand?" Grover stared at the master in rapt joy. "That would square accounts. I'd be satisfied with that."

Doyle interlaced his fingers behind his head. When he leaned back, his nosebleed started again. *What the hell?* He hadn't done a line in weeks. Money was too tight now for coke, hotel suites, or the LaRue sisters.

He grabbed a tissue and pressed it to staunch the flow.

The study door swung open and Pam stepped into his inner sanctum. "You could be more Christian toward her, Henry."

What? She never came in here. He forbade it. "And why would I do that?"

"Faith, hope, and love, Henry. But the greatest of these is love. First Corinthians."

That church had turned her into a zombie. "Money, sex, and power. But the greatest of these is power. Henry Doyle."

She saw the nosebleed. "Oh, my."

As she stepped forward, he raised his hand to stop her. She glanced at the open drawer. Her eyes darted away, and she stepped back. Had she seen something?

He pushed the drawer closed. "Shouldn't you be feeding the homeless or helping at the battered women's shelter or doing something Christian?"

Pam stared at him, shaking her head. "She's carrying your children."

He snorted.

"I'm praying for you, Henry. And for the dark spot on your soul." She stepped from his domain and closed the door.

He didn't need her prayers. He needed his money.

"Her faggot preacher boyfriend is one of them too, Grover. He thinks he can take my wife." He called up his email. Compose. *Ms. Fontaine*, he typed. *Another job. Prepare a dossier of Milton Cole, associate pastor at my wife's church. The usual terms. HMD.* Send.

He settled back as the dog circled, matting down the ancient grass of his ancestors and collapsing into the imaginary nest. "No one steals from me."

CHAPTER 39

Wednesday evening, Bob guided the Honda Civic along the dark street. Next to him, Darryl drummed his fingers on the door armrest.

"Why not get the law on him?" Darryl said. "Tell his parole officer he's threatening Mrs. Hargrove."

Bob shook his head. "He hasn't actually done anything." Lights from the trailer park came into view. "Being scary isn't a crime."

Darryl gazed out the side window. "In Missouri, someone shot the town bully in front of thirty witnesses, and no one saw a thing." He took a swig of his beer. "They made a movie about it."

A country singer from a passing house wailed about his baby.

"You don't give a rabid dog a treat," Darryl said. "You put it down."

"No violence," Bob said.

They pulled into the trailer park and eased down the narrow lane, past mostly-dark mobile homes, to the isolated trailer in back. The screen door lay in Hector's vegetable garden.

"Wait in the car," Bob said.

"No, sir," Darryl said. "Johnny's too dangerous to meet alone." He tilted his bottle up and drained the beer. "You might disappear forever, like the others."

Darryl had a point. It was a lamebrain plan.

They got out and Bob knocked. Johnny opened the door. From beneath his yellow-stained sleeveless undershirt, tattoos spread out along his arms and neck like creeping gangrene. His lips clutched a cigarette, and his hand, a beer bottle. He squinted.

"What the hell do *you* want?"

Bob swallowed hard. "I have a proposition."

"Get lost." Johnny pushed the door, but it did not close. Bob had wedged his shoe between the door and the jamb. Johnny glared. "You're living real dangerous, my friend."

Bob reached into his pocket and exposed a stack of bills. "You might want to hear me out."

Johnny's eyes widened. He licked his lips. "I might." He pulled open the door. "Why don't you come in and we'll talk."

Bob squeezed past, followed by Darryl. Hector's trailer was in shambles. Dirty clothes, beer cans, and adult magazines lay about. Bob stepped through the litter and lowered himself onto the ratty sofa. Darryl remained standing.

"Want a beer?"

"No, thanks."

Johnny brushed past Darryl and got himself another beer. "This your bodyguard?" he said. "You ain't afraid of old Johnny, are you?" He popped the top, downed half the can, and collapsed in the overstuffed chair. "You mentioned a proposition."

Bob forced himself to look into Johnny's eyes. "I want to buy this place."

"My trailer? I don't know. I got a lot of good memories here. What have you got in mind?"

Bob took a breath. "I'll give you ten thousand dollars right now, and pay you a thousand a month on a mortgage for twenty years."

Johnny leaned back in the chair, his gaze at the ceiling. "That's two hundred fifty thou." He cocked his head. "This shithole ain't worth five grand." He grinned his jagged-tooth grin. "Why so generous? You wouldn't want to get rid of old Johnny, now would you?"

Bob remained silent.

"Okay," Johnny said. "Deal." He bent forward, his upstretched palm bouncing in the air awaiting payment.

"There's a condition," Bob said.

Johnny cocked an eyebrow. "And what would that be?"

"You have to leave town. If you return, the payments stop."

Johnny grinned and leaned back with his beer. "You know, I ain't such a bad guy." He took a swig. "Except for that one thing they got me for, I didn't do none of those crimes they said I did." He winked. "You see, if there ain't no witness, it didn't happen."

Bob straightened up and tilted forward. "Is this something you'd be willing to do?"

"No, but you give me that ten grand and you have my word I won't bother no one. After all, I'm on parole. I don't want no trouble." He grinned. "Is that something *you'd* be willing to do?"

"Come on, Johnny. You know that wouldn't work."

Johnny smiled and stood up. "What's to keep me from taking this money and throwing you out?" He glanced at Darryl. "Him?"

Darryl stood stone-faced.

Bob rose. "Because there's more where that came from, and I'll send it as long as you stay away." Bob swallowed hard. "And because the smart move is to leave. You're not popular around here. And every man and boy in this town has a gun, and most of the women too."

Johnny stepped forward.

"Bob," he said. "That's your name, right? Bob. Let me tell you something." He put his hand on Bob's shoulder. Bob recoiled but Johnny held him. "I spent twenty years locked up with the meanest, sickest bunch of degenerate animals in the West." His yellow teeth showed through his tight lips. "Do you think I'm afraid of anyone in this pussy town?"

Bob shook his head. "You have to leave."

"And why's that?" He put his nose an inch from Bob's. "So you can keep fucking my wife?" In a flash, a beefy hand snatched the front of Bob's shirt. "I seen you arm-in-arm at the funeral."

Darryl leaped forward and grabbed the back of Johnny's massive shoulders.

Johnny released Bob's shirt and raised his hands. "It's okay. Just joshing with you." He grinned. "No need for an altercation."

Darryl released him.

Johnny spun around in a lightning-fast pivot and cold-cocked Darryl in the forehead with the beer bottle, shattering the glass and sending Darryl reeling back. A gut punch doubled Bob over, and a massive fist uppercut against his jaw sent him sprawling against the wall. Johnny turned again to Darryl, who stood dazed, his hands at his sides. Johnny sent a flurry of jabs to Darryl's head, who collapsed to the floor. He began kicking him.

Stunned and wheezing to catch his breath, Bob heard the crunch of a breaking jaw. He struggled to his feet. Johnny bent over Darryl.

"Are you banging my wife, too, you little punk?" He beat Darryl in a fury. His ham-hock fists were blood red.

"Stop," Bob yelled. He jumped on Johnny's back, grabbing his bicep to stop the blows.

Johnny brushed him off like a gnat, throwing him against the wall. Bright colors flashed as Bob's brain bounced against his skull. He slid down the wall, dazed.

Slowly, the room came into focus. Johnny hovered over Darryl, beating him. A broom lay on the floor. Bob grabbed it, stood up, and whacked Johnny on the shoulder. He didn't even react, like a grizzly slapped with a fly swatter. Under a crescendo of rapid jabs, Darryl appeared unconscious.

Bob scanned the room. Hector's filthy rake stood beside the refrigerator, mud clods still impaled on the tines. He struggled to his feet and reached for it.

"Stop," Bob yelled. "You're killing him."

Johnny didn't even slow down.

Bob lifted the rake with both hands. Through a bloody blur, and with all his strength, he swung the rake in a wide, horizontal arc like a six-foot baseball bat. The iron rake head connected solidly with the right side of Johnny's neck, several of the three-inch prongs buried to the hilt, knocking him off Darryl.

Johnny rose in a satanic fury.

"Now it's your turn." He took a step toward Bob. He grabbed the head of the rake and yanked it out of his neck, opening gaping wounds. Blood spurted out from what had to be his carotid artery. Bob stumbled back as Johnny came at him. The pulsing dark red goo became a torrent. Johnny reached out, then stopped. His jagged-tooth smile contorted. His eyes lost focus, his mouth dropped open, and he crumpled to the floor like a sack of barley. His neck muscles spasmed, slapping his head in a growing pool of blood on the linoleum floor.

Bob stared until the convulsions stopped, then staggered to Darryl. His face as raw as hamburger, he groaned in a daze, seated against the wall, his head bent over.

"Darryl, can you hear me?"

Darryl grunted. His bloody face was swollen and deformed, and his jaw clearly broken, but Bob spotted no arterial bleeding.

"Hang on," he said.

He returned to Johnny. His motionless face lay in a pool of blood. His open eyes stared unfocused into the void. Bob felt for a pulse. Nothing.

He knelt beside Darryl. "I think Johnny's dead. I'll get help." He reached for his cell phone and punched in 9-1-1.

Darryl's bloody eye half opened. "No."

"You're hurt. I'm calling an ambulance."

"911 operator. What's your emergency?"

Darryl grabbed the phone, brought it to his half-open eye, and hung up. "No."

"No? Why not? You need help."

"They'll say…" He winced in pain and put his hand on his jaw. "They'll say we murdered him."

"No, Darryl. We have to report it. We acted in self-defense. He would have killed us."

Darryl shook his head. He was missing a tooth. "They'll say I came over here to his house and killed him. I've said some things. Things I didn't mean. But I said I'd get him."

"I don't understand. Why?"

Darryl winced in pain and squeezed Bob's arm.

"He killed my father."

Bob stared at Darryl's bloody face. Then it struck him. Bobby Wise, the murdered Shop-N-Go clerk. And the six-year-old son who witnessed it. Darryl Wise.

Bob collapsed against the wall next to Darryl. His mind raced. He gawked at the dead man and remembered what Johnny had said. If there ain't no witness, it didn't happen.

"Can you stand?"

Darryl nodded.

Bob helped him up, led him out of the trailer, and settled him into the passenger seat. He buckled Darryl in and stumbled back inside. He found a carpet in the bedroom, rolled up Johnny, and dragged him to the door, leaving a wake of blood. The package bounced down the trailer steps and left a furrow in Hector's garden. Bob fumbled for his keys and popped the trunk. No, not the trunk. No blood in the trunk. He opened the rear door, shoved Johnny and the carpet onto the backseat, and threw in Hector's shovel.

The car eased among the dark trailers and out onto the highway. It followed the mountain crest road and turned onto an overgrown dirt trail. Branches and bushes scraped its top and sides. They entered an aspen grove and stopped. Darryl's head lay back against the headrest. He held a towel to his bloody face. Bob pushed the door open against the high grass, grabbed the shovel, and dragged the carpet through the underbrush. A few yards off the road, he came upon the hole that once hid his treasure. He set to work, the music of the fluttering aspen leaves accompanying his labor.

Thirty minutes later, Bob drove back onto the highway and headed toward Memorial General Hospital. Five minutes out of the county seat, he pulled to the side of the road. He helped Darryl out and pushed the car over the embankment. It fell twenty feet before hitting a boulder, demolishing the front end. He pulled out his phone and dialed 9-1-1.

In the hospital ER room, they took Darryl immediately.

"I swerved to avoid a deer. I know you're not supposed to. It was a reflex."

The young deputy sheriff wrote on a pad. "I have to cite you. Your friend is pretty messed up. I never seen so much blood."

The ER nurse came in. "We're ready for you," she said to Bob. "You finished here, Travis?"

The deputy smiled at the young nurse. "Sure." He ripped the citation off his pad and handed it to Bob. "I hope your friend is okay."

Later, Bob sat in Darryl's room. Grace raced in. She leaned over Darryl's heavily bandaged head and teared up. "How is he?"

"He lost some blood. Broken jaw, broken nose, broken orbit. And lots of cuts. I'm so sorry."

She collapsed into a chair. "And how are *you*?"

"A knot on my head and a mild concussion, but I'll be okay."

When Darryl awoke in the morning, they were both still there. Grace pulled a chair up to his bedside and put her hand on his arm. "How are you doing, Darryl?"

He whispered through a wired-shut jaw. "He won't bother you no more, Mrs. Hargrove."

She looked at Bob. "You won't bother me? What does he mean?"

Bob shrugged, his eyes downcast. "It's the Percocet."

CHAPTER 40

A powder-blue overnight bag sat next to Heather on the park bench. She filed her nails, occasionally glancing up at the mini-mansions across the street, their yards immaculately kept, save one, several houses down. Weeds grew in the lawn, and the bushes were unkempt. Near the sidewalk, a for-sale sign tilted with its *Bank Foreclosure* appendage hanging beneath. First National wasn't taking good care of her old home. How did they expect to sell it with that sorry curb appeal? She shook her head and returned to her nails.

Heather had always been a problem solver. Whenever adversity appeared, she drew upon a simple strategy: Define the problem. Devise a solution. Implement.

Her immediate challenge was finding a home. She had managed to move her possessions from the condo after visiting a mid-level, mid-life bureaucrat at the IRS office and persuading him with her tale of woe and her legs. But she couldn't live in the Happy Days storage locker, and returning home to her mother in that hayseed town would never happen. Henry wouldn't help, Bob remained missing, and Pam was so ga-ga over that church guy, her judgment was clouded.

"Our church sponsors a refugee mission," Pam had said. "I could find you a place there."

Heather scrunched her nose. Sleeping on a cot with Burmese farmers and their chickens?

"Do you have family?" Pam said. "Friends?"

Heather shook her head.

"You must know someone."

The garage door squeaked open, catching Heather's attention. Millie's Mercedes backed out, pulled onto the street, and motored away. Heather grabbed her bag, hurried across the road, and strode to the front door. She checked her hair, face, and cleavage in the window, and knocked.

Mike pulled open the door, his eyes wide.

"Why, Mrs. Baldwin. What a pleasure."

An orange football jersey hung to his knees, giving way to gray sweatpants that draped onto blue crocs. An open newspaper dangled from his fingers.

"Thank you, Mike." She blushed. "And it's *Heather*." She tilted her head. "May I speak to Millie, please?"

"She left a second ago." He peered down the street. "You just missed her."

"Oh." Heather pouted. "I needed to talk to her."

"She won't be gone an hour." He raked his hand over his skyward-pointing white hair, untamed and merging at his temples with a week's growth of gray on his face. "Why don't you come in and wait for her?" He stumbled to get out of the way as he opened the door wide.

"If it's not too much trouble." She smiled and stepped in.

She sat on the sofa and sipped the sparkling water he had insisted on getting her.

"I'm sorry to intrude like this. I wouldn't do it unless, unless..." Her eyes glistened. "I'm so embarrassed."

"Don't be. It's okay." He jumped up and got a box of Kleenex. "What's wrong?"

"I should wait for Millie." She pulled a tissue and dabbed her eyes. "It's just that...I know we're not close, but I had no place else to go." A tear coursed down her cheek. "I always wanted to come over and get to know you and Millie better, but Bob worked so much, we never did. I'm sorry. We weren't good neighbors."

"I understand. You're young, you have busy lives."

"Thank you, Mike." She touched his arm. "You're too kind."

He shifted.

Beyond the window, the disarray of her old backyard disturbed her. The pool was green, the deck covered in leaves and branches, and the pool house dark.

"He deserted me, Mike." Tears filled her eyes. "I became lonely and did a foolish thing. Now I have no place to go."

An hour later, Millie had returned, and muffled voices came through the closed study door.

"It's only for a few days," Mike said.

"That woman is not staying in my house," Millie said.

Heather fished in her purse for the emery board.

"She has no place to go. Bob deserted her."

"Hah."

"We have plenty of room."

"The guest room is right next to our bedroom, Mike. For all we know, she'd bring that Mexican with her."

"The mother-in-law suite is on the other side of the house. You'll never see her."

"No."

He lowered his voice and whispered.

"Pregnant?" Millie said.

"Shhh. She'll hear you."

They mumbled on for a minute.

"What if it were Kathryn?" he said.

The conversation stopped.

"A few days," Millie said. "And I don't see her."

Mike came in and delivered the good news.

"Our daughter Kathryn is about your age. She just had our first grandchild. A girl. Melissa. She's the light of Millie's life."

Heather sat on her bed, searching employment sites on the laptop. Beside her rested three large suitcases she had retrieved from the storage locker. Having found a home, her next challenge would be getting money. She had decided against an abortion. Henry was bluffing with his custody threats. He no more wanted a new family than he did his last, all of whom were estranged from him. Plus, the babies were cute. She looked at the picture of two amorphous blobs. And when the children came, so would the child support. But that would not be enough.

"What's she doing?" Millie said in the hall.

"Looking for work," Mike said.

"Why?"

"Because Bob abandoned her. She's penniless."

Heather pushed the door closed. The condo lockout had shocked her to the core. She had never been treated like that, and never would again. Counting on a man for money was like opening your mouth and counting on rain for a drink. She needed to fill her own cistern. Problem, solution, implement.

Two weeks later, Heather sat on the barstool at the granite kitchen island drinking her breakfast juice and eating freshly cut fruit. Her brow furrowed as she tapped on the laptop, scrolling through employment sites, her long, tan legs emerging from her short shorts.

"Good morning, Heather." Mike strode in, sporting a crisp Polo, khaki slacks, and deck shoes. His neatly-trimmed hair had been combed, and his clean-shaven face smelled of Christian Dior.

Millie came in, looked Mike up and down, and snorted.

"I'm not going to be banished from my own kitchen," she mumbled as she poured her coffee and left.

Mike scowled and sat across from Heather.

Heather sighed and closed the laptop. "I can't find anything, Mike."

His frown evaporated. "It takes time, Heather. What job experience do you have?"

She shook her head. She hadn't worked since her waitressing days in New York while awaiting her big acting break.

"Ever done any office work?"

"No."

"Bookkeeping?"

She pouted.

"Retail?"

"No." She tapped her nails on the counter with a thoughtful gaze. "But real estate interests me."

Mike's eyes widened. "That sounds perfect for you. Selling real estate is mostly selling yourself."

Heather tilted her head. She had been selling herself all her life.

"After thirty years with the bank," Mike said, "I have a lot of real estate contacts. I could make a call."

She placed her hand on his. "Could you, Mike?"

The day Heather left, Mike had a hangdog look. He was sweet. Naïve, really. A lot like Bob.

The studio apartment came rent-free, compliments of Mike's broker friend Barry, as one of several vacant rentals he couldn't move during the market slump.

Heather's beautiful face adorned the refrigerator magnet. *Barry Atwater Realty, Heather Baldwin, Sales Associate.* She helped stage homes for open houses while she worked toward licensure. She had jumped the gun on the magnets and business cards, but the world was forgiving toward attractive people.

The magnet held the black-and-white picture of the kids dangling in her uterus like caterpillars in their cocoons. She ran her hand down the front of her stomach. Her tummy hadn't seen such a bulge since she lost her baby fat before puberty. But once the children came, she'd get back to her fighting weight.

CHAPTER 41

In the early morning darkness, Bob snuck out the brewery back door and loaded Lester's pickup with a mop, bucket, and a garbage bag full of cleaning supplies. He drove to the trailer and parked in the woods behind. Inside, as he mopped his victim's blood, the full impact of what he had done hit him. He had killed a man, an act that he could never negotiate away. Whether he ran or gave himself up, his life here had ended.

Later, in the diner, Bob lifted the mug and drank around his swollen lip. He winced as the hot coffee touched the raw skin. He sighed and put it down. The detective stared back at him from across the booth.

"I heard about the accident. You okay?"

Bob nodded. The knot on his forehead still throbbed.

"My new buddy, Milo, told me about it," Dawson said. "He doesn't like you much."

Bob took another sip. It hurt, but he sucked it down anyway. This guy was playing the good cop today.

"Look, Baldwin," the detective said. "You come back, get a lawyer to negotiate with Doyle not to file criminal charges, and return the money. Four million dollars buys you a lot of leverage." He leaned forward as if to share an intimacy. "Doyle needs the money. He'd agree to anything. Might even let you walk."

As if that were possible. In truth, Bob was back to square one. Worse than square one. If he ran, he ran with no money. At least he would leave Grace free of Johnny and with a profitable brewery to provide for her. He had no choice except to sacrifice love. But he didn't have to sacrifice his freedom.

"I can leave tomorrow."

Dawson's eyes widened. "I'll get the tickets."

Bob stared into his coffee. "I need to wrap up a few things."

They went silent as a teenaged waitress appeared and refilled both cups.

Bob took a sip and stood. "I'll meet you tomorrow morning in the brewery parking lot. Ten a.m." He took a step toward the door. "Four million? Is that what Doyle said?"

"Yeah. Three withdrawals within several weeks."

Bob laughed, grimaced, and brought his fingers to his cut lip.

Bob hovered over Grace, seated at the desk with papers spread about. The open blinds of the glass-walled office afforded a broad view of the brewery floor below.

"These are our suppliers," he said. "And these are our customers, and these are the sales numbers since we started. You can handle it. It's like keeping the books for the diner." Bob inhaled the fragrance of the shampoo she used that morning, and the ache in his chest grew stronger. Lester had been right. She was easy to love. "Milo is obnoxious, but he's an okay brewer if he'll follow the recipe."

She watched his face as he pointed at the papers. "Where are you going?" Her voice quavered, but remained controlled.

"And Hector is ready to take over when Milo's contract is up."

"Will you be back?"

"Hector knows a lot about the finances, too. He can help and—"

Her fingertip touched his lips. Her eyes glistened. "The business needs you, Bob." She withdrew her finger. "*I* need you." She put her hand on his. "Please stay."

He withdrew his hand and shook his head. With Grace safe, business booming, and the town recovering, everything would mend. Except this hole in his heart.

"I can't, Grace."

"But you'll return?"

"I don't know."

She bowed her head. "It will be hard without you." She dabbed her eyes with a tissue. "How can I reach you?"

Bob drew in a breath. Revealing one of his phone numbers would make him trackable. But her pleading eyes made him scribble it onto a scrap of paper, press it into her palm, and curl her fingers around it. "In case of an emergency," he whispered.

As Bob and Grace descended the stairs, Candy entered, taking off her coat. When she spotted Bob, she angled toward him. "I'm furious with you," she said. "Poor Darryl. How could you be so careless? Were you drunk?" She poked a finger into his chest. "Go visit him. He asked for you."

Work stopped as other employees watched the show.

Candy tied her fraulein apron and turned toward the tasting room.

"Wait," Grace said. "Please, everyone."

A small group encircled them.

She took a deep breath. "Bob will be leaving us for a while."

Hector gasped. "What?"

"No," Candy said.

Milo smirked.

"I'll be handling the upstairs office work. Milo will remain as brewer and Hector will become assistant brewer. Milo, I trust you'll be generous in sharing your knowledge of the brewer's art with him."

"Is the business in trouble?" Candy said. "Our jobs?"

Grace shook her head. "No. The business is fine, but we need to pull together."

"When do you leave?" Jane asked.

"Tomorrow." Bob swallowed hard. "I'll miss you all." He headed for the door. "I'm going to see Darryl."

Hector followed him.

Bob stopped at the door, rested his hand on the younger man's shoulder, and squeezed. "Take care of Grace."

CHAPTER 42

Milo didn't have to be a weatherman to know which way the wind blew. They wanted him gone. But who was gone now? One down, one to go. *Assistant brewer? He* didn't need no stinkin' assistant. And it would be a cold day in Hell before he would go back to Coeur d'Alene Middle School. Milo Bender still had a few tricks up his sleeve.

"Hey, Martinez," he said, as Hector returned and mounted the forklift.

Hector stopped.

"I wouldn't be ironing your brewmeister frock yet."

Hector shook his head, started the forklift and drove off. "You're crazy, man."

Like a fox. Milo tapped on his phone. "Immigration and Customs Enforcement," he said. "Salt Lake City." He watched Hector disappear through the plastic drapes onto the loading dock. Assistant brewer? That wasn't going to happen to a sleuth like Milo Bender. "Agent Chastain, please."

Friday morning, Dave arrived two hours early and parked in the corner of the brewery lot. The tracking device he had slipped into Bob's jacket pocket at their meeting showed him already in the building, so Dave waited. Employees began to arrive and go in.

A white Grand Marquis pulled in and backed into a spot. The car screamed *government*. Instead of getting out, the driver, a bald man in a white shirt, worked to open a potato chip bag. He pulled at the top. He tugged one side, then the other. He bit the seal. Nothing. Finally, he pulled on both sides at once like Atlas himself. The bag exploded and chips showered down in the passenger compartment. He retrieved them one at a time and popped them into his mouth.

A white pickup entered the lot. Dave recognized it as Lester Hargrove's truck. Hector Martinez sat behind the wheel. The Grand Marquis fired to life and squealed across the lot, before braking and skidding to a stop, blocking the truck's path.

"What the hell?" Hector mouthed.

The bald man jumped out and rapped on Hector's window, smirking and spinning a set of hand restraints. "Hello, Hector," he said. He pulled out an ICE cap and put it on.

Hector rolled down his window. "Chastain," he said. "You still driving that same car, man?"

The ICE agent cuffed Hector, put him in the rear seat of the Marquis, and drove off.

Dave checked his watch. 10:15. The tracking monitor showed Baldwin still in the building.

Dave ran the math again and wondered how Baldwin could have all the money left, especially with the stories of the costs of start-up and operation, including the purchase price of the corporation, the lease of this large facility, the initial slow sales, equipment failures, and Milo's bad formula.

The thought hit him like a jab to the solar plexus. He sprang from the car, jogged to the building, and raced through the tasting room onto the brewery floor.

"Hey, my man," Milo said, raising a hand.

Dave hurried by, leaving Milo's hand un-fived, and trotted up the stairs to the perch. In the middle of the large desk, the tracker rested on a folded piece of paper. He opened it and read, *I changed my mind.*

"You lost him?" Doyle said.

"Yes, sir," Fontaine said, her head bowed as she sat in the client chair.

Doyle trembled as he tried to maintain control. "He's not coming back with my money?" His face was afire.

She remained silent. This dyke's horseshit contrite act didn't help. Neither did this inflatable cast. He unstrapped the walking cast boot and massaged his calf.

Fontaine stared.

"Splinter fracture," he said. "Skiing accident."

"In July?"

"In the Andes, okay?" His voice quavered. "Ms. Fontaine, this is not a good time for this news."

Artie and his goons might jump him again at any time. His computer was filled with emails and calls from the state bar requesting information about trust account "irregularities." The IRS stuck to him like a tick. And he had no money for life's pleasures. His head might explode at any moment.

"But there's a ray of hope, sir."

He sipped the bourbon. Hope? The only hope he saw was in jumping out that window. He put the cold glass against his forehead. Thank God for this. He took another sip.

"We suspect he invested some of your money into a business. A brewery." Fontaine slid an inch-thick folder onto his desk. *Confidential,* in bold red letters, emblazoned the cover as though it contained national security secrets.

Doyle flipped it open and rifled through the notes her man Dawson had written. *I believe Baldwin injected cash into the brewery. He had a good position there and was well-liked. Plus, the operation enjoyed unusually rapid growth from a hobby business.* Two full pages of numbers backed up his analysis.

Doyle froze. "He sank my money in physical, immovable assets?"

"Looks like it, sir."

What a moron. When Doyle had money, he always kept it fluid. Cash, gold, offshore accounts. "I'll seize everything in that God-forsaken town and sell it for scrap."

"The plant is a lease, sir. She doesn't own the real estate."

"She?"

"Grace Hargrove. The owner. We also suspect Baldwin has a thing for her."

An idea blossomed, fully formed. He punched a button on his desk phone. "Martha, get me Nelson on the phone."

"Henshaw? The federal prosecutor?"

"Yes," Doyle said. This would get that son of a bitch Baldwin back.

A week later, Bob awoke to the sun leaking in through the randomly-crimped blinds of the old motel. Ten blocks off the beach, the Destin Traveler's Retreat was a cluster of eight tiny huts set amid an ancient grove of palmetto trees and out-of-control bamboo. The state road upon which it stood had been abandoned shortly after the place had been built in the 1920s, and the almost-hundred-year-old concrete road had crumpled into gravel. Its faded paint, rotting eaves, and wild undergrowth made the property as disheveled as the octogenarian proprietor. And perfect for Bob.

He had just spent his third night working at Der Wienerschnitzel, a place where he cooked hot dogs and ate for free. Ronaldo, the night manager, wasn't a stickler for employment paperwork and spent most evenings smoking weed behind the store with high school girls ten years his junior. "You're doing a great job, Bob," he had said, shoving a Schnitzel Supreme into his mouth after coming in the back door. "You have a bright future here."

As he had done every morning for the last three weeks, Bob lay still in his bed, watching the beam of sunlight pierce the blinds and land on the stucco wall. Though alone, broke, and missing Grace, knowing she was safe gave him solace. He missed his home. Funny. He thought of LaPlante as home.

Beside the butt-filled ashtray, a box buzzed on the nightstand. He sat up, rifled through it, and pulled out one of the "burner" phones. Only one person had this number.

A panicked voice pleaded. "Bob, the police are here. And federal marshals." Grace sobbed. "They've arrested me."

Bob bolted upright.

"They said we financed the brewery with stolen money. Is that true? They say I'm an accessory." She paused. "Bob? Are you there?"

"Yes," he whispered.

"I'm the sole owner of the brewery. They say it's a criminal enterprise and I'm an accomplice in laundering stolen money. That I participated in the negotiations with Alvin." She sniffled. "Bob, say something."

"Don't talk to anyone. I know a lawyer. And tell Hector to keep quiet too."

"Keep quiet? I could lose the diner. And my house. We mortgaged it to finance the brewery." Her sniffling stopped. "And Hector's gone. The Iceman took him away."

Silence floated about the room.

"Is it true, Bob?"

He didn't answer.

Her voice became stern. "I see." She paused. "I never want to see you again."

"I...I'll take care of it."

"Goodbye, Bob." The phone clicked.

CHAPTER 43

Bob circled the polished black stone, examining its somber streaks of gray and brown minerals. The human-sized sculpture, mounted on a pedestal, was one of several artworks scattered throughout the cavernous Law Offices of Gifford, Farnsworth, and Associates. What had been a rundown brick warehouse near the wharf now housed the luxuriously appointed law firm. Several of George's client-partners were doing well, and one, a scooter-sharing start-up, had skyrocketed.

Bob lifted his arm and touched the object's smooth surface. "What is it?"

"What do you think it is?" George said from behind the large cherrywood desk, dwarfed by the backdrop of a huge brick wall.

Bob shrugged. "Failure? Despair? Death?"

"You need to see a therapist. It's a woman's torso." George held his glasses to the light. "An original LaSalle. Know who he is?" He popped a tissue from the box and cleaned his lenses. "Me neither, but he's dead, and that's good, art-wise."

Bob collapsed into the client chair, engulfed within the tomb. Around him hovered the ghosts of longshoremen, seamen, and ladies of the evening, cavorting in raucous bars that never closed. Beyond the window, nearby warehouses were being converted into boutique shops, residential lofts, and professional offices. "How did he have Grace arrested? Isn't that for the prosecutor to decide?"

George interlaced his fingers and leaned forward across the desk. "Doyle owns the prosecutor. Nelson Henshaw plans to run for state

213

attorney general next year, and then, who knows? Governor? With political ambitions, he needs powerful allies, and Doyle's been a kingmaker for years. So, Doyle gets his pal Henshaw to file RICO charges claiming a criminal conspiracy to launder stolen money through the brewery, and, voila, they have you and Grace, and can seize the brewery when you're convicted."

Bob dropped his head into his hands. "Okay, I'll confess to the theft if they'll drop the charges against Grace."

George shook his head. "Not good enough. Besides a pound of flesh, Doyle wants his money. Are you prepared to make restitution?"

Bob didn't answer.

"Besides, they didn't hold her," George said. "She's out on bail."

"I know. She had to put up her house." Bob's shoulders sagged. He missed his friends. He missed the mountains. He missed Grace. He stared out the window at the old wharf. He'd left a lot of damage in his wake. "I've hurt people who trusted me. Even Hector stuck his neck out by coming out of the shadows, and now has to pay the price."

George pursed his lips. "That, we might be able to do something about." He reached toward his keyboard, punched up his contact list, and scrolled to *Homeland Security*. He scanned the names and dialed.

"Ed," he said. "George Gifford. How are you doing? … Oh, fine… What? … No need. I was glad to help." He took a breath. "Listen, Ed…"

George laid out the story of Hector's capture, his value to the brewery, and Agent Chastain's personal vendetta.

"Thanks, Ed. I appreciate anything you can do. My best to Margaret." He clicked off. "He'll look into it. They have some prosecutorial discretion." He tilted his head. "Now, can we talk about *you?*"

"I'm dead, George, boxed in. All that's left for me is prison." His gaze locked on George's. "What'll I get? Ten years?"

"I'm not a criminal attorney, but maybe six, out in three." George picked up the file on his desk. "What we need is a bargaining chip. With restitution off the table, what do we have? Doyle's own culpability? He's been playing fast and loose with the clients' trust account for years. He must be nervous about that."

"What if I confess to taking the whole four million? That would get him off the hook for embezzling the eight-hundred-thousand difference."

"It's not enough. We need to twist his arm until he squeals." George expelled a gust of air that flapped his lips. "With all these consolidations, thousands of working stiffs lose their jobs while he makes millions. And even that's not enough, so he screws his partners out of their share. And now he'll do it again with the Bradley merger."

Bob furrowed his brow.

"Bradley Manufacturing," George said. "It's the biggest industrial merger approved in the last decade. And K&D handled it." George's old social-injustice scowl crossed his face. "And Bradley makes your Worthington guys seem philanthropic. They're shutting down four sites in the U.S. They've already sent out termination notices. It's a bloodbath." He shook his head. "It's too bad we can't help those workers like you helped that town."

Bob stiffened. "When did Bradley close?"

George shrugged. "Several weeks ago."

"What did K&D make on the deal?"

"A huge fee. Bigger than your Worthington deal."

The two men disappeared into their own thoughts until Bob broke the silence.

"He's holding Grace hostage. I need a hostage, too." And there was only one hostage that Doyle loved enough to negotiate for. Bob took a deep breath. "If Doyle will get his prosecutor pal to drop all charges against Grace, I'll come clean and they can do with me what they like."

George shook his head. "It doesn't work if you can't offer restitution."

"What if I can?"

George eyed his friend. "Do you know what happens when a client lies to his lawyer?"

"The lawyer gets blindsided in court and the case explodes?"

"Bingo."

"I can make restitution, George."

"I don't believe it."

"It's what Doyle believes. And he'll take the meeting if there's any chance of getting something back."

George drummed his fingers on the table.

"I'm going to return the money, George. Set the meeting."

George didn't move.

"I return the money, and Doyle calls his dogs off Grace."

"How are you going to do that?"

"That's not your concern."

"Yes, it is. I'm your lawyer."

"Set the meeting."

George tossed the file on his desk. "Lawyers are the worst clients." He pulled up his contact list again and dialed.

Bob listened in as George set the details with Doyle's secretary.

"Eleven a.m., Wednesday, thirtieth-floor conference room, Kravitz and Doyle." George rocked back in his swivel chair, his fingers interlaced behind his head. "Thank you, Martha," he said toward the speakerphone.

"You're welcome, Mr. Gifford," the box squawked. "I look forward to seeing you—"

Doyle's voice interrupted her. "Baldwin returns every penny, or I'll burn down that brewery and lock up that Hargrove bitch until her tits look like flapjacks." The phone clicked off.

The two men stared at each other in silence. Bob knew he had made the right decision.

"Well," George finally said, holding up his hands, "there you have it. You give him three point two million, and Doyle agrees to drop the conspiracy charges against Mrs. Hargrove. We'll sign the agreement Wednesday, just before the transfer."

"I should be ready by then."

George eyed him. "Please, Bob, play it straight. Doyle is unhinged. You could get hurt."

That night, Bob lay on the sagging motel bed with a phone cradled on his shoulder, working to fit in the last piece of the puzzle. "I need it by Wednesday."

Only silence came from the phone.

"Pam?"

A throat cleared. "I don't think I can help you, Bob."

"The meeting is set, Pam. It's now or never."

"I can't. Henry is a dangerous man."

"He won't know. It'll be like last time."

"When I helped you before, I was drunk. Heck, I was always drunk then. I regret what I did."

"Because that was revenge. This is to save an innocent person."

"You're not innocent, Bob."

"Not me. He wants to send an innocent woman to prison. You could save her."

"A woman?"

"Yes, a woman I care about. Pam, please, will you think about it?"

"It's unchristian. Even Henry deserves forgiveness."

"Forgive him for the past. But don't let him do more harm."

She drew a deep breath.

"I'll think about it, Bob, but I don't know that anything would change my mind."

CHAPTER 44

Doyle rocked on the swivel chair, his feet on the desk and a cold glass of scotch in his hand. He looked over the city below. His domain. And on Wednesday, Salvation Day, all debts would be paid and accounts reconciled. It was biblical.

At the meeting, he'd get the stolen money from Baldwin. Then, he'd transfer the Bradley fee. He'd be awash in cash. He'd pay off Artie and his goombah pals. He'd pay off the IRS. And he'd even take a long weekend in the islands. He deserved a break, and that new, hot little receptionist Stephanie had given all the right signals. But even better than sex would be the revenge he would extract from Baldwin. Sure, he'd let Baldwin's bitch go for several million. What did he care? Baldwin would get his comeuppance when gang raped in prison by tattooed animals for years to come. Or maybe he'd have Artie make him disappear.

The thought of Artie reminded him of the ache in his leg. He popped another Advil. Baldwin bore responsibility for that, too.

But on Wednesday, the sun would shine again. The state bar would drop the investigation on trust account irregularities. The partners would get their bonuses and stop their incessant whining. And a long weekend on the beach with Stephanie. How old was she? Nineteen? Twenty?

He sank into the soft leather of the big swivel chair. Fontaine's confidential Baldwin report lay on his desk. Beside it lay another large manila envelope that had just arrived by courier. He sliced it open and withdrew the contents, labeled *Milton Cole.*

As he read the report in on Pam's boy toy, his lips stretched over his teeth. "Excellent."

He shook the envelope. On his desk landed several eight-by-ten glossy photos graphically depicting marital infidelity. His face reddened and meandering veins bulged from his temples. This would be sweet revenge. The only question was whether to wait until he nailed Baldwin. Nah. He would clear the accounts now.

He dialed the church number. "Good morning, Reverend. I have some information about your associate pastor that might interest you."

"You hacked into my account, Frankie?" Dave slapped his stapler repeatedly. The old envelope had dozens of staples in it already. "Those were my private notes. Not for you or anyone else, certainly not the client. How could you give it to him? You had no right."

"I'm afraid I did. You work for me, Davie boy, so your work product belongs to me. Besides, I had to give him something or there would have been blood on the walls."

Dave knew the story. When Frankie delivered the bad news that Bob had slipped away, Doyle had hurled a golf club across his office, hitting and shattering the mirror above his bar. "It could have been me," she said. "Plus, he's the customer. He paid for the information." She put her hand on Dave's shoulder. "And it got the job done. It brought Baldwin in."

He shook off her hand. "Yeah, by criminally charging an innocent woman."

She shrugged.

"Grace Hargrove is a nice person, Frankie." He threw his hands in the air. "She got arrested because of my speculation. And she didn't do anything wrong."

"That's not for us to decide. We're not judges, we're detectives delivering a product. Information. That's how the market works."

"Then the market stinks." He finished with a flourish of whacks and threw the riddled envelope into the trash.

"It's just a job," she said.

He snorted and picked up Tracy's picture. At nine, she had thought he was perfect. Now, at thirteen, she knew better. He set it down. He knew better, too.

Frankie's cell sang. She peeked at it. "Ooo, the whale." She answered and listened. "Thank you, Mr. Doyle," she finally said. "I'll tell him."

"That my case?" Dave said.

"Nah. Something else."

"What'd the pervert do now?"

"Nothing. The usual domestic dispute. Trash the boyfriend."

"Pamela Doyle? Doyle's wife? I met her. She's a nice lady. She got with God."

"She also got with her preacher-boyfriend. And they weren't exactly careful, if you catch my drift. I put Jake on it. He got some good pics." She chortled. "Plus, the boyfriend has a past."

Dave stared up at Frankie, his mouth open.

"What?" she said. "The client was pleased."

He didn't move.

"Don't wig out on me, Dave."

"I already have." He put his arm over Frankie's shoulder and kissed her cheek. "I'll miss you, Frankie."

He grabbed an empty box from the shelf, set it on his desk, and put Tracy's picture in it.

Basking in the joy that tomorrow would bring, Doyle looked up when Pamela barged into his study, her nose raw and eyes swollen.

"What did you do?"

He snipped the cigar tip and flicked the lighter. "You mean your boyfriend?" He lit the Arturo Fuente. "Why, I outed him."

She broke into sobs.

"Seems he has quite a past." He blew smoke that billowed like a cannon discharge. "It turns out he impregnated a sixteen-year-old girl."

"I know. That was a long time ago. He was nineteen, just a boy."

"And a rapist."

"It was consensual."

"Not in the eyes of the law. Did he also tell you he gave her cocaine? That he spent a year in prison?"

"Yes, he did. And when he got out, he found Christ and turned his life around."

"After a decade of alcoholism and drug use." He blew a smoke ring toward the ceiling. "The man was a junkie, my dear."

"He told me all about his past."

"Well, he didn't tell the elders of your Church-of-What's-Happening-Now. We had a long talk. They found it relevant. Especially since he ran their youth program."

"He's a different person now."

"Perhaps they didn't want their parishioners to find out who was watching the kids."

"That church meant everything to him." She dabbed her eyes with a tissue. "Now, he'll never work in a church again."

"Nor should he. The man's a pedophile." Grover came in and plopped down at the master's feet.

"He is not. Who wasn't reckless in his youth? How is it possible to be that cruel, even for you?"

Doyle reached down and massaged Grover's ear. "Because no one steals my property, sweetheart." He took a long drag and blew a column of smoke toward her. "And *you* are my property."

Her tears stopped, and her eyes narrowed.

"I have photographs," he said, fingering a manila envelope. "Want to see?"

She trembled. "You had us followed?"

He shrugged.

She stiffened, growing two inches taller. "I see." She walked away. "I'm sorry it's come to this, Henry." She stepped out and closed the door.

CHAPTER 45

Three-ring notebooks, colored markers, and post-it notes littered the card table in Heather's dining area as she plowed through her real estate certification course. "Dining area" would be an exaggeration. It was more like a location, a geographical point in space, like the south pole, between the living area and the kitchen area and the sleeping area that formed the studio apartment.

Barry, her broker, had provided the apartment and gainful employment, and would soon demand his reward. But after Bob and Henry, Barry wouldn't even be a lateral move. And she had never in her career taken a pay cut.

She turned the page of the white notebook. Curb appeal. Mow the lawn, trim the bushes, slap on a coat of paint. But this couldn't be painted over. Her hand glided over her growing tummy. Besides, she wasn't a flip. She was a buy-and-move-in.

The walls began closing in, so she grabbed her notebook, headed for the office, and settled into her small metal desk next to the supply cabinet to resume studying. It didn't take long for Barry to sniff her out.

"Mind if I come over to make sure you're settling in all right? I want the space to be comfortable for you."

"Oh, thanks Barry. I can't tonight. Lamaze class. But you can come with me if you like. I need a partner."

Barry remembered a previous engagement and returned to his office.

Across the room, Lucinda chattered on the phone. "Yeah, Barry's cute," she said, "but that comb-over's a real turn-off…"

Heather shook her head. Lucinda spent her days talking to friends rather than chasing down sales leads. How could she achieve anything? Heather buried her head in her workbook, trying to block her out.

"…a foreclosure on Willow Lane."

Heather blinked. Willow Lane? Heather's house was on Willow Lane.

"Janet promised me the listing," Lucinda said. "It's a big one."

Heather tuned in on the conversation.

"Janet? She's the lawyer…"

Her face buried in the real estate manual, Heather absorbed chatty Lucinda's every word. She even took notes. Information is power. Janet Lieberman was an attorney who ground out foreclosures for First National, which held the mortgage on Heather's old house. Ms. Lieberman's boyfriend, a lawyer at Kravitz & Doyle, told her that their missing partner was returning and owned a house she had been trying to foreclose for a year. She could now nail him with service of process and wrap up the foreclosure, at which time Ms. Lieberman would use her best efforts to direct the listing to Lucinda.

"Those were her words," Lucinda said. "Best efforts. And that place is worth a million." Lucinda said that the listing brokerage got three percent and the listing agent got one and a half, and that Lucinda could buy a lot of school supplies for her kid with fifteen hundred dollars.

Heather snorted. "Fifteen thousand," she muttered. This would be like taking candy from a baby.

She dialed the phone.

"Law Offices of Gifford and Associates."

The receptionist put her through.

"Is he back?"

George stammered. "Heather?"

"Yes, George. Ask him to call me. I have a business proposal."

The tumblers of Heather's mind clicked and pinged. She had spent a lifetime chasing men. But she hadn't wanted the men, she'd wanted the financial security they provided. And she was far more reliable than any of them. If a frumpy part-timer who can't multiply could make $15,000 just for securing a listing, think what Heather could do. She didn't need a man, she needed his business. Like the late-night mattress factory commercials, she too could bypass the middleman and keep the savings.

Heather went into the ladies' room and tapped her cellphone.

"Ms. Lieberman, this is Heather Baldwin. I have a proposition."

"I'm listening."

Heather and Bob would execute a deed to the bank in lieu of foreclosure, thus ending Ms. Lieberman's headache, and making her look good to the bank client.

Ms. Lieberman paused. "And what's in it for you, Mrs. Baldwin?"

"I want the listing."

CHAPTER 46

The morning sun radiated through the sheer curtains, casting a cheery glow throughout Doyle's bedroom. The suite occupied an entire wing of the house, and included a separate dressing area, a room-sized walk-in closet, and a luxuriously-appointed bathroom with granite shower and jacuzzi tub that would be ideal for entertaining guests.

He admired the reflection as he stood before the full-length mirror. The creases on his navy-blue trousers were as sharp as a letter opener, his crisply-starched shirt blazingly white, and his red power tie domineering. He lifted the suit coat off the polished wood valet, slipped into it, and pulled the French cuffs from the jacket sleeves to ensure the diamond cufflinks were visible. When he tightened the knot of the Hermès silk tie and inserted the royal-blue sapphire tie pin, he achieved perfection. Ready to accept the surrender, he was Lafayette at Yorktown, Grant at Appomattox, MacArthur on the battleship *Missouri* in Tokyo Bay.

He strode down the open staircase, unlocked the door to his study, and woke the computer on his desk. As the banking program loaded, he unlocked the desk drawer and removed a green cellphone with a shamrock decal, his secret phone for "special" communications. Originally for clandestine liaisons, but now, with no need for any pretense of marital fidelity, he used the phone strictly for financial matters.

A text read, *Funds Deposited. Og.*

Oglethorpe liked to personally announce deposits, as though he provided the money. Doyle snorted. The man may have been the bank president, but he was just another clerk.

When the bank page opened on the computer screen, a thrill shot through Doyle. The Bradley fee had been deposited. $5,200,000. He glanced at his Rolex. 10:15. No time. He'd transfer funds right after the meeting. He locked the phone in the desk drawer, shut down the computer, and grabbed his briefcase. This would be a red-letter day.

As he locked his study door and pocketed the key, he looked up the open staircase. Pam's bedroom door on the second-floor landing was cracked open, and a shape moved within. Her skulking about had become tedious. He'd had enough. Though still his property, she'd have to go as soon as he finished today's business.

In his underwear, Bob hoisted himself from the sagging motel bed. His head drooped as he staggered into the seedy bathroom and started the shower. How had this happened? He lathered, rinsed, and toweled off. At forty-two, his life was over. His hand shook as he shaved his cheeks and neck. He trimmed his now-gray Van Dyke and combed his shaggy hair. And for what? In the last year, he had aged five. He pulled on his jeans, cowboy boots, and tan corduroy jacket. He should run. Right now. He could disappear again. He knew how.

He sighed, picked up his computer satchel, and called a cab. Stepping into the glare of a merciless sun, he pulled the motel door closed behind him with the click of a jail cell locking.

As he entered the office building lobby, four beefy security guards fell into position around him and marched him to a waiting elevator like he was the center pip on the five of spades. They shot straight to the thirtieth floor. The gleaming doors swung open with a melodious ding, and they trooped down the corridor toward the conference room.

Startled former coworkers gaped. When he passed his old office, Doris's mouth dropped open. "Bob?"

A ping of nostalgia coursed through him as his entourage swept past. Some good memories lingered here.

Ahead, Martha guarded the inner sanctum of Doyle's corner office, a tight smile frozen on her face. "Good morning, Mr. Baldwin," she said when they passed her desk. "Welcome back."

As they approached the glass-walled conference room, he saw Doyle and three senior partners seated at the huge oak table. The view of the city and river was as magnificent as it had been those many months before when they celebrated the closing of the Worthington deal. Bob brought his fingers to his forehead, remembering the errant Champagne cork. He was surprised that the memory struck him as pleasant, and it helped calm his nerves. He steadied his knees, took a deep breath, and summoned his energy. The glass door swung open and Bob bounded in.

"Good morning, gentlemen," he said. "It's been too long."

The partners appeared startled. The four guards positioned themselves at each of the two doors out.

"Armand, Kevin," Bob said, greeting each. The two partners rose and he shook their hands vigorously, clasping each man's forearm with his other hand. He turned to the third partner, who had remained seated. "Tony. How's Bea?"

Tony looked at Doyle. "Fine," he said as Bob grabbed his hand and pumped it with enthusiasm.

"Great. Give her my regards."

Doyle remained seated.

"Henry," Bob said, slapping him on the shoulder as he passed.

Doyle recoiled from the touch and offered neither a hand nor a nod.

Bob rounded the table and took a seat opposite the four men, his back to the picture window and his shaking knees hidden by the oak table. He placed his computer satchel on the floor and his phone face down on the table.

Martha appeared with a cup of coffee and a saucer. "Black, Mr. Baldwin." She set it on the table and scurried out.

Bob looked across at Doyle. The two men locked gazes.

Bob smiled. "Good to see you, Henry."

"Where's Gifford?"

"I came alone." George had made a fuss about not coming.

Doyle shrugged. "Suit yourself."

The long, polished table sported futuristic tripod phone speakers, glass pitchers dripping with condensate, and crystal water glasses. He folded his hands and leaned forward. "How have you been, Henry? You look well."

Doyle scowled. "Are we here to chit-chat or to close a deal?" He opened the folder in front of him, spun it around, and slid it across the table.

Bob reached out, drew it to him, and turned to the last page of the six-page document without reading. He held up his hand. "Pen."

Doyle exhaled a long sigh. "If your lawyer were here, he'd tell you to read it."

"He already read the one you emailed." Bob raised his eyebrows. "You didn't change it, did you, Henry?"

Doyle fumed and shifted in his chair. "That's not how we operate around here."

"Right," Bob said. He wiggled his fingers of his upturned hand.

Doyle grunted, reached into his coat pocket, and slapped onto the table a gold pen, engraved with *H. Meriwether Doyle, Esq.*

Bob picked it up and signed the agreement. He spun the papers around and offered the pen to Doyle, who took it and signed.

"Okay," Doyle said, returning the pen to his pocket. "No conspiracy charges against anyone else. You want to admit what you did?"

"I admit to nothing," Bob said. He inhaled deeply. "But if I had withdrawn funds from the firm trust account..." He took a slow sip of his coffee and sighed with pleasure. "I would have transferred the money offshore, then brought it back, and buried it in the earth."

"All four million?" a partner said.

"No, Armand," Bob said. "I wouldn't have taken four million." He took another sip and replaced the cup on the saucer. "Just three point two million."

The partners looked at each other. Then at Doyle.

"You stole four million," Doyle said.

"Four million, three point two million. Speaking hypothetically, why would I lie at this point?"

"So you can pocket the difference." Doyle glanced at the others.

Bob chuckled.

"Can you explain the discrepancy, Bob?" Armand said.

"Maybe the extra eight hundred thousand was already gone."

Their brows furrowed. They looked at Doyle.

"And how could that happen?"

Bob shrugged. "Who had access?"

"How did *you* get access?"

"Ask your boss."

Doyle became crimson. "That's enough of this nonsense. Let's get on with the transfer."

Bob took a final sip and put down the coffee cup. He lifted his phone off the table, checked it, and put it back. He reached into his satchel on the floor, removed the laptop, and set it on the table in front of him.

"It'll take a few minutes to set up," he said.

He opened the laptop and began typing, backspacing often to correct the errors of his trembling fingers.

Three minutes went by as Bob kept typing and regularly glancing at his phone. Then five minutes. "Okay," he finally said. "I'm linked to my account. Where do you want the funds sent?"

Doyle grinned. "Into the firm trust account." He slid a piece of paper across the table.

Bob read the account number and punched it in. "Hmm," he said, and spun the laptop around toward Doyle. "I'll need your fingerprint."

Doyle snorted and reached across the table. The partners seemed agitated.

"Henry." Armand stood. "He'll have access to our trust account."

"Only to make a deposit," Doyle said, pressing his thumb against the fingerprint pad. "Besides, he's not going anywhere." He sneered and tilted his head toward the massive security guards.

Bob stopped typing, checked his phone again, and put it down.

"But Henry," Armand said. "He stole from us before."

"It's a different account. I'm not an idiot."

"But…"

"Shut up, Armand. He can't do a goddamned thing. Withdrawals require a code. No one has it except me and the bank." Doyle froze.

The partners looked at each other.

"Code?" Kevin said. "What code? Expenditures over twenty thousand require signatures of two members of the finance committee."

"What's going on, Henry?" Armand said.

"Shut up. All of you."

Bob checked his phone again. 11:20. Seconds ticked past and nothing happened. Perspiration freckled his forehead and soaked his shirt. More seconds went by.

"What are you pulling here, Baldwin?" Doyle glanced at his watch. "You've got three minutes to return my money, or your girlfriend is going to prison." He held up his phone. "Should I make the call?"

Bob expelled a deep sigh of failure.

Bzzzt. The cell phone vibrated once, against the table. He picked it up, studied it for several seconds, then replaced it facedown.

He resumed typing.

Login failed.

He looked at the phone again.

Login failed. Three failed attempts results in a lockout.

Perspiration trickled down Bob's temples. He checked the phone again. Nine numerical digits and the letter "S." Shouldn't it be ten digits? His heart pounded. Perhaps the "S" was a "5." His last chance. He typed in the number.

Login Successful.

Bob's fingers danced across the laptop in a flurry of keystrokes.

Another cell phone jangled. Doyle jumped up and pulled it from his pocket. "What?" He listened. "Of course, it's authorized, Oglethorpe, goddammit. Let the transaction proceed."

He sat back down.

"Goddam bankers. They act like it's *their* money."

Bob typed his final keystrokes with a flourish and hit the send key with élan, his hand with finger extended bouncing into the air, like a concert pianist finishing a movement.

A few seconds passed. They all watched the laptop screen. As small deposits appeared in the account, Doyle leered at Bob in delight.

Bob relaxed and stared across the table. "Why the guards, Henry?"

Doyle snorted. "To block your escape route. Only a suicide bomber would allow himself to be trapped like this."

"Precisely. A suicide bomber sacrifices himself to take out the target."

Doyle's brow furrowed.

At that instant, the small deposits stopped, and money started to disappear. Doyle watched in horror as the account funds drained away.

Bob leaned forward. "Initial deposits are just the accounts shaking hands to verify authorization."

The anguish on Doyle's face became rage. He grabbed Bob's phone and focused his bloodshot eyes on the text message showing the ten-digit code. And it came from Doyle's secret phone. The one locked in his desk at home.

The laptop showed $5,200,000 transferred from the trust account and into the ether.

"It's all gone, Henry." Bob pushed the laptop toward Doyle to give him a better view of the now-zero balance. "You have a hostage, and now *I* have a hostage. Care to negotiate a prisoner exchange?"

Throbbing veins bulged from Doyle's purple temples. A guttural howl filled the room. Doyle threw himself across the conference table and clutched Bob's throat, sending Bob careening back in the wheeled swivel chair against the plate glass window. "I'll kill you, you son of a bitch!" Maniacal red eyes burned into Bob's, and fingers clawed at his throat.

Two guards grabbed Doyle's ankles, while the other two ran to Bob and pried Doyle's fingers from his neck. They dragged Doyle back across the table and stood him up. He swung his arms free of their grasp and pointed at Bob. "You're a fucking dead man." He stormed through the door and down the hall. A stunned silence filled the room.

Bob stood up, gasping, his hands on his throat.

A guard looked at the others. "What do we do now?"

As they stared at each other, the door slammed open and an explosion obliterated the silence.

A sharp pain shot through Bob's leg, glass shattered, and a sledgehammer whacked his chest. He was thrown back, slid down the wall into a seated position, and watched the mayhem. He counted five rounds fired before a thousand pounds of security guards piled on Doyle and wrenched the gun from his hand. The three partners rose from beneath the conference table and dashed from the room. Cool air flooded in. The plate glass window was gone, save jagged shards spiking from the edges.

He found the pungent smell of gunpowder pleasant. Where had he smelled that before? Oh, yes. Grace. When she chased the bear. He smiled. She had spunk. He slumped over onto the royal blue pile carpet. Warm goo pooled around his face as the room turned black.

CHAPTER 47

The discharge of Doyle's rage in an explosive crescendo surpassed the best mind-blowing, cocaine-fueled sex he had ever experienced. Watching the bullets throw his tormentor against the window. The explosions, the smoke, the acrid smell. The massive arms tackling him. And when the four no-neck security guards hog-tied him for the police, the afterglow of his revenge was as satisfying as any other.

Having a cadre of defense attorneys, a golf-buddy judge, and ties to the community that negated any flight risk, he secured release on bail before dinner. A staccato of camera clicks peppered him as he pushed his way through the crowd on the courthouse steps to the waiting cab. At home, the double oak doors to the study stood open, wood splintered around the lock. He entered slowly. The drawer lay upside down on the top of the desk, one side chewed apart. A claw hammer lay on the carpet. The envelope remained taped to the bottom of the drawer. The card had been removed and lay on the desktop, next to the green cellphone with the shamrock. He pressed a button for sent text messages. On the screen appeared his secret ten-digit code.

His chair reeked of her perfume and her boot scuff marks marred the polished desktop. She had sat on his throne and savored her victory like a lioness spraying her territory. A brilliant light of clarity flashed in Doyle's mind. A year earlier, jealous and drunk as usual, the bitch had unlocked the drawer and given the code to Baldwin, and then concealed her crime, returning the card to the envelope, and locking the drawer and the study. This time, she used no such stealth. This time, she proudly left her mark for him to see.

His pulse pounded in his temples. He picked up the claw hammer and slowly ascended the stairs.

"Oh, Pamela," he sang, pushing open her bedroom door. "I'm home."

CHAPTER 48

When Bob opened his eyes, a blur hovered over him. His lips parted to speak, but his throat was raw. A straw touched his lips and he greedily sucked in the cool liquid.

"Can you hear me, Bob?" A tender hand took his.

He heard himself croak. "Grace?"

The haze became Heather's face. "No, Bob. It's me." A tear coursed down her cheek.

His eyes moved about the room. A hospital.

"Thank God," she said. "You had me so worried." She touched his arm. Her scent permeated his sinuses and the memories flooded back.

She dabbed her eyes.

He sucked in more cool water. "How long have I been here?"

"A week. They just moved you here from intensive care." Her lips twitched into a smile, but her eyes were sad. She had such blue eyes. "It's a private room."

He licked his lips. "What happened?"

Her eyes grew wide. "Henry shot you. Don't you remember?"

He shook his head. "I thought the building exploded."

"One bullet went through your abdomen." She poked herself below her ribs. "The doctor took part of your liver." She pointed at his leg. "Another bullet shattered your left femur. That's going to take a lot of rehab."

"Is that all?"

"Don't be like that. This is serious."

She looked healthier than he remembered, her face fuller and eyes kinder.

"You also lost half your left index finger, probably in a defensive move." She held up her hands to demonstrate. "It was gone so they couldn't reattach it."

"Anyone else hurt?"

"No." Her eyes moistened. "Just you." Her face was pinched with pain. "I'm so sorry about everything."

He shook his head, hoping to clear the befuddlement. The surreal scene seemed another dream.

"I wish I could do everything over," she said. "I made such a mess of us."

The fog began to clear. This was no dream. He looked into her eyes. With effort, he placed his bandaged hand on her arm. "Heather, we can't get back together. Too much has happened."

"Oh, I know," she said, patting his hand. "I've come to peace with that." She watched him for a moment, smiling with affection. He understood the silence to be a transition, an ending. She took a deep breath and sat upright. "I have a business proposition." She opened the folio on her lap and removed some papers. "We can help each other." Heather explained her work in real estate, the foreclosure, the promise of a big listing. They should be allies during these difficult times. Determination filled her eyes. "You can help me in business, and I can help you with Henry." She held up a pen.

Bob smiled. He couldn't help it. This new Heather was a pip.

He took the pen with his undamaged right hand and scrawled his signature on the deed in lieu of foreclosure.

"George will notarize it." She tilted her head. "He's outside."

As Heather left, George toddled in and plopped onto the bedside chair. "You going to eat that?" He picked up the spoon and pointed at a custard cup. George had gained weight in the last year.

Bob pushed it toward him. He wet his lips to speak. "I got my bargaining chip."

George peeled off the top and attacked the pudding with the spoon. "Five million of them, I hear."

"Talk to the prosecutor. Here's the deal. I'll return it and plead guilty if they drop all charges against Grace."

"They already have, buddy."

Bob didn't understand. Grace was cleared?

George spooned the last of the custard. "They found your finger. Next to a hotdog stand on Fourth Avenue. It took a while because of the glass everywhere." He tossed the spoon on the table. "Do you want it?"

"I don't understand."

"Well, it's your finger, so you're entitled to it."

"No, I mean Grace. What about Grace?"

"Oh, Henshaw, the prosecutor, dropped all charges against her."

Bob looked into George's eyes. "Thank you." He touched his hand. "But how?"

"Someone called a reporter at the *Tribune*."

"You?"

George held up his hands in protest. "Apparently, this lady reporter doesn't like Doyle much and wrote an exposé on prosecutorial abuse. It called for a state bar ethics investigation on whether Henshaw used his position to advance a personal vendetta of his crony Doyle. Henshaw got clobbered all over the news and held a press conference. Said he was shocked to learn that the city's leading law firm had given him inaccurate information. Shocked. That's what he said." George giggled. "And if we elect him attorney general, he would vigorously root out such perversion of the criminal justice system." George shook his head. "Politicians."

"So, Grace is in the clear?"

"Completely. Henshaw is now praying she doesn't make trouble."

Bob's head fell back against the pillow.

George stared at him. "Bob, did you ever intend to return the 3.2 million?"

Bob closed his eyes. "I *did* return it. Just not to Doyle."

After Bob signed the deed in the hospital, Heather and her five-month baby bump wasted no time striking a deal with Ms. Lieberman and getting the listing. No doubt Lucinda chafed at being outmaneuvered on her own deal, but business was business.

The yard sign read Excelsior Realty, and the appendage hanging below it, *Heather Baldwin, Sales Associate*. A muscular man shoveled mulch from a wheelbarrow into the flower beds beneath the manicured shrubbery. The freshly mowed lawn and edged sidewalks blended in with the surrounding posh homes. Inside, Heather finished staging the house, featuring the aroma of brewing coffee, the strains of a classical quartet, and open-curtained rooms, bright and inviting.

She inspected herself in the foyer mirror, the dark skirt and gray jacket with pink chemise. No cleavage and a subtle baby bump made her non-threatening to women, who made the call when house hunting. A car pulled up and she stepped out the front door to greet the first of the open-house visitors. Across the yard, the Simpsons stood in their picture window, a scowl on Millie and a wistful gaze on Mike as though admiring a tropical isle. Heather smiled, raised her hand, and gave it a quick wiggle.

The house sold in three days and closed in a month. Heather's 1.5 percent as listing agent and 1.5 percent as selling agent became $30,000. Her first commission. She bought a business wardrobe, leased an upscale condo, and resolved never to be dependent on a man again.

CHAPTER 49

In the days and weeks that followed, as they weaned him from the drugs, Bob became more alert, but the malaise remained. He couldn't help it. Everything seemed without purpose. Reading. Eating. Talking.

"Doc says you're not trying, buddy." Pain showed in George's face. "Time to snap out of it."

Bob stared at the white ceiling tiles, as bleak as his future. Nothing remained for him.

One evening, as NBC's new hit reality show *Gay or Straight* approached the big reveal, Bob's door cracked open and George's face appeared.

"Thought I'd bring something to cheer you up, buddy."

Bob muted the squealing studio audience.

George entered with a paper bag and a Cheshire-Cat grin. He reached in and came up with a bottle of Lester's Lager.

Bob's eyes brightened.

George popped the top and offered it.

Bob took the cool bottle. "Where'd you get that?"

George gave a head tilt toward the door.

Bob squinted at the backlit silhouette.

"You're not drinking that now," Grace said, coming in and taking the bottle from Bob's hand. "That's for when you're better. We'll celebrate when you get out of here."

Bob's chest froze mid-breath. Finally, words came. "How did you know?"

She handed the bottle to George. "He called." She sat and took his hand in both of hers.

George took a long swig, made an approving face, and left the room.

Bob's heart raced. "How long can you stay?"

"As long as it takes." She massaged his hand. "Is it true, Bob? You did this to protect me?"

Damn George. "I didn't think I'd get shot."

She caressed the back of his hand with her cheek.

He sighed. He couldn't lie to her. "It was the only way."

She leaned forward and spoke in a low tone.

"Bob, you need to fight this thing."

"For what?" He shrugged. "Painful rehab? Disbarment? Prison?"

She peered into his eyes.

"No, Bob," she said. "For me."

During Bob's second month in the hospital, Grace flew in every other week, staying several days each visit. He objected because of the cost. And the stress. But she insisted.

"With Hector back, things are running smoothly," she said.

Of course, George took all the credit and retold the story often. After Chastain had hauled Hector to Salt Lake City, the office director received an inquiry asking why Agent Chastain utilized government resources and time to settle a personal vendetta. The embarrassed director released Hector, reprimanded Chastain, and reassigned him to Nome. "So, Chastain says, 'Do we have an office up there?' And the boss says, 'Yes…you.'" George always ended the story with a guffaw.

Hector's return sounded the death knell for Milo's hope of a contract renewal. That and his beer consumption, which had catapulted him over the four-hundred-pound threshold. Plus, everyone knew he had ratted out Hector.

With a good job and the Iceman no longer hovering, Hector rented a garage apartment. He said he didn't feel right living in Grace's basement, and he wasn't about to go near the trailer park.

Grace's visits soothed Bob's soul and healed his body. They shared his custard and watched the soaps and played cards. His fever disappeared as the infection waned. His finger healed over. His yellow pallor returned to pink. And when he finally stood on his shattered femur following several surgeries, he shuddered at the intense pain, but remained upright. Walking would still be a while, but with Grace's help, the storm clouds of depression had lifted.

The state charged Doyle with aggravated battery and attempted murder. It would have been worse if Pam had been home when he entered her bedroom, claw hammer in hand. But she had left, run off with her pedophile boyfriend. Just as well. Good riddance.

As the months rolled by and he prepared for trial, life became unbearable. With the firm in chaos, partners in revolt, and clients jumping ship, Doyle needed his money. Money for Artie, for the IRS, for his life. And now, money for his criminal defense. The only option left was to negotiate, so he called George.

"I want my goddamned money back," he said. "What does your client want?"

"This is your lucky day, Henry," the arrogant son of a bitch said. "Bob is willing to deal."

Gifford offered to make restitution of five million as part of a plea agreement he was negotiating. In addition, Doyle and the firm would relinquish all other claims against Baldwin, and Baldwin would not file a personal injury action against Doyle or firm.

"He stole *eight* million from me."

"And you shot him three times. Consider the 3.2 million as compensation for his injuries and call it even." Doyle could almost hear the smirk. "The man spent two months in the hospital, lost a quarter of his liver, half a finger, and now hobbles around on a shattered leg. A jury might give us a lot more."

Gifford was a worm.

"Plus, as far as anyone knows, *you* took the three million."

Doyle gritted his teeth. He had no choice. If he didn't get his five million back, he was dead.

After two months in the hospital, Bob moved to a wheelchair-accessible apartment near the airport, and Grace's visits continued during his rehab. They had picnics on the patio, board games on rainy days, and dinner and a movie on the sofa. They laughed, remembering the antics of Hector and Milo.

Bob missed his friends in LaPlante. He regretted the choices he had made and thanked her for her forgiveness. He didn't deserve her kindness. She prepared meals, helped him with his exercises, and drove him to rehab.

In the third month of Bob's convalescence, Grace came to his bed. His heart pounded as her warmth pressed against him.

"You know I'm still married," he said.

"Yes," Grace said. "So am I." She buried her face in his shoulder. "And I miss him every day."

He looked into her weary eyes.

"And now I'm going to lose you, too," she said.

His trial would begin next month. "I'll come back," he said, holding her close, "as soon as I can."

And "soon" meant no trial and no appeals. It meant a plea agreement.

"Doyle's ready to deal," George said. "You were right. Five million is a powerful bargaining chip."

"I need this to be over. What do they want?"

George cleared his throat. "If you make restitution of the five million, the prosecutor will drop that charge. You plead guilty to one count of grand theft for the 3.2 million."

"What about my civil liability?"

George grinned. "The law firm will forego action in civil court for the 3.2, and you forego the personal injury claim against them. Net result, you keep the 3.2 million for your injuries and do some jail time."

"How much jail time?"

"Seven years."

Bob expelled a long breath.

"Eligible for parole in four. Maybe less."

Bob dropped his head into his hands. Four years without Grace.

CHAPTER 50

When Doyle got his five million back, he had to spread it around to shut up the whining partners. With his share, he paid off Artie, the IRS, and all his howling creditors. Then came his defense costs.

With prosecutor Henshaw out of the picture, Doyle had lost control of the criminal process. So he had to hire the most expensive criminal defense lawyer in the East, with his Gordon-Gecko slicked-back hair and double-breasted suit. He might have been Artie, had Artie gone past the eighth grade. The lawyer showed up with a couple of minions and assured him he'd get the charges reduced. With no priors, he wouldn't spend a night in jail. But the tide had turned against Doyle. The state bar had opened an investigation, lawyers of the firm were in open mutiny, and his political allies headed for the hills.

His attorney wanted to dress him up with an attractive and supportive family. Estranged from his ex-wife and adult children, Doyle had to be creative. Pam had run off with her faggot boyfriend, so she was out, too. Heather said she loved hearing from him, and, should he ever need a home or commercial space or run across clients who do, please call. But sorry, her business consumed all her time. His supportive family became the matronly Martha and a demurely-dressed LaRue twin. Twin One, perhaps. Her fee came to $2,000 per day for the five-day trial.

"The evidence will show that the defendant, Henry Meriwether Doyle, took Mr. Baldwin into custody, held him in a room with four security guards, then shot him."

Doyle would put this smug prosecutor on his get-even list when this ended.

"Yes," Doyle's lawyer said, "there were eight eyewitnesses in the room at the time of the shooting, but Mr. Doyle suffered from psychosis due to the enormous stress he had endured, and was unable to distinguish right from wrong."

What? This guy would get him hanged. Doyle had to salvage this. His attorney howled when he insisted on taking the stand.

The prosecutor smiled. "Mr. Doyle, did you have sexual intercourse with Mr. Baldwin's wife?"

From the jury box, twelve heads turned in unison toward Doyle.

"Objection," Gordon Gecko said, leaping to his feet. "Irrelevant."

The jury returned a guilty verdict after deliberating two and a half hours, including lunch.

"We'll get it reversed," his crackerjack lawyer said. "We have great grounds for appeal. You won't spend a day in prison. We'll take it to the Supreme Court if necessary."

Of course he would, with the meter ticking at $500 per hour.

"Don't worry, Henry," he said. "Powerful men don't go to prison."

Bob struck a plea agreement with the federal prosecutor, still smarting over the recent Grace Hargrove unpleasantness and anxious to make this go away. At the sentencing hearing, Heather dutifully upheld her end of the bargain. Demurely dressed, with no cleavage, no glam makeup, and clearly thirty-seven weeks pregnant and ready to pop, she sat behind Bob and touched his shoulder several times when the judge was looking.

"I just want to get on with my life," Bob told the bench, standing with the help of his cane.

Heather groaned, stood, and waddled out, her spine arched to counter-balance the huge belly, her hand on the small of her back.

Though hardened by seventy-two years of life and forty of them on the bench, the judge was still a man. And a grandfather. "Counsel, approach." The lawyers moved forward. "This man won't see his sons until they're five years old."

Whispered negotiations followed.

"Step back."

George and Bob's criminal attorney returned to the defense table.

"Five years," the judge said, striking his gavel. "Eligible for parole in two and a half."

Monday morning, Bob surrendered himself for transport to the minimum-security Medford Correctional Facility, where lawyers, politicians, and other white-collar thieves played tennis and wrote their memoirs.

The next day, Liam and Tomás entered the world thirty minutes apart at Women's Hospital. Heather had waved off the suggestion of a cesarean. "No scars," she said.

One baby was pink and bald and cherub-faced. The other was caramel-skinned, with a full mane of fine, black hair. She looked at the two infants in her arms. "These are twins?"

"Not identical," the nurse said. "Fraternal twins, like regular brothers. Each comes from a different egg. And a different sperm."

Heather stiffened.

"Different sperm?" She grabbed the nurse's wrist, bobbling Liam. "Different fathers?"

The nurse shrugged. "It happens." She cocked an eyebrow. "You tell *me*, sweetie."

As Doyle watched the cash dwindle, the falling-glass cases were scheduled for trial. Some piss-ant ambulance chaser had filed a class action lawsuit against the hot dog stand and Kravitz & Doyle, LLC. Of the 132 plaintiffs in the class, two claimed cuts from falling glass, thirty-seven claimed psychological trauma, and the rest said they ingested hot dogs tainted with glass powder. And while the hot dog vendor had long since disappeared, the real target was the silk-stocking law firm, which possessed the critical element of all personal injury law: deep pockets.

Smelling blood in the water, other PI sharks rounded up hundreds of new clients under creative theories of liability, such as a cloud of glass dust that had wafted across the city causing eye irritation and respiratory problems as far away as the suburbs. Every bloodsucker in town wanted a piece of him.

The spate of lawsuits was dubbed *Kristallmorgen* by a World-War-II-buff reporter in his story, *The Morning of Falling Glass*, a series which entertained the paper's readership for weeks.

Like the airship *Hindenburg*, the once-proud name of Kravitz & Doyle became a synonym for "disaster." Under the weight of the onslaught, the firm lost decades-old clients, fees plummeted, and lawyers and staff fled. The final straw came when Kravitz & Doyle's liability insurance carrier declined coverage, pointing out that intentional torts committed by partners were not covered. Liability coverage was for negligence. "We're very sorry." They closed their briefcases and promptly exited the building, leaving the law firm holding the bag for all losses.

The firm imploded, leaving a vacant thirtieth floor and King Doyle without a kingdom.

The expectant-mom look proved so successful in residential sales, Heather switched to a dual papoose carrier when the boys appeared. After twenty-four home sales in eighteen months, she said goodbye to Barry and opened *H. Baldwin and Associates*.

The working-mom persona earned Heather an invitation from The Women's Business Council to speak on "sisterhood empowerment," featuring her stylized life story as the model.

"I once judged my self-worth in terms of how attractive I was to a man."

"No, no," the women chanted.

"But now men judge *their* self-worth in terms of how attractive *they* are to *me*."

The ladies of the Council went wild.

Heather rode the crest of a prolonged real estate boom. Salesperson-of-the-Year plaques, certificates of achievement, and a World's-Greatest-Mom trophy adorned her office, as did a photo of Heather in a hardhat with a shovel, a beautiful smile toward the camera, the standout in the picture of five men in suits.

Her business acumen and other attributes so impressed the bank president, he began funneling much of their work to her.

"You're too kind, Phillip," she said, touching his sleeve at the annual Realtors' ball.

She sold new condos and offices renovated from warehouses in the now-chic wharf district, and expanded into commercial leasing and property management.

"This is perfect for us," one of the men said. The three hedge fund partners stood in the thirtieth-floor conference room, admiring the panoramic view of the city in the bright April sun.

"Indeed," Heather said. "It's the city's premier address." She opened her portfolio and removed the lease for the men to sign. "It once housed a prominent law firm."

Doyle stood next to his criminal defense attorney as the judge entered the courtroom. "Ten years," he said, and banged his gavel.

Ten years? Maybe Doyle would be joining Baldwin at the Medford country club.

"Stafford Correctional Facility," the judge said.

Two and a half years of appeals had ended, his money and friends had run out, and he was headed to the state maximum security lockup. As the deputy led him away in cuffs, he turned to his attorney. "You said powerful men don't go to prison."

The grease ball lawyer looked him in the eye. "They don't."

CHAPTER 51

Bob walked through the front gate of the Medford Correctional Facility like a butterfly emerging from a cocoon, its wings unfolding to a new world. His debt to society was paid, his body mended, and his personal life free. He and Heather had quietly divorced a year earlier, neither wanting her growing assets to be jointly owned.

Grace and George greeted him. His reception at the offices of Gifford and Farrington gathered several familiar faces. George had hired two former K&D associates, Bob's former secretary Doris as a paralegal, and an investigator.

"You remember Dave Dawson," George said. "He was with the detective agency K&D used. Fontaine & Associates. He works here now."

"Of course," Bob said, shaking Dave's hand.

Grace smiled at Dave. "Jane said you're coming out for another visit." She raised her eyebrows. "This is becoming a regular thing."

Dave blushed. "Yes, Madam Chairman."

At contract's end, Grace sent Milo packing back to Coeur d'Alene Middle School, and Hector became brewmeister and Chief Operating Officer. He gave shares of the brewery to the employees. Everyone in town pulled together to brew, sell, and drink Lester's Lager. Under Hector's stewardship, production quadrupled and Cascade MicroBrew became the second largest brewery in the state. *Immigration Magazine* featured Hector as a rags-to-riches tale, "From

Dishwasher to COO," and CEO and Chairman of the Board Grace Hargrove was voted Idaho's Businesswoman of the Year.

"And my partner Susan comes to town every month," George said. "To touch base at the office."

Susan offered her hand. "I never got a chance to thank you."

"Thank me?" Bob said. "I turned my back when Doyle fired you."

"And you recommended me to George. Best thing that ever happened. Now I have my dream job, live in a small town with my family, and have a great work-life balance. I even remarried. He's an associate professor at the college where I live."

George beamed.

"Winnie has a little brother. And another on the way." She patted her belly.

Bob hugged her and whispered his congratulations.

George produced a tray of bubbling champagne flutes, and took one. "A toast."

Bob smelled Grace's strawberry shampoo as she clung to his arm, and the celebrants raised their glasses.

"To Bob and his new life."

The cell door slid open with a bang. Doyle stood, gaping in at the chipped paint, stainless-steel toilet, and double bunk bed. He held a towel, bar of soap, and a change of clothes. A massive man sitting on the lower bunk looked up. The guard's club pressed into Doyle's back. He shuffled in and the door clanged shut behind him.

Veins bulged from the man's massive biceps and neck, beneath the tattoos snaking out from his prison smock.

Although Doyle had kept himself fit at the club, this place had no golf or squash or tennis. It had weights. And his new acquaintance appeared to have spent a lot of time lifting them. Twenty-pound weights, fifty-pound weights, hundred-pound weights.

"Name's Doyle. I'm a lawyer." He planned to spend his days preparing writs of Habeas Corpus, appeals, and all manner of legal paperwork. It was his best hope for survival here, short of becoming a close friend of the notorious Achilles, a powerfully-built inmate of high rank in the jailhouse hierarchy. So what if Doyle had been disbarred? A jailhouse lawyer needed no license. And so what if he had no clue how to prepare those documents? These animals wouldn't know the difference. Everything gets denied anyway.

"I don't need no lawyer," the man said. "I need me a mental healthcare professional."

Doyle took one step back and hit the opposite wall.

"They say I'm a sociopath." The man's eyes scoured Doyle up and down. "And a sexual predator." His grin revealed several missing teeth. "Not that any of them gals didn't enjoy it."

Doyle's Adam's apple bobbed. "Yeah." He forced a sick smile. "Women have been the bane of my life." He climbed onto the top bunk and cocooned himself in the blanket. The lights went out, but sleep would not come. As he lay staring at the flaking ceiling, a low voice broke the silence.

"I ain't no homosexual, just so you know."

Doyle shivered amid the stench of body odor, urine, and prison antiseptic.

"But a lot of them animals in here been screwed by a lawyer." A deep chuckle rose from below. "Some may want to return the favor."

CHAPTER 52

"Read us the Prince and the Ogre," Tomás said, as Heather tucked in the boys.

"Yes, Mommy," Liam said. "Please."

Heather opened a book but looked beyond the pages. "Once upon a time there was a beautiful princess. She was in love with a handsome prince. He had dark hair and a gorgeous smile, and he pleased the princess greatly. But the ogre had a big castle with gold and jewels, and he bedazzled the princess with his wealth. So she chose the ogre and sent the good prince away."

"I want to be the ogre," Liam said, his pink cheeks glowing.

"Okay," Tomás said, his dark mane belying his tender years. "I want to be the prince."

"But the ogre chained the princess to the wall in the dungeon." She turned the page. "She languished in the dark, waiting for the prince to save her. But he never came. So she dug out the mortar with her locket, pushed out a stone, and escaped."

She closed the book.

"And now the ogre is in the dungeon."

"What happened to the prince, Mommy?"

She sighed as she stroked the boy's hair. "He went back to Miami, sweetheart."

Bob settled into Grace's bungalow on Second Street. From the south-facing porch, he watched the arc of the sun shine its promise into his life. His journey had been a dark tunnel. Hunted, shot, and imprisoned, he had lived without love, and upon finding it, endured separation. The black memories lingered, but he said nothing about the trailer, or Darryl's disfigured jaw, or the discoloration where the plastic surgeon had removed the "JP" burn scar from Grace's leg. They never spoke of Johnny. Like asbestos in the basement, some toxic agents were better left undisturbed.

But his morning walk drew him to an empty lot, weeds overgrown and the forest encroaching. Only the mailbox remained, dented and rusting, but the lettering still legible. *Paxton.*

"Bob," a voice behind him said. "I heard you was back."

Hose nozzle in hand, the manager of the Mountain View Mobile Home Park sprayed her flower beds.

"Hello, Maggie."

"You ain't looking for the trailer, are you? When Johnny run off, Grace had the thing hauled away and crushed. Said she didn't want him bothering her no more."

A shiver shuddered up Bob's spine. He remembered Darryl's drugged-up words in the hospital three years earlier. *He won't bother you no more, Mrs. Hargrove.*

After church on Sunday, Bob and Grace stood on the windswept hillside among the grave markers.

Grace stepped forward and touched Lester's granite headstone. "I told you he'd come back."

Bob watched as the breeze sent wisps of her hair dancing in all directions.

She stepped back, wiping a tear, and hugged Bob's arm. "I promised Lester I'd take care of you." She rested her head on his shoulder.

Bob kissed her hair. "We both promised him."

A minute passed in silence.

"He led a good life, Grace."

"Yes, he was a wealthy man."

Bob squinted. "I thought you doubted that."

She shook her head. "I never doubted his wealth. I doubted his money." She squeezed Bob's arm. "A man's wealth is his love for others." She looked up and met his gaze. "His willingness to sacrifice for another."

Though Bob's limp slowed them as they walked hand-in-hand down the hillside, the sun cast a warm glow on the path ahead.

About the Author

Ken Hubona has been a naval aviator, attorney, engineer, and bureaucrat. He lives and writes in suburban Richmond, Virginia.

KenHubona@comcast.net

43417289R00154

Made in the USA
Middletown, DE
24 April 2019